It's Not PMS, It's You

Rich Amooi

D0287483

Copyright 2019 © Rich Amooi
http://www.richamooi.com
Edited by Meg Stinson

You are a rare bird, so don't let this story ruffle your beautiful feathers. This book is a work of fiction, remember? Seriously. References to real people, monster wedgies, bagels, companies, dead people, restaurants, sushi, events, products, stress, services, karma, businesses, corporations, panties in bunches, near-death experiences, drones, organizations, or locations are intended only to provide a sense of authenticity and are used fictitiously. Characters, names, story, locations, incidents, and dialogue come from the author's imagination and are not to be construed as real. WARNING: Reading this book may lead to an abundance of positive feelings and oxytocin in your body. Please consult a professional to find out if you are too happy for your own good.

No part of this book may be reproduced, scanned, recorded, eaten, or distributed in printed or electronic form without permission from the author.

To Deb Julienne.

CHAPTER ONE

RUTH

I have orchestrated multi-million dollar business deals and have butted heads with Fortune 500 CEOs and some of the biggest corporate lawyers in the country, but my biggest challenge by far was trying to remove a monster wedgie during my spinning class without the gorgeous guy behind me noticing.

Casually turning my head to the right, I checked my periphery, confident I looked like some halfwit who was thinking of changing lanes on a stationary bike.

I couldn't tell if the man had his eyes focused on me or on the instructor in front of the class, but it didn't matter at this point. I had real-world issues here and needed to solve the dilemma before my butt sucked all my clothes inside my body and turned me inside out.

With every revolution of my bike's spinning wheel, the

wedgie seemed determined to go deeper, like a burrowing squirrel who hadn't found a suitable place for habitation.

I got up at five in the morning for this torture?

To make matters worse, the instructor—Manson, Mussolini, or whatever his name was—appeared to be on a mission to send us all into cardiac arrest. And don't even get me started on the chafing from a bike seat that was obviously manufactured with materials excavated from the surface of Mars.

I needed a distraction for the extraction.

Glancing down at my water bottle in the drink holder, I came up with the perfect plan. I would wait for the instructor to get us up off our seats again for the next sprint, then drop my water bottle on the floor to create a ruckus.

If the man behind me was a gentleman—no wagers, please—he would get off his bike and get the water bottle for me, thus taking any attention away from my derrière long enough for me to perform the embarrassing and delicate wedgie-removing procedure without him seeing.

Ironically, the song changed to "Shake Your Booty" by KC and the Sunshine Band.

"Off your butts!" the instructor barked out like a psychotic sea lion with Tourette's. "Take it up to level five for a sprint. Thirty seconds. Go! Go! Go!"

Perfect timing.

I slammed my water bottle to the floor behind me for the distraction.

It crashed against the back wall with a loud BOOM.

Never let it be said I did anything half-assed.

No pun intended.

I checked my periphery again to see if the guy fell for the trap.

Bingo.

He slowed his pedaling and glanced behind him at my bottle on the floor.

After he made a move to get off his bike, I lifted my butt off the seat, leaned forward on the handlebars, shifted all my body weight over to my left hand, and used my right hand to reach behind me and remove the mother of all wedgies.

Oh, no.

Completing the task was proving to be difficult since it was almost impossible to pedal while standing up on the bike with only one hand gripping the handlebars.

I used one finger, then two, then three, but still couldn't dig out the wedgie that must have been halfway to China by now.

Losing confidence with every second that passed, I wobbled back and forth like the Elvis bobblehead doll on the dashboard of my dad's 1977 Cadillac Coupe deVille.

Things were heading south in a hurry.

There was a sharp pain in my left wrist.

My elbow buckled.

Timber!

The fall to the floor was not graceful.

I banged my shoulder on the handlebars on the way down, slid off the bike sideways, and hooked my foot on top of the pedal. My other leg flew over my head and got wedged in between the bike seat and the drink holder.

Great.

Now, I had two wedgies.

Before I had a chance to untangle and upright myself, two hands gripped me from under my armpits and lifted me to my feet in one swift motion.

I looked up, dazed, confused, blinking a few times.

It was the guy who had been on the bike behind me. "Are you okay?"

There was genuine concern in his voice, but I was a big girl and could take care of myself.

Flustered, I said the first thing I could think of. "I do that all the time."

A smile tugged at the corner of his lips. "Of course." He chuckled and grabbed my water bottle from the floor, sticking it back in the drink holder on my bike.

"Thank you." I opened and closed my left hand, wincing from the pain.

He pointed to my wrist. "Get some ice on that."

"Okay . . ."

It was good advice since my schedule was full today and a swollen wrist would throw everything out of whack.

I grabbed my towel hanging from the handlebars and wiped my forehead, preparing to leave the class early.

"Okay, bring it back down to level two as we start the cool down." The instructor got off his bike and rushed over. "What happened?"

"Don't worry about it. Everything is fine." I took a step toward the door.

"Hang on—I need to fill out an accident report. It's gym protocol."

I stopped and turned back. "There was *no* accident."

The instructor pointed to the wedgie maker. "I saw you fall off the bike."

"You saw me *get off* the bike."

"Head first?"

I crossed my arms and winced from the pain. "Who wants to get off the bike like a normal person? Not me, I'll tell you that much."

He shook his head. "A report is necessary. Especially since it looks like you hurt yourself."

This guy had no idea who he was dealing with.

I had an MBA from UCLA and have brought a conference room of testosterone-loaded men to their knees. This spinning class instructor was small potatoes on the way to becoming mashed.

"Fine." I placed my hands on my hips and felt another bolt of pain from my wrist. "But be forewarned that I will have *a lot* to say in that report of yours. We'll need to discuss the class in general, your song choices, the specifications, aerodynamics, and comfort of the bikes, and your skills as a teacher and how they may or may not attribute to accidents and the likelihood of death."

He just stared at me.

"Don't worry, we should be able to avoid a lawsuit here and there's a fifty-percent chance you'll still have a job when all is said and done. So! Let's get to that report. If we start now, it shouldn't take more than four hours." I crinkled my nose. "I'm a perfectionist and a little long-winded."

More staring from him, but now his mouth was slightly open.

"I mean, unless we can both agree that there was *no* accident, which there wasn't."

He blinked and could finally form words. "What accident? I came over to tell you to have a great day. Good job in class today." He returned to his bike in front of the class.

I felt a smidgen of guilt for scaring the instructor like that, but what else was I going to do?

The man was trying to kill us, plus I just needed to get out of there.

I turned to thank the man who helped me off the floor, but oddly he was nowhere in sight. It was better that way since I was already embarrassed enough. And luckily, I would never see him again since this wasn't my regular gym and I wouldn't be returning before the turn of the next century.

Two hours later, I had showered, eaten breakfast, popped eight hundred milligrams of Ibuprofen, iced my injury, and walked to the pharmacy on the corner to buy a compression sleeve for my wrist.

Just like that, I was busy at work in my home office in Del Mar, California, a gorgeous beach town known for horse races and former residents Desi Arnaz, Burt Bacharach, Angie Dickinson, and Jimmy Durante.

I glanced over at my vibrating cell phone on the desk.

It was a text from Dee, my administrative assistant and best friend.

Dee: We need to talk ASAP about the Amsterion deal. Video conference?

Ruth: Give me two minutes. I'm in desperate need of more coffee. Got up early today for a spinning class.

Dee: You + spinning class = disaster. I'm surprised you made it out alive.

Ruth: Barely.

Dee knew that I wasn't a fan of high-intensity workouts. In fact, she knew everything there was to know about me in my personal and professional life.

That's why she got paid the big bucks.

As a partner in my firm and a corporate takeover investment specialist, I couldn't afford to have someone who wasn't on top of things. I needed someone who had my back and was smart enough to think for me when I was too stressed out or operating on four hours of sleep, which was almost always.

Dee was that person.

I prepared another cup of coffee, sat back down at my desk, and then connected to the video conference on my laptop. "Good morning." I adjusted the compression sleeve on my wrist since it felt a little too tight.

"Good morning." Dee lost her smile and pointed. "What happened to your wrist?"

"Don't ask."

She nodded. "Does this have anything to do with the other thing I'm not supposed to ask about, the spinning class?"

"I thought you had something urgent regarding the Amsterion deal."

Dee sighed. "Fine, but the conversation about your wrist is not over."

I laughed. "Believe me, I know. Talk to me."

"Stewart Peters is going to try to make a play for Amsterion."

I sat up in my chair. "You're kidding me."

Dee shook her head. "I wish I were."

"How reliable is your source?"

"If he or she weren't reliable, you and I wouldn't be having this conversation."

Stewart Peters was the enemy and my biggest pain in the butt, always trying to steal my clients out from under me. I would be fine with it if he did it fair and square, but the guy was an unethical weasel.

"Okay, looks like I have to move quickly on this. Can you set up a call with Teddy Markston? I need to close the deal today and get him to sign the papers."

Teddy was the CEO of Amsterion, the man I had been negotiating with.

"That will be difficult since Teddy is at the BioWorld conference in Phoenix," Dee said.

"Of course. I knew that."

"I'll check flights to—"

I shook my head. "No."

Dee nodded. "You're right, you're right. Let's forget about it. It's no big deal that Stewart is at the conference at this very moment, trying to woo Teddy away from you. No big deal at all. You're just flushing millions of dollars down the drain. Okay, I'll let you go then."

I blinked. "Reverse psychology . . . well played."

Dee smirked and gestured to me. "I learned from the master."

"How do you know that Stewart Peters is at the conference?"

Dee arched an eyebrow.

"Of course, you know."

Dee knew just about everything about every deal I was involved in, inside and out. I was certain she could read my mind. And more than anything, like me, she wouldn't take crap from male colleagues who thought they could do or say whatever they wanted just because they were packing two olives and a cocktail weenie in their shorts.

She was the closest thing to being my clone, which probably explained why we got along so well. She was the only person who seemed to understand me, which would also probably explain why she was my only friend.

Dee held up a finger and leaned in closer to the camera. "I also know that *Stewart* is having an affair with Markston's daughter. The only reason he has a chance of stealing Amsterion from us is because he has insider information from the owner's offspring."

I nodded my appreciation of the bomb she had dropped on me. "What does he know?"

"I'm not sure, but it most likely has to do with financials and a way for Amsterion to get more money on the deal. Whatever it is, it can't be as useful as what *you* know now." Dee grinned. "Stewart needs to be put in his place."

"I don't want to spend the night in Phoenix."

"How long have I known you?"

I opened my mouth to answer and—

"It was a rhetorical question." Dee took a sip of her tea

and then typed on her computer. "I can get you on a flight that leaves in three hours, which gives you ninety minutes to leave your house since you won't be checking baggage. That gets you into Phoenix in time for the welcome reception at the conference this afternoon, where you should find Teddy by the bar with his vodka tonic. You'll have about four hours to work your magic."

"I only need two."

"I know. I gave you that buffer so you can stop by Harumi Sushi on your way back to the airport."

Have I mentioned how well Dee knows me? She remembered that I raved about Harumi Sushi when I had eaten there six years ago. I was always interested in eating sushi. Unfortunately, there was zero interest on my part in flying to Phoenix at the moment, but I needed this deal. And I wouldn't mind the sushi at all.

My goal from day one was to become the top dog of the company, managing partner of Stansfeld Investments. I was so close I could almost taste it. I had been at the firm for over ten years and had worked my butt off to get to where I was today. There was no way I would let up now. Plus, Teddy Markston told me he wanted to meet in-person at some point. It was either a one-hour flight to Phoenix or a five-hour flight to Miami to meet Teddy in his office after he got back from the conference. Even if I preferred Miami, I didn't have the luxury of time being on my side.

I sighed. "I don't like that Stewart Peters is fishing in my waters again."

Dee smirked. "He doesn't know that you're a shark." She

continued typing on her computer. "You've been taking it easy on him."

"Not anymore." I nodded, knowing what I had to do. "Book it."

"I already did. And I just registered you for the conference. Check your email for the confirmation."

I shook my head at her. "What did I do to deserve you?"

"Your checks don't bounce."

I laughed, but then stopped when I thought of something else important. "I'm supposed to meet Nick Morris this afternoon."

"For a date?"

"*No*. To give him the key to the house."

Nick was the landscape designer I had hired for my backyard project that would start tomorrow.

Soon, I would have french doors in my home office that open up to palm trees, a fountain, benches, chimes, cactus, succulents, rocks, as well as flowers that attract butterflies and hummingbirds. He had already lined up someone to come lay the foundation for the fountain and gazebo a few weeks ago. The project also included waist-high planter boxes to grow organic vegetables, plus the gazebo would have comfy chairs for relaxing, reading, working outside, and even taking afternoon naps.

Okay, I'm pretty sure I hadn't had a nap in my entire life, but Dee told me that sleep experts believe that daytime naps would increase my alertness, boost creativity and memory, ease stress, improve perception, enhance my nonexistent sex life, help me lose weight, reduce the risk of heart attack, and brighten my not-so-sunny disposition.

According to Dee, naps were like a miracle drug.

I was willing to give them a shot.

"For an older guy, Nick looks delicious."

"Older guy?"

Dee nodded. "Yeah—he must be up there in his forties."

I glared at her, even though I knew it would have zero effect. "Excuse me? *Up* there? I guess that means I'm up there, too. Careful or I'll bounce your next paycheck on purpose."

I was forty-five years old and didn't have a problem with getting older, but I didn't consider myself to be *up there*.

Dee smiled. "Yeah, but you don't look a day over thirty-five. I hope I look half as good as you when I'm your age."

"You're forgiven." I smiled. "I don't understand how you get anything done when you get off topic so much."

"I'm a multitasking queen. By the way, I already sent Nick a message to let him know I would meet him instead of you."

Dee had met with Nick the last two times he had come to my house to take measurements and do some calculations in my yard, since I'd been out of town on business. All of my communication with Nick had been through email and phone calls because my schedule had been crazy lately.

He sounded professional when we talked and it appeared that we were on the same page, but I knew from experience that many business owners were trained in the skill of telling the client exactly what they wanted to hear so they could get the job. That's why I had a rule of meeting everyone I did business with in person, to make sure there weren't any negative vibes, red flags, or personality conflicts. I wanted to look that person in the eyes and trust what I felt in my gut. I had one of the best bullshit detectors around and could determine almost immediately when a person wasn't being sincere.

My gut is always right.

"Maybe I should tell Nick to hold off and I can meet him after I get back from Phoenix."

"No." Dee was adamant, as usual. "I'll take care of everything and give him the key. And remember, he's the best in the business. You have *nothing* to worry about."

"Just because Nick Morris is the best doesn't mean he can't be a pain in my butt. I already have enough stress in my life and don't need more."

"And *that's* why you hired him in the first place, remember?"

Dee had come up with the idea of the backyard project. She claimed that the stress in my life would kill me and that I needed a place to disconnect and destress. My backyard would be transformed into a tranquil space, my little zen garden. Yes, I only lived three blocks from the beach, but sometimes I needed just a minute or two to step right outside my home office, take a few deep breaths, clear my head, and lower my blood pressure. Hopefully, my new zen garden would be a game changer, but I wasn't going to worry about that right now. I needed to get ready to fly to Phoenix.

I downed the rest of my coffee. "Okay, gotta run."

"Wait!" Dee scooted closer to her camera again. "Before you go, tell me what happened to your wrist. And the spinning class. What was that all about?"

I stared at her, not wanting to tell her, but knowing she would keep insisting. "Okay, but don't you dare laugh."

"I would *never* do such a thing."

"Right." I sighed. "Well . . ."

"Just tell me." Dee took a sip of her tea.

I sighed. "I hurt myself in the spinning class trying to remove . . . a wedgie."

Dee's eyes went wide and tea sprayed from her mouth straight onto her computer monitor. She coughed and snorted, her laugh building until it became hysterical. I could no longer see her since her camera was obviously covered with tea. Waiting for her to get it out of her system was my only option. Hopefully, it wouldn't take all morning.

"At least your problems are behind you!" Dee laughed harder as she started to come back into view, furiously wiping her monitor like she wanted nothing more than to see how embarrassed I was.

I'm glad somebody thought it was funny because it wasn't to me.

After she finished wiping her computer screen, she wiped her eyes. "You made my day. I'm not sure if I ruined my monitor, but it was worth it."

"I'm glad my pain is your gain. May I go now?"

Dee nodded, her bottom lip quivering from trying to

hold in more laughter. "Keep me updated on Amsterion, and good luck."

I nodded and disconnected the video conference, knowing luck would not help me one bit.

I could attribute the success in my career to hard work, determination, experience, and knowing how to deal with men's super-sized egos. It was also about having the right information available to make the right decision at the right time.

Teddy Markston was a brilliant businessman who believed in honesty and integrity.

Stewart Peters was a lying, cheating douchebag.

That was all the info I needed to make things right in Phoenix.

CHAPTER TWO

NICK

"Careful!" I said to Brandon, who was laughing and on the verge of dropping the brand-new french door he was carrying to my truck. "If you drop it, you're paying for it."

I pointed at the door and gave him my best serious look, even though I could never get mad at him. He was one of the nicest and hardest working guys I had ever met. I was lucky to have him working for me.

"Relax. I'm not going to drop it." Brandon continued to laugh but got a better grip on the door. "And it's *your* fault. Don't tell me things like that when I'm in the middle of something that requires my attention. That's hysterical."

I had just mentioned to him that a woman in my spinning class fell off her bike while she was trying to remove a wedgie.

"Maybe she was falling for *you*."

I shook my head. "Not funny."

Brandon was a rare man, a hopeless romantic. They weren't very easy to spot in the wild, but he assured me that there were many more out there if I looked close enough.

Maybe I needed to buy binoculars.

"Is she okay?" Brandon asked.

I nodded. "She'll be fine. She injured her wrist, but I'm guessing the bruised ego is what's bothering her. Talk about embarrassing. Hang on." I opened the tailgate of my truck and stepped out of Brandon's way. "Okay, go for it."

Brandon laid the edge of the second door on top of the first one and slid it into the bed of my truck. Then he closed the tailgate and wiped his hands on his jeans.

We were headed to a client's place to get the key to her house, but had to make a stop to pick up custom-ordered french doors for the job.

Brandon was my employee, even though he felt more like an equal partner because of everything he did, including the grunt work that my doctor ordered me not to do. The same doctor who told me the spinning class was okay for me.

It didn't make much sense for a forty-five-year-old man who had gone through what I had gone through, but maybe that's why I was a landscape designer and not a doctor.

Brandon leaned against the back of my truck. "You didn't ask her out then?"

"I don't go to the gym to pick up chicks."

"I know that, but that doesn't mean you need to avoid them. You're a good man and you deserve love. Everyone does."

"Thank you and I'm confident I'll meet someone. When the time is right, it'll happen."

"Not even a hello?" Brandon asked. "That's all it takes to start, you know. Then next time another hello, and by the third hello you can introduce yourself. Nice and slow is the way to go, but it always starts with a hello."

"Now, you're a poet. And if it makes you feel any better, I told her she should put ice on her injured wrist."

"Great! But I still think you should've asked her out."

We both got in the truck and I started the engine, turning to him before I pulled out of the parking lot. "Asking her out was the last thing on my mind. She could be married with five kids."

Brandon fastened his seatbelt. "I get it. You're holding the wedgie against her."

I chuckled. "Yes—that's it. Exactly." I pulled onto the street and headed toward my client's home. Luckily, it was only a few minutes away.

"Everybody gets wedgies, you know." Brandon moved his butt around on the seat. "I think I have a little one right now."

I shot him a quick look and then got my eyes back on the road. "I don't need to know things like that. And true, people get wedgies, but not everybody falls off a bike in a spinning class. Not that I would hold *that* against her, but you need to give it a rest. Trust me—there's no doubt in my mind that she's hoping to never see me again after what happened."

"Well, as long as you keep an open mind. You can't let

what happened between you and Crystal stop you from finding someone special."

Crystal was my ex-wife.

She had worked too much, I had rarely seen her when we were married and when I had, she only wanted to talk about her work. She was the one who pushed my career path into a direction I hadn't wanted it to go, which led to my health problems. We ended the marriage on good terms and we have a beautiful daughter together, Lindsey, who's in her last year of college now.

"Crystal wasn't a bad woman," Brandon said.

"I know that." I turned down the next street and slowed down since we were approaching my client's house. "Crystal was a workaholic, and it takes a certain person to live with and be in a relationship with a workaholic. I'm not that person. Call me crazy, but when I'm in a relationship with a woman, I like to see her regularly. I gave it a shot, tried to be as supportive as possible, but being *career-minded* differs from being *career-obsessed*."

"Can't argue with that." Brandon pointed to the driveway. "Back into the driveway, so I don't have to carry the doors so far."

"Of course." I backed in, stuck the truck in park, and turned off the engine.

Brandon opened his door and was about to jump out, but then stopped. "I still think you should've asked out wedgie girl."

"She seemed a little too serious for me. She didn't even smile."

"I don't think anyone smiles in a spinning class."

"Fair enough."

"And most people aren't filled with joy and happiness and smiles when they have something stuck up their butt."

"Another fair point, but there was also a tiny incident of her threatening to sue the gym and get the instructor fired, even though it was her fault she fell off the bike. I heard the whole thing since I was right behind her. She knew exactly what to say."

"Did it work?"

I nodded. "The instructor looked terrified."

"She's smart, too."

I chuckled. "Yeah. I did love her confidence, I'll give her that much. Anyway, she looked like she was out to bulldoze anyone who stood in her path. I snuck out of the class before she killed me for leaving fingerprints on her water bottle."

Brandon arched an eyebrow. "What were you doing with her water bottle?"

"She dropped it. I picked it up for her."

He nodded and scratched his chin, thinking about it. "Like when Cinderella lost her shoe . . ."

"Not even close." I laughed and headed to the front door, Brandon trailing right behind me. "Oh . . . remember Ruth is the client, but she's out of town on business again. We're meeting with her assistant, Dee." I knocked on the front door.

Brandon leaned closer and whispered. "Maybe that's not a bad thing that she's out of town since she works from home. There's nothing worse than a client watching us as we work. Especially a control freak who keeps changing things on the fly."

I put a finger over my lips to quiet Brandon since I heard footsteps on the tile approaching the front door inside the house.

Dee swung the door open. "Hi, Nick."

She did a double-take with Brandon, like she recognized him.

"Hey, there. Good to see you again." I gestured to Brandon. "This is my partner, Brandon."

"Nice to meet you." Brandon shook Dee's hand.

"You, too." She led us to the kitchen where she grabbed a key ring from the counter and began removing one of the keys from it.

I glanced around the kitchen and got the same feeling that I had the last time I had been there. It almost felt as if a woman didn't live in the house. There was barely a hint of feminine touches and style. Very neutral colors, too.

Nothing on the refrigerator.

Nothing on the counters.

No picture frames.

No flowers.

No plants.

No lively decor like sunflowers, roosters, cows, or vibrant colors.

Dee handed me the house key. "Here you go. Just a couple of things and I'll let you do whatever you need to do to prepare for tomorrow. Ruth asked me to stock the refrigerator with various drinks and juices for you both. Please help yourself." She pointed to the coffee maker. "And you have unlimited coffee there. Just pop in a pod and press start." She pointed to the cupboard. "And nuts and dried fruits there. Don't be shy. Grab something if you ever get the urge."

"Thank you."

I could say without hesitation that no client had ever offered me nuts and dried fruits on the job in the past. It was thoughtful and generous, albeit a little weird at the same time. Not weird enough for me to not partake since I loved nuts and dried fruits. There was no doubt in my mind I would be raiding that cupboard over the next couple of weeks.

"Okay, follow me." Dee led us past the family room toward the hallway.

Ruth had an amazing house, roomy, clean, completely remodeled, and very modern. Too modern, if I was being honest, almost like it was a place rented out as corporate housing. If I didn't already know it was a woman's house, I would've been certain it belonged to a businessman with no life. It was almost as if Ruth only used the place to work and sleep.

What about living and enjoying your home?

"Okay," Dee said, leading us into the office and turning around to face us. "Just a couple of housekeeping items to go over with you before I go." She pointed to the large window that I would be removing tomorrow morning to install the french doors that would give Ruth direct access to her backyard from her office. "I know you have to do some work in here, but I want to make sure you know that this is Ruth's sacred workspace, so just a heads-up to not touch anything. Please keep it tidy."

I nodded. "I promise. This will be a clean installation. As I shared with Ruth in the design, the window is the same width as the two doors, so we won't have to cut. We'll use the same header for support above the doors, and we don't need to remove any king studs or reroute any electrical wiring."

Dee blinked. "King studs?"

I chuckled. "Sorry, I'm getting technical on you."

"That's okay. I'm actually surprised a landscape designer is installing french doors."

"It's not normal." I gestured to Brandon, chuckling. "Brandon used to do construction before he started working with me, so I threw it in as part of the deal. We enjoy this stuff. Anyway, the installation of the doors will be quick and easy, let me say that. We will make sure to leave Ruth in peace and quickly move on to the backyard."

"Great. One more thing . . ." Dee walked toward the large window and pointed to the row of rose bushes on the other side of the glass. "Just a reminder that Ruth's rose garden is the only thing of value to her in the entire backyard. For now." She gave us a knowing smile. "Anyway, those roses are her pride and joy. I wanted to warn you. I know you have a lot of work to do back there, but please take extra care and caution when you're working anywhere near the roses. Unless you have a death wish, that is." She laughed.

I stared at her.

"I'm kidding. Sort of . . ." Dee snorted. "Look—Ruth is

my best friend and is one of the kindest and most generous people I know. I love her to death, but she can be a little hardcore and blunt when things aren't going as planned. She's a perfectionist. As long as you remember that and deliver what you promised, there won't be any problems at all."

If Ruth was anything like my ex, I knew what I needed to do. Just do my job and do it right. Avoid confrontations and mind my own business. The best thing I could do was keep as much distance as possible between me and a woman like that.

The problem was that she worked from home.

I was most likely going to hear things, things related to her personal life and her job. Since I'm a natural problem solver, I'm always looking for ways to help. Some people look at that as sticking my nose where it doesn't belong, but I like to think I'm being kind and looking for ways to help others. If Ruth was a perfectionist, maybe she would be way ahead of me and come up with solutions before I could. Either way, I didn't see any issue there.

I grinned. "Good thing I'm a perfectionist, too."

Dee nodded. "I got that feeling when I saw the meticulous work you had done on some of your previous projects. And I know you're the best in the business—that's why we hired you. Anyway, forget I even mentioned it. Okay, I need to get back to work. I do pop in on occasion to help Ruth with things. I'm sure I'll see you around."

"I look forward to it," Brandon offered, but then cleared his throat. "I mean, yeah, we'll see you around."

Dee blushed. "Lock up when you're done."

After Dee left, Brandon brought in the doors from my truck.

I pointed to a spot in the corner. "Lean them against the wall over there. Gently."

He carefully set the doors on the floor and leaned them against the wall, turning to me. "Dee is cute, don't you think?"

I nodded. "It looked like you two had a little connection going on there."

He grinned. "Yeah, I got the same feeling."

I decided to play with him a little. "How come you didn't ask her out?"

Brandon stared at me. "Well, I, uh . . . I just met her and . . ." He shrugged.

"I didn't ask out wedgie girl at the gym because I had just met *her*, but you seemed to have a problem with that. What's the difference?"

"There's a *huge* difference."

I crossed my arms. "Do tell."

He thought about it for a moment. "Because you have much less time left on earth than I do. You need to meet someone sooner."

I laughed, since I wasn't that much older than Brandon. "Not if I kill you for saying something like that."

He pointed to my chest. "Your heart wouldn't be able to take not having me around."

"Lucky for you." I gestured with my thumb to leave the office. "Let's check out the backyard again before we head out."

25

Brandon followed me through the house to the sliding glass door in the kitchen that led to the backyard.

I slid the door open and stepped outside, surveying the area and visualizing what we had to do over the next few weeks. We had several deliveries scheduled for the next morning and I was excited to get my hands dirty again. This was what I lived for. Starting a project from scratch, from my vision, and transforming the backyard into something special for my client.

Brandon pointed toward the ground near my feet. "You're standing mighty close to the roses. Do you have a death wish?"

I glanced down and chuckled. "I'm at least thirty inches away."

He laughed. "Ruth sounds like a ball-buster to me. We need to be careful."

"We're careful with every job, it doesn't matter who the client is."

"I guess I'm trying to say that we need to be *extra* careful."

I nodded. "Maybe you're right, but why is she so protective of these things when she's not taking proper care of them?" I pulled one leaf off the rose bush closest to me and showed it to Brandon. "I mean, look at this?"

Brandon gasped, as if I had committed the biggest sin in the history of mankind. "I can't believe you did that. Are you crazy? She's going to kill you."

I chuckled. "Relax. She has a problem with the roses and I'm sure I know what's going on. See how the leaves are brown and appear scorched?"

Brandon leaned in and inspected the leaf, nodding. "Yeah."

"She's over-fertilizing them and if she keeps it up, she'll kill them all. Lucky for her, I have just the thing that'll help."

"Ask first before you do anything."

"It's no big deal. These roses have been neglected. I'll give them something to revive them. Believe me, Ruth will thank me."

"I don't know . . ."

Brandon was worrying about nothing.

Ruth was too busy being a workaholic to take care of her own roses.

How sad was that?

If I sat back and did nothing, the high stress and ammonia on the plants would kill them and there was no way I was going to let that happen.

I was going to save the roses.

How could Ruth have a problem with that?

CHAPTER THREE

RUTH

Inside the Phoenix Convention Center, I checked in at the registration booth to get my conference badge and hung the lanyard around my neck.

I made a beeline for the welcome reception in the atrium lobby, weaving in and out of the conference attendees, on a mission to put someone in his place.

Most men were intimidated by a strong, confident woman.

That was their problem, not mine.

And it was definitely going to be Stewart Peters' problem in a couple of minutes.

I spotted Teddy Markston near the bar with a vodka tonic in his hand, as usual. Stewart was right next to him, a cocky grin on his face like he had just found out his penis was two inches long instead of one.

Teddy's eyes lit up when he spotted me. "Ruth." He

stepped past Stewart to shake my hand enthusiastically. "I thought you weren't coming."

"I hadn't planned on it, but I wanted to chat with you, if you don't mind."

"Of course. I wanted to talk with you as well. I was going to call, but it's always better to talk about these things in person." He gestured to Stewart. "You two know each other, if I recall correctly."

We both nodded, but then Stewart gave me the stink eye when Teddy wasn't looking.

I glared right back, then included a few poisonous darts and a kick to the nuts.

"Please excuse us for a moment, Stewart." Teddy gestured to an open spot away from the attendees.

I stepped in that direction and stopped near the wall. "What's going on?"

"Well, you know how fast things can change in our industry." Teddy nervously glanced over at Stewart and then back to me, which wasn't a good sign. "I appreciate all the time, hard work, and research you put into your offer, but unfortunately we have to go in a different direction."

I glanced over at Stewart's grin that seemed to be wider, then got my eyes back on Teddy. "What changed? I thought we had a deal and were waiting to take care of the paperwork."

"Well, since the papers were never signed . . ." He cleared his throat. "Look, I'm not at liberty to get into the specifics of everything. I'm sure you understand that plans change. I'm sorry. Nothing personal. You know that I like your style. You've always been a straight-shooter with me and that means more than any business transaction, but sometimes it does come down to hard numbers, facts, and dollars."

I nodded. "And Stewart? He's been a straight-shooter?"

"Very much so. He opened my eyes to a few things that we overlooked, money we left on the table. Quite frankly, I was surprised that he knew so much about our company, but it was refreshing that he did his homework."

He didn't do any homework. He did your daughter.

I was tempted to mention to Teddy what the douchebag was up to, but I didn't think it was my place to do so. Plus, I didn't want to break the man's heart since he and his daughter were very close. I was sure I could solve this problem without him finding out about his daughter's indiscretions.

"Did you already sign a contract?" I held my breath as I waited for his answer.

He shook his head. "I'm going to review the offer tomorrow and—"

"Mr. Markston!" a man called out.

Teddy gestured to the man approaching us. "Sorry, but I need to talk with Pete Jackson. Don't leave without saying goodbye."

"I won't." I forced a smile and turned, walking toward Stewart Peters, ready to stick it to him.

He downed the rest of his beer, placed the empty bottle on the bar, and motioned to the bartender for another.

He turned to me, grinning. "No hard feelings?"

I shrugged. "*You* tell *me*. You're the one who's going to come out on the losing end when all is said and done."

He laughed. "Right . . . *That* is not going to happen."

"Just watch."

He took a step closer and stuck his chest out, like it was supposed to impress me. "You lost this round. Accept it. Now why don't you run along like a good little girl?"

Here we go.

I took a step toward him. "You're messing around with the wrong person."

He eyed my admittedly impressive cleavage, bit his lower lip, and ran his finger along my arm. "Messing around with you isn't a bad option at all. How much do you want this deal? Maybe we can work something out." He winked.

His words were like a verbal tongue depressor.

I held off the gag reflex, grabbed his finger, twisted it, and clenched my teeth. "Touch me again and I will kick your balls so hard you'll have to have them surgically removed from your stomach."

He winced and yanked his finger from my grip, shaking it. "No need to go all psycho on me. Is it that time of the month?"

Another one who went there.

"It's not PMS, it's *you*. Now, here's the deal, so listen up. *You* are going to tell Markston you're rescinding the offer."

He laughed. "That's not going to happen. It's already a done deal and there's nothing you can do about it."

"Really? Because he told me he hasn't even looked at the paperwork yet. And there is *plenty* I can do about it."

The bartender placed another beer in front of Stewart.

"Yeah? Like what?" He took a swig of his beer.

31

I shrugged. "I guess you'll find out soon enough. In the meantime, why don't you tell me how his daughter is doing? I hear you two are *very* chummy. Wait, that's odd, aren't you married?" I arched an eyebrow and stared at the wedding ring on his finger, waiting for my information to sink into his pea-sized brain.

Stewart glanced down at his wedding ring and then took a step back, like he had let out some gas and didn't want me to smell it.

I gave him my best pouty face. "You don't look well. Can I get you some water? Or if you're hungry, how about a serving of crow?"

"You're playing with fire."

I smirked. "I've got a big hose and I'm sorry that's not something you can relate to. Rescind the offer now or your life will implode before your eyes. Everyone will know who you really are. Markston. Your boss. Your wife. You have five minutes."

His nostrils flared. "You little—"

I held up my hand. "I changed my mind. You have *three* minutes. I think you'd better get moving." I winked. "Run along . . . like a good little boy."

He tapped his shoe on the floor several times, thinking. Then he slammed the rest of his beer, set the bottle on the bar, and muttered a few swear words before turning and walking toward Markston.

~

On the flight back to San Diego, I relaxed in my seat in

business class, feeling productive and content that everything in my world was back in order again. Teddy Markston had told me that our deal was back on, fewer than ten minutes after I gave Stewart the ultimatum. He even shook my hand and said he wouldn't change his mind again and would send the signed contract tomorrow after his lawyers went over it. I didn't bother asking what happened to the offer he had received from Stewart even though I was curious of the excuse he used to rescind it.

It didn't matter.

I wanted to get back home where I felt most comfortable.

Business travel did nothing for me. The only thing I enjoyed were the drinks on the flight and being able to use the wifi in business class to work and communicate with Dee while I was 35,000 feet in the air.

The announcement from the flight attendant about the descent let me know I was almost back home.

I took a deep breath and relaxed for the last part of the flight.

Fifteen minutes later, the plane pulled out of the descent and turned away from San Diego.

"What's going on?" I mumbled to myself, looking out the window, confused.

"I have no idea," the man next to me said.

The flight attendants were already seated, and there were no announcements, but I was starting to get worried when we circled around San Diego instead of landing.

I looked out the window again and didn't see any smoke or a missing wing. It didn't appear that we had any mechanical issues. And the flight was just as smooth as it was when we had left Phoenix. Maybe there was a lot of traffic on the ground at the airport and we had to delay the landing or wait for a gate to open up.

After the plane circled around San Diego for the third time and destroyed the possibility of an on-time arrival, I was sure my assumptions were wrong.

Something was going on.

The pilot confirmed it.

"Ladies and gentlemen, this is your captain speaking. A mechanical malfunction is preventing me from extending the landing gear, and that's why you probably noticed we've been circling the aircraft above San Diego. I was hoping the problem would work itself out, but that hasn't been the case. We'll need to make a belly landing, as we call it. We don't have any strong crosswinds and the visibility is very good. I don't anticipate any problems. I'm going to circle around one more time to burn off a little more fuel before we land. I'll keep you updated. Please remain seated and follow any and all instructions from the flight attendants."

I glanced around the cabin; the worried faces of the other passengers didn't help the uneasy feeling in my stomach.

The two flight attendants in front of me were avoiding eye contact with the passengers.

But what happened next is what really made me think this was serious: the female flight attendant looked toward the ceiling, close her eyes for a few seconds, and then made the sign of the cross.

Not good.

I turned to the guy next to me. "Please tell me a belly landing isn't what it sounds like."

He leaned closer and whispered. "It's *exactly* what it sounds like. I watched one happen live on television last year during the local news. He's going to land the plane without the wheels."

"Without the—"

"Like a baseball player who steals second base. He goes headfirst, you know? He slides on his chest and belly to the second base bag. The metal underside of our plane is the belly."

I blinked twice, not exactly sure I understood his baseball lingo. "Wait, are you telling me he's going to slide the actual belly of the plane against the cement until we come to a stop?"

"Yeah . . ." He nodded. "Pretty much."

My heart rate picked up. "What are the risks with the continuous friction of the metal against the tarmac at high speeds?"

"I remember this well because the news reporter was being very dramatic about it. The plane can disintegrate, flip over, or catch on fire. That's why he's burning fuel, to try to prevent an explosion."

I swallowed hard.

He was pretty much saying that there was a chance we all could die.

I stared out the window for a few seconds, then turned back to the man. "And why didn't the pilot mention *that* part?"

"He obviously doesn't want to freak everybody out. I'm

sure there are ten fire trucks already waiting down there for us."

"And why aren't *you* freaking out?"

"Believe me—I am." He gestured to his clothes. "It's all happening inside of me, mentally. Plus, I'm sweating like a pig underneath this suit."

I nodded, leaned back in my seat, and took a deep breath.

I didn't want to die.

Not like this.

I never even became managing partner of the firm.

All that work for nothing.

A few seconds later, I pulled my phone out of my purse and quickly sent a text to Dee and then another to my parents, telling them I loved them.

Dee responded almost immediately.

Dee: I love you too, but why are you randomly telling me this now? Is something wrong? Did you land yet?

I opted to not answer, knowing it would worry her.

I turned off my phone, stuck it back in my purse, and slid it underneath the seat in front of me.

Then I leaned back in my seat again, gripping the armrests, thinking of how helpless I felt at the moment. Unlike my business life where I was able to calculate risks and make strategic decisions to minimize the chances of a disaster, this scenario was completely out of my control.

My life was in the pilot's hands.

There was nothing I could do now.

I sat back and waited to find out if I was going to die.

CHAPTER FOUR

RUTH

After what had to be the longest descent in the history of aviation, I held my breath as the pilot finally touched down on the tarmac with the belly of the plane.

The scraping, rumbling, and vibration of the metal against the asphalt got more unbearable with every second that went by. It was almost too much for my ears and mind to handle as thoughts of what the passenger next to me had said earlier.

The plane can disintegrate, flip over, or catch on fire.

I kept my head down as the flight attendants continued to yell, "Brace!"

Their screaming was driving me insane.

What I needed was positive affirmations to block out their voices.

Everything is going to be fine. Nobody deserves to die this way. We're all going to be okay. We're going to walk away from this. I will never take life for granted again. I want to live. I promise to be a better person if I get through this. I promise to put my shopping cart back where it belongs after I unload the bags in my car at the grocery store.

We had been instructed earlier to stay in the crash position until told otherwise, but I couldn't help lifting my head and peeking out the window to see if the plane was catching on fire as we slid down the runway.

The sparks, smoke, and small flames that shot up from underneath the plane were too much for me to handle.

I dropped my head back down and closed my eyes.

We're going to live. We're going to live. We're going to live.

The plane finally came to a stop on the runway and the cabin erupted in cheers.

Why were they cheering?

We still needed to get out!

My heart was banging in my chest.

There was an announcement for us to stay in our seats. Soon, we would use the emergency chutes to slide out of the airplane one person at a time. Then we would take a shuttle bus to the special terminal that would have a holding area for us until we received further instructions.

I stared out my window at the fire and rescue crew surrounding the plane with their trucks and emergency vehicles. Shuttle buses were not that far behind them in the distance.

There was no way we could leave the plane yet since there was still smoke right outside the door. Something was still on fire, although I couldn't tell exactly what it was. One of the larger fire trucks was already spraying liquid underneath the plane and on the wings and engines.

Did I cheat death?

I turned to the man next to me after I heard sniffling.

His hands were covering his face, and he was shaking.

As if he knew I was watching him, he removed his hands from his face and wiped his eyes, shrugging. "Sorry." He sniffled again.

I shook my head. "Please . . . there's no need to apologize."

"It's just . . ." He pulled out his phone and showed me his screensaver, a wedding picture of a bride and groom kissing at the altar. He held it closer for me to see. "I got married three months ago. This was my first time away from my wife."

I smiled. "She's beautiful."

He sniffled again. "She's my soulmate and the thought of not seeing her again rips my heart in two."

I nodded. "Of course."

Dee was the only one in my life.

Yes, both of my parents were still alive and I loved them to death. I knew they loved me, but would they miss me? That may be a dumb question for a lot of people since parents are supposed to love their children no matter what, but it wasn't like I had made much of an effort to see them on a regular basis, even though they lived ten minutes from me.

And I had always been unlucky when it came to love.

Yes, I was picky as hell, but why shouldn't I be? If the men weren't good enough for me, they never got a second date. Dee said I was looking for the wrong type of man. She also said that I was too quick to judge and never gave the men a chance, but time was precious because of my demanding job.

Cheers and clapping filled the plane again when we were finally given clearance to evacuate.

"Ladies and gentleman, please take smaller items with you that are under your seat, but please do not open the overhead bins. All carryon items in the overhead bins will be delivered to you in the baggage claim area. Slide down the emergency chute one person at a time. Please stay calm. Wait for the person in front of you to clear the bottom of the chute before sliding down yourself."

After we slid out of the plane, all the passengers—including me—ran toward the shuttle buses, like a scene out of a movie where we thought the plane might explode.

Some passengers kissed the ground before getting on the shuttle bus, but I opted to look up into the blue sky and whisper, "Thank you."

The shuttle bus took us to a terminal close by where we were given bottles of water, cookies, and pretzels, although it didn't look like many people cared about eating.

We waited there for hours while airline employees offered emotional support to whomever needed it. Just about everyone was on their phones at one time or another, arranging for pickups, letting loved ones know they were okay, but I sat there staring, in shock.

My parents didn't even know I went out of town, so they couldn't have been worried about me, and Dee was probably too busy tackling my to-do list.

When they finally gave us the clearance to leave the secure area, everyone jumped to their feet and ran out as fast as they could to the baggage claim area where many friends and family members were waiting.

Hugs and kisses were exchanged.

Tears were shed.

News crews were on the scene, approaching passengers, trying to get interviews.

I stood there, looking around.

Everyone seemed to have someone, except for me.

I glanced around again and spotted an older woman standing by herself. If I had to guess, I would say she was around eighty years old. She stood there, head down, shoulders slumped, biting her fingernails as she waited for her bag to come out.

Like me, all alone.

She glanced over in my direction, locking eyes with me.

A hint of a smile formed on her face and I forced a smile back at her.

"You're going to end up like me if you continue on the same path," her eyes seemed to be saying. "Old and all alone."

I was losing my mind.

Why would I end up like her?

Because your life is pathetic and you have nobody.

I glanced around the baggage claim area again, suddenly

jealous of the couples who were holding hands, the families who were kissing and hugging, the smiles of relief and gratitude that they hadn't lost that special someone they loved.

I glanced back over to the older woman, and for some unknown reason I walked in her direction.

I stopped next to her and gestured to the baggage carousel. "Do you need help looking for your bag?"

"Thank you, that's very kind of you, but I'm fine." She pointed to a vintage avocado green suitcase that passed us and was circling back around. "That's my suitcase right there."

"Oh . . ." I watched it disappear out of sight around to the other side. "Do you want me to grab it when it comes back around again?"

I had never offered to grab anybody's bags because I was always in such a hurry. I admit that this was strange behavior on my part, and I wasn't quite sure why I wasn't in a hurry like I normally was.

The woman didn't seem to be in a hurry either.

She shook her head. "That's quite all right, dear. I'll grab it when I'm ready."

When she was ready? Ready for what? She wasn't doing anything at all. She was all alone, and she wasn't even on her phone.

What was she waiting for?

I nodded, not knowing what else to say to her, but for some reason still not feeling the urge to do anything else but stand next to her.

Was I that desperate for company?

Was this where the lonely people hung out in the airport?

Was I still trying to process what had happened to all of us on the plane?

Maybe the near-death experience had affected me somehow.

I saw my carryon come around and then watched it go right by.

What am I doing?

Something was off.

I felt odd.

I wasn't even sure why I approached the woman or why I was still standing next to her. I usually kept to myself when I was in public, to avoid distractions and to stay on schedule, unless someone was pissing me off, of course. Then, I always found time to tell them what was on my mind. That was different though because nobody should get away with being an idiot.

The woman turned to me. "Life is like a box of chocolates."

I smiled, thinking it was cute she was quoting something from *Forrest Gump*. I loved that movie because there were many hidden messages that I didn't get until the second and third time that I had watched it.

I decided to play along. "You never know what you're going to get."

She shrugged. "Or maybe we *do* know what we're going to get and that's why we keep doing the same thing over and over again."

I nodded. "Consistency is a good thing."

"Consistency is the quality of a stagnant mind."

"Is that also from *Forrest Gump?*" I didn't remember that quote from the movie.

She shook her head again. "John French Sloan."

I had never heard of John French Sloan, but I was curious about something. "So . . . why don't you want your suitcase?"

"Everyone grabs their suitcase the moment they see it, like their lives depended on it. If they can't get it the first time, they huff and puff, disappointed, as if it was the biggest inconvenience in the world to wait one more minute for it to come back around. I used to be like that, I admit. I wanted to see what would happen if I let my suitcase go around again, on purpose. I wanted to see how I would feel."

I had no idea what she was getting at or if the woman was crazy.

I thought about it for a few moments and finally asked, "And? How do you feel now that you had a chance to grab your suitcase, but didn't?"

She nodded. "It's quite liberating, I have to tell you. To see everyone rushing back and forth while I myself am *completely* relaxed, not having a care in the world. No hurries. No worries. I quite like it." She pointed to her suitcase coming by again on the baggage conveyor belt. "Here it comes again *and* there it goes! I think I'll let it go around a few more times. This is fun. Not a care in the world!"

The blank look on her face said otherwise.

I was tempted to ask her if the reason she thought she

didn't have a care in the world was because she had nobody in her life. Because it would seem to me that if you had people in your life that you cared about, you would have *many* cares in the world.

Was it possible that I would end up like this woman for keeping myself isolated from relationships? Alone and convinced that it was liberating to not care about anything?

I wanted to care about something.

I wanted to care about *some*one.

I hadn't been honest with myself or Dee about this, but it was the truth.

Which got me thinking about how many cares in the world I *did* actually have, if I wasn't including my career.

It didn't take long to figure it out.

I basically had three people in my life that I cared about: Dee, my mom, my dad.

It was my mom's fault that I didn't have many friends. I didn't want to end up like her, so I did the complete opposite of everything she had done in her life.

She got married. I didn't.

She had a child. No kids for me.

She gave up on her dreams. I gave up a social life and shot for the stars.

I still didn't know how she could've given up on all her dreams and desires when she was younger. She gave up everything for my dad, including a bright future as a talented artist. Why?

Because she got pregnant.

That wasn't an excuse.

Yes, the pregnancy was planned, and yes, I'm happy that

I was born, but why did she throw everything away when I came into the world?

Anyway, three people in my life was indeed pathetic.

I definitely needed to do something to get the numbers up.

After what had happened on the plane, I needed some perspective on what was most important in life. My career was still number one, but I was smart enough to be able to figure out a way to have a man at the same time. And I needed to quit avoiding my parents, just because I wasn't happy with the way their lives turned out.

I still enjoyed their company and loved them dearly.

"Take care," I said to the woman who didn't have a care in the world. Before she could answer I turned back, curious. "Actually, I have a question for you."

"What is it? I've got all the time in the world."

"Is there another reason why you're not in a hurry to get out of here?"

She thought about it. "You don't buy my excuse?"

I shook my head. "I'm afraid not."

She nodded again. "Okay, then . . . Most of my friends have moved away to a quieter life in another state. I rarely hear from them anymore or I've outlived them. I've outlived my husband *and* my daughter. Honestly, my home feels kind of lonely. While my home is my residence, it reminds me of a shell on the beach that nobody wants to turn over. It reminds me of how lonely I am when I'm there. Do you know what I mean?"

"I get it. I mean, my parents are still around, but I've never been married myself, don't have any kids, and I don't have many friends either. I can honestly say that my home feels lonely, too."

"But the difference is . . . you're young. You still have plenty of time to meet a man and make new friends."

"Everybody does—age doesn't matter."

I think the near-death experience definitely affected me because I would have never said that in the past. But I truly believed it now, and I wanted this woman to believe it, too.

For some reason, I didn't want her to give up on life, even though she was a complete stranger.

"It's never too late to make a new friend, and it's never too late for love," I added.

"If you say so," the woman said, clearly not convinced.

"I'm Ruth, by the way." I held out my hand.

She shook my hand. "I'm Judith, but my friends call me Judy."

"Well, looks like I need to call you Judy then, because *you* just made a new friend. See how easy that was?"

She smiled. "We just met in the airport. I would say you're more like a passerby or an acquaintance, not a friend."

"Looks like we need to change that, now don't we?"

"How are we going to do that?"

"How about joining me for a cup of tea tomorrow?"

Judy seemed to perk up at the idea. "Tea? The two of us?"

"Yeah, why not? We lonely people need to stick together and figure out a way to *unlonely* ourselves." I pulled a business card from my purse and handed it to her. "Give me a call or send me a text and we'll get together tomorrow afternoon for tea."

Judy stared at my business card. "Really?"

"Yes. And I won't take no for an answer. And one more thing." I walked over to the baggage carousel, pulled her suitcase off the conveyor belt, and lugged it over to her. "Here. Now, go home. It's time for both of us to get a life."

CHAPTER FIVE

RUTH

After Judy left, I stood by myself in the baggage claim area, looking around. All the passengers from my flight had gotten their bags and had left the airport. The only bag on the conveyor belt was mine, going around again.

"This is pathetic." I grabbed my carryon bag as it came around the carousel this time and followed the signs to ground transportation.

My Uber app said the nearest driver was seven minutes away, which normally wasn't bad, but suddenly I was in a hurry and didn't want to wait that long. Luckily, there wasn't a line for taxis.

I stepped up and grabbed the first one.

I gave the taxi driver the address of my parents' home, surprising myself, but surprising my mom even more after I walked in the front door.

It was the first time in over a decade that I had showed up to my parents' house unannounced.

"Sweetheart!" My mom moved toward me, then stopped, analyzing my eyes. "Something's wrong. What's wrong?"

Always a mom.

I hadn't seen her since last Christmas, I think, but she could still read me like a book.

"Nothing's wrong," I lied, hugging her and immediately beginning to sob.

"What's going on?" my dad said, coming into the entryway. "My baby is home! What a surprise. And what's all this crying for?"

My dad moved closer and wrapped his arms around me and my mom.

I missed this.

I missed them.

I finally pulled away from them and wiped my eyes. "I'm sorry."

My mom leaned to the side to get a better look at my face, then tucked some of my hair behind my ear. "Sorry for what, honey?"

"For not visiting more often."

My dad shook his head. "Don't be silly. We know you've been busy trying to become the ruler of the universe. And it looks like you're kicking some serious butt! I read about that last deal of yours in the business section. Half a billion dollars!"

"We're proud of you, honey." My mom rubbed my

back. "And of course, we understand." She pointed to my wrist. "What happened?"

I shook my head. "It's just a mild strain from the gym."

I couldn't believe the bike incident at the gym was only this morning.

This felt like the longest day of my life.

"Have you eaten?" my mom asked.

I nodded. "Sushi."

I would need to tell them about what happened at some point, but that could wait for now. They watched the news every night. They had probably heard about it, but they had no idea that I was on that plane.

I followed them into the kitchen and stopped in shock, not recognizing a thing. "You already remodeled?" I glanced around at the playful pastel colors throughout, the bay window over the sink, the huge kitchen island, the new quartz countertops, new stainless steel appliances, and the ceramic tile floor. "Wow. I love it. I thought you were going to remodel next year."

My dad laughed. "We told you that *last* year, so *next* year is actually *this* year. Well, technically six months ago." He winked. "Time flies, huh? Let me give you a tour."

The house was beautiful.

There was so much light from the two new skylights and a lovely array of colors, including the yellow kitchen. It was completely opposite of mine because my parents' place felt like it was full of life and love.

It was a home.

My house felt sterile and boring, like the waiting area at

my dentist's office. The only things missing were the year-old copies of *People* and *Better Homes & Gardens* magazines.

I'd designed it that way since I didn't want any distractions. Anything that caused feelings and emotions would take my focus off my work. That's what my boss had told me countless times, and I had drilled it into my brain, so I wouldn't forget it. Nothing was more important to me than my work and I needed my home office to be the most important room in my house if I wanted any chance of becoming managing partner.

I wondered if I had been making a mistake all these years because my parents' home gave me positive energy, and it felt wonderful. Yellow was my favorite color, but you wouldn't have found it anywhere in my house.

At least I was working on my backyard. That was a start.

After my dad showed me the rest of the house, we headed back to the kitchen.

I slid onto the bar stool on the other side of the kitchen island.

My mom moved closer, rubbing the top of my hand on the counter. "Why are you so emotional today? We got your text and were worried. We called twice and left messages both times, but never heard back from you."

"Oh—sorry. I didn't even know I had messages since my phone was off."

My dad blinked. "Your phone was off? Your phone is never off."

He had a good point.

I couldn't live without my phone. My head was

obviously in the clouds since I hadn't even once thought about my phone since I had gotten off the plane.

"I turned it off after I sent you the text, when we were landing. I came straight here in a taxi from the airport. I had to fly out of town on business."

"Did you fly into San Diego?"

I nodded, wondering how I was going to tell them that I thought I was going to die.

"Not sure if you saw it, but a plane had to land without the landing gear. Imagine that! The news had live coverage of the landing and it looked scary as hell."

"I was on that plane." My eyes burned. Soon I was sobbing like a baby again.

Why was I so weak today?

Because you almost died, you fool.

I couldn't remember the last time I had cried, and there I went again, crying for the second time in the same day.

It was a bit jolting and hard to comprehend because I considered myself the strongest woman I knew. I had trained myself not to get emotional, especially working in a field dominated by men, men who didn't treat me with respect and had called me just about every name in the book to try to intimidate me. I'd been called the A word, the B word, and the C word more times than I could count. I'd developed thick skin in the process, but that obviously didn't count when your life was on the line.

"You were on that plane?" My dad kissed me on the top of the head. "I can't imagine what it was like. Thank God nothing happened, and you all walked away."

I sniffled. "It was horrible. I had no idea if we were all

going to die or not. I had no idea if I was ever going to see you again. And then I felt guilty."

"Why would you feel guilty?"

"I haven't been visiting enough. I haven't been telling you how much I love you, and how much I appreciate everything that you've done for me."

"Now, now," my mom said. "We know how you feel. That's all that matters. I wish you would've told us you were going out of town. You used to always tell me when you were going out of town and would *always* send me a text after you landed, just to let me know you arrived safely."

I nodded. "I know, I know. And I promise I'll start doing it again." I glanced over to the family room and saw one of my favorite pictures of my parents, in front of Big Ben in London on their anniversary.

I froze and my heart banged against my ribs.

Did I forget my parents' fiftieth wedding anniversary this year? I did. I totally forgot. How could I? I am such a horrible, horrible person.

My dad pointed to my face. "Are you going to cry again?"

"I'm sorry."

"Now what are you sorry for?"

"I forgot your anniversary! I have to be the most horrible child in the world. You'd think at the age of forty-five that I would still have a decent memory, but obviously I have completely lost it."

My mom stepped toward me. "Honey, you didn't forget our anniversary this year."

I blinked. "I didn't?"

"No!" She pointed toward the family room and the new HD television mounted on the wall. "You sent us a beautiful card and gave us that TV as an anniversary gift, remember?"

I stared at the TV. "That was this year? I thought it was last year."

My mom rubbed my back. "Oh, honey. You need a vacation."

I sat there, deep in thought.

I felt weird again.

It was hard to explain, but it was like I had a sinking feeling deep inside of me telling me that there was something wrong with me.

And even weirder, once again, I wasn't in a hurry to go anywhere.

I was craving carbs.

"Do you have any . . . cookies?" I asked, knowing it would probably surprise my parents.

They both stared at me.

I never ate cookies.

I loved them, but I had always tried to avoid carbs since my body had this annoying habit of storing them in my thighs when I finished.

"Cookies?" my mom finally said. "Yeah, we always have cookies around here because of your dad's sweet tooth. In fact, I made a fresh batch yesterday." She walked over to the pantry and pulled out a plastic container, pulling the top off and showing them to me.

My dad pointed at me. "*Don't* eat them all."

My mom laughed. "We have a real live cookie

monster living in our house. Here." She stuck the container under my nose. "Chocolate chip. Your favorite when you were a little girl. Honey, pour Ruth a glass of milk."

My dad poured me a glass of milk and set it on the counter in front of me.

"Thank you." I grabbed three cookies from the container.

I slowly ate the first cookie while my parents watched me in silence, both with smiles on their faces. Then I ate the other two cookies, washing them down with milk.

"Are you sure you're okay, honey?" My mom frowned.

I must have looked ridiculous to them. Here I was, some hotshot corporate partner of a prestigious firm who didn't take crap from anyone, asking her parents for cookies and milk.

I felt needy.

I needed to suck it up.

I waved them off. "I'll be fine."

"What you went through was a traumatic experience, you know?" My mom rubbed my back. "Do you want to spend the night?"

I hadn't spent the night with my parents since my freshman year at college, over twenty-five years ago. I had been lonely in the dorms during my very first week of school and ended up calling my parents to see if I could go home for the weekend. Back then, even one week was a long time to go without seeing them. Now, a whole year could go by, even though I lived close to them.

My dad came around to my side of the kitchen island

and hopped on the stool next to me. "When was the last time you had a vacation or a day off?"

I laughed. "Two thousand and . . . hmmm, I can't remember."

"Life isn't just about work, you know."

"Don't start, Dad."

This is what he always said whenever I came over, one of the reasons why I probably didn't visit often. Well, that, and the fact that he asked my mom to give up her career when I was born.

They did look happy, though, I'd give them that much.

Still, I was sure my mom had regrets, giving up on her dreams like that.

I had made a promise to myself that I would never let a man dictate how my life should be.

Not even if that man was my dad.

He wrapped his arm around my mom. "You need love in your life. Love is what makes people feel whole."

"Stress goes down when your love goes up," my mom chipped in.

"It's only natural. And Lord knows you have too much stress in your life."

I couldn't argue with that.

"You need love!" My dad sounded like a cheerleader now.

I couldn't believe my parents were trying to sell me on love.

"You work too much, honey," my dad added. "You need to take a day off. Then you need to meet someone special."

I crossed my arms and smiled. "I agree."

My dad cocked his head to the side. "You do?"

I nodded.

"You're going to take a day off?"

"That's right."

"You."

I nodded again. "Yup. Me."

They both stared at me again, and I couldn't help but laugh out loud.

I was scaring myself, too.

For the first time in a very long time, I agreed with my dad.

I needed a day off.

And I did need someone in my life.

I didn't want to die alone.

I wanted to be married.

Like the man on the plane, I wanted to meet my soulmate.

All men couldn't be douchebags. I needed to figure out a better way to meet them instead of at work-related events and conferences.

Someone perfect had to be out there, just waiting for me.

And when I wanted something, I always got it.

Dee could help me.

I pulled my phone from my purse and turned it on. A few seconds later, it began buzzing like crazy, one text message after another after another kept coming through.

All the messages were from Dee.

Dee: Fine. You tell me you love me and then you don't answer back.

Dee: What's going on? Where are you?

Dee: Holy crap, I'm watching the news and that's your flight that's having the landing problems, isn't it?

Dee: Everything is going to be okay! Think positive.

Dee: I'm watching your plane about to touch down and I want to throw up!

Dee: Please land safely.

Dee: I love you, Ruth! Do you hear me? I love you!

Dee: Yay! The pilot did it!

Dee: I can see you on TV! You're sliding out of the plane! You're wearing your favorite blue blouse, the low-cut one that shows off your girls.

Dee: I can't wait to see you and give you a hug. Call me! I don't care how late it is, just call when you can.

Dee: It's been two hours. Why haven't you called me or replied to my text messages?

Dee: This is ridiculous. I'm going to have a coronary. Call me!

Dee: Okay, that's it. You didn't die on that plane, I know that for a fact, but I am going to kill you if I don't hear from you in the next hour.

I laughed out loud.

"What?" my mom asked.

"I had thirteen text messages from Dee. She was worried."

"Of course, she was worried. She's your best friend."

"She's my *only* friend."

I tapped in my response to Dee.

Ruth: I'm fine.

Dee: There she is!

Ruth: Sorry, I had my phone off.

Dee: You never turn off your phone. Are you drunk?

Ruth: I should be. Hey, I need your help.

Dee: Anything.

Ruth: I'm ready to meet the love of my life.

Dee: Good one!

Ruth: I'm not joking. Listen up, you're going to help me find my soulmate.

I waited for Dee to respond, but there was nothing from her. No moving dots like she was replying to my last message. Nothing.

Ruth: Hello? Are you there?

Dee: I'm here. It took me a while to pick myself up off the floor. Do you really want to meet your soulmate?

Ruth: Tomorrow we start the search. I'm taking the day off.

Dee: You have never taken a day off since I've known you. Are you sure you didn't hit your head during that landing?

Ruth: Not funny.

Dee: Did they spray the plane with hazardous materials to put out the fire, and you inhaled too much?

Ruth: Also not funny. You're going to help me put together a business plan to meet the right man. We'll spend all day on it if we have to.

Dee: A business plan to meet a man? Wow, you're seriously out of practice. No, no, no. If you're going to do this, you're going to do it right. I know exactly what we need to do, but you have to trust me.

Ruth: If I don't like your way, we're going to do it my way.

Dee: No.

Ruth: ???????

Dee: It's my way or the highway. Take it or leave it.

Ruth: You're pretty pushy for someone who works for me.

Dee: You taught me not to take crap.

Ruth: From men.

Dee: You've got bigger balls than most men.

Ruth: Flattery will get you everywhere. How early can you be at my house in the morning?

Dee: 7:30 if you have croissants. Otherwise, expect me between 8 and 8:30.

Ruth: No problem. See you at 7:30. Plan on spending the entire day at my house. Love you.

Dee: Love you, too.

I tucked my phone back in my purse and smiled. "Okay, I'm heading home. I'm going to open up a bottle of wine and take care of a few business things, since I won't be working tomorrow."

My dad arched an eyebrow. "You're really taking the day off tomorrow?"

I nodded. "I sure am. Who knows? I might even introduce you to the new man in my life."

"You met someone?"

"No. Not yet, but I'm going to make it a priority. And I also want to make a habit of seeing you more. In fact, let's get together soon and I'll make some pancakes, like I used to."

"Deal," my dad said. "I must say, I like the new you already."

"*Thank* you. Having a brush with death can change your perspective on a lot of things."

I hugged and kissed them both and caught an Uber back to my place.

After entering my house, I closed the door behind me, then turned around and screamed, dropping my bag on the tile floor.

A man stood there with a screwdriver in his hand.

It was the man from the gym.

The man I thought I'd never see again.

I dropped my purse and put up my fists. "You have five seconds to explain why you're in my house or you will feel my wrath."

I had taken countless self-defense classes and was trained for this exact scenario.

This guy was going down.

"Whoa, whoa, whoa!" He threw his arms up over his head like I was the police. "Sorry to scare you. You must be Ruth. I'm Nick Morris. You know, your landscape designer? Glad we finally get to meet in person."

I dropped my fists back down to my sides.

Another man approached and stopped next to Nick, smiling.

"And this is my partner, Brandon. We were working late to finish the doors today since Dee told us you were out of town. I assumed you weren't coming back until tomorrow." He studied me for a moment and then saw the brace on my wrist. "Wait a minute. You're the woman from the gym this morning."

"No way." Brandon pointed at me with his index finger. "You're wedgie girl?"

I wasn't ready to die on that plane, but now I was all for it.

CHAPTER SIX

NICK

I elbowed Brandon on the side of his arm and cleared my throat. "Why don't you go put this in my truck and wait there for me. I'll just be a minute." I handed the screwdriver to Brandon, his eyebrows squishing together, not understanding that I was trying to get rid of him.

Run, you fool! There's a chance you are going to be killed! Never call a woman wedgie girl!

On second thought, maybe I should have been the one hightailing it out of there since Ruth was smart enough to know that he had found out from me about her wedgie in the gym.

Brandon finally caught on, his eyes opening wider, his head nodding up and down like he was listening to his favorite song on the radio. "Right, right, right! I would *love* to put the screwdriver in your truck! I was hoping you would ask!"

Acting was not his forte, clearly. That was a ridiculous performance.

Thankfully, he snuck out the front door without another word or head bob.

Ruth stared at me, tapping her foot on the tile floor.

I was pretty sure I saw steam coming off the top of her head.

I jammed my hands in my pockets. "Anyway . . . welcome back. We made a lot of progress today."

Her face was flushed, her eyes beady, her jaw clenched so tight she looked like she'd just sucked on a lemon.

I swallowed hard. "I can go since I'm sure you've had a long day with the traveling."

Ruth crossed her arms. "Wedgie girl? Really?" She articulated so well, like she was an ESL teacher and I was hearing the words for the first time.

My first impression was not one that I would ever be proud of.

"Don't listen to him." I pointed to Ruth's brace. "How's your wrist?"

She hesitated. "Not that I want to talk about my wrist or anything associated with what caused my wrist to get this way, but it's not bad. Thank you for asking."

A thank you was a good sign, but I decided my best course of action would be to change the subject. "Would you like me to show you what I did today before I leave? I think you'll be quite pleased."

She hesitated. "Please do."

"Great." I made my way down the hallway, wondering if it was a mistake to turn my back on her. Fortunately, I made it to her office alive and stopped, waving her through. "After you."

"Actually, could you give me two minutes to change before you show me?" Ruth asked. "These shoes are killing me."

I was tempted to glance down and look but resisted. "Of course. Take your time."

"Thank you." Ruth disappeared down the hallway and returned a few minutes later, stepping inside the office. She had changed out of her business clothes and shoes and was now wearing a casual white summer dress and sandals.

"Much better." Ruth looked around the office and then glanced down at the oscillating fan on the floor.

I pointed to it. "The fan is there to speed up the drying process of some touchup paint that I applied around the doorframe. It's almost dry, and don't worry, it's non-toxic paint." I smiled proudly and gestured to the french doors. "I hope you like them."

Ruth stared at the doors, a blank look on her face.

Unfortunately, I couldn't get a good read on her at all.

Say something. Anything. Tell me you love them.

If she didn't like them, I would have made it right. I always made sure my clients were one hundred percent happy.

Finally, her shoulders and face relaxed. She took a few steps closer toward the doors, running her fingers along the smooth wood and nodding.

The oscillating fan rotated in her direction and—

Ruth screamed as the bottom of her dress flew up toward her head. She shoved the dress back down with both hands, holding it close to her body in the front and the back as she stepped away from the fan.

"Sorry about that." I lunged forward to yank the fan cord out of the wall, dropping it to the floor. I stood there, not sure what to say at that point. For fear of sticking my foot in my mouth, I did the safe thing and waited for her to say something.

She smoothed out her dress, obviously not having to worry that it was going to fly up again since the fan was no longer on.

Ruth turned to me slowly. "Did you see anything you weren't supposed to see?"

I blinked, surprised by the question. There are certain things that women ask men that are problematic and have to be dealt with properly and delicately.

Some are legitimate questions.

Some are tricks.

To this day, most men haven't figured out which is which. It's like playing a game of Russian Roulette when answering, only there is a bullet in every chamber.

No matter how you answered the question, you lost.

As I see it, the man always has three options:

1) Avoid answering the question and run far away, as fast as possible.

2) Answer the question honestly and hope that was actually what she wanted.

3) Lie.

Obviously, this scenario doesn't apply to all questions from females, but here is the shortlist of questions that have proven to be troublesome for men:

* Does this make me look fat?
* Do you think that woman over there is pretty?
* What are you thinking?
* Do you notice anything different about me?
* I know we had plans, but would you be mad if I went out with my girlfriends tonight?

I have to admit that the question, "Did you see anything you weren't supposed to see?" was a tricky one and I was on the fence as to which way to answer.

Ruth was glaring at me. I needed to quit stalling.

I opted to tell a lie. "I didn't see anything at all."

Except those gorgeous legs and cute pink-laced panties.

She stared at me.

This is another problem.

When they don't believe you.

Women are such wise creatures that they can get a man to admit to just about anything, even something they didn't do.

Ruth seemed to be an expert in this category because I was beginning to cave.

Oh, hell.

I decided to give in. "Okay, I saw something, but it happened so fast that I already forgot what I saw."

This is yet another problem guys have. Someone like me who is not used to lying will always look like he's lying when he gives it a shot. And that will lead to saying the most idiotic things.

Change the subject again. Now!

I gestured to the french doors. "What do you think?"

She nodded. "I like them. A lot."

Great! Now we were getting somewhere.

Ruth looked through the glass on the doors to the backyard.

I quickly flicked on the light switch, so she could see outside since it was already dark.

She took a step back and cocked her head to the side, glancing at the wall. "I'm pretty sure I didn't have a light switch there before."

Uh-oh.

Ruth wouldn't have a problem with me adding something that wasn't part of the original plan, would she? Most clients would be thrilled that I had thought of that extra detail at no charge. Dee had warned me that Ruth wanted things the way she wanted them, and the way things were agreed upon.

I hadn't asked her permission to install the new light switch.

Dee's words about Ruth bounced back and forth in my head.

She's a perfectionist. As long as you remember that and deliver what you promised, there won't be any problems at all.

Hopefully, I hadn't overstepped my boundaries here. Ruth was a workaholic. She should have been able to appreciate anything that would save her time, even if it was thirty seconds. That had to be my angle for the explanation.

I cleared my throat. "I installed it in case you ever wanted to turn on the backyard light from here in your office and enjoy the view outside while you're working at night. I linked this light switch to the other one next to your sliding glass door in the family room. Now, you can turn the backyard lights on and off from either room. Convenient *and* a time saver."

She did that staring thing again.

"No charge," I added, in case she was thinking that she had to pay extra since it wasn't part of the original plan. I had no plans on charging her for it anyway, but it was good to spell things out for my clients so there were no misunderstandings.

"I like it. Good call, but"—she shook her finger at me —"You will get paid for all the work you do here." She gestured to the doors. "May I?"

"Of course."

She opened both of the french doors, swinging them all the way open, and standing back to inspect what I had done. I had also installed the screen doors to keep the bugs out, but that wouldn't keep her from hearing and enjoying the crickets singing.

A wonderful ocean breeze entered the office.

"I needed this badly today."

I nodded. "Rough day?"

"You have no idea." She watched the blinking lights of a plane fly by and her face and shoulders tensed up again. "If you'll excuse me, I need to get some work done."

What was that all about?

Who knew what she had going on? It certainly wasn't my place to ask. The best thing to do was get out of her hair.

"Of course," I said. "I'll be back in the morning at eight to get started on the backyard, starting with installation of the fountain."

"Thank you. Oh . . . and I do hope that Brandon was able to get that screwdriver to your truck without any difficulties."

"I'm confident he succeeded." I grinned, appreciating her sarcasm. "Sometimes, I let him carry three or four at the same time."

The bottom of her mouth curved up just enough to let me know she wasn't mad about Brandon's wedgie comment.

Still, we needed to be careful.

Ruth seemed to be the type of woman who could snap at any moment.

CHAPTER SEVEN

RUTH

The first thing I did when I woke up the next morning after I washed my face and got dressed was walk over to the local bakery around the corner to grab my favorite croissants.

I told people—and myself multiple times every day— that I was trying to watch my carbs, but breakfast didn't count. Neither did lunch or dinner, for that matter.

In fact, the only time I felt guilty about eating carbs was when they were the in-between-meal snacks. Like those wonderful cookies I'd eaten at my parents' house last night.

Luckily, I had trained myself to block out the guilt of carb eating with each bite of the buttery, flaky pastry by drowning myself in work up to my eyeballs. Of course, that wasn't going to work today either, since I had decided to take the day off, so I splurged and got two croissants instead of my usual one. I also got two croissants for my petite freak of nature friend, Dee, since she ate whatever she wanted without putting on any weight.

I ate the first croissant on my walk back to the house.

After arriving back home, I pulled my chair closer to my desk with the second croissant and the first of four cups of coffee that I would be drinking that morning.

My only goal today was to officially start my search for the perfect man. Well, that, and meet my new airport friend, Judy, for a cup of tea in the afternoon.

Maybe it wouldn't hurt to check my business email before I got started.

My phone vibrated before I could open the email app.

Dee: You'd better not be working right now.

I don't know how she did that, but it always weirded me out. It was like the woman had ESP or a hidden camera in my office.

Ruth: Me? Come on! I have the day off!

Dee: I don't believe you. Be there in five minutes.

I sighed, knowing that I would feel too guilty checking my email now. I opened up the document that I had started working on last night with the list of qualities that I was looking for in a man.

If my potential suitor didn't match any of them, he had zero chance of being compatible with me. Yes, I was on a mission to meet a man so I wouldn't die alone, but I wasn't going to settle for an inferior specimen who did nothing but annoy or bore me.

I was sure Dee was going to love my list because I had spent a lot of time thinking about what I wanted in a man.

I needed a high-powered executive who understood how important my career was to me. Someone who understood business.

I took a sip of my coffee, analyzing the list of traits I was looking for.

1) Confident: I liked a man who walked into a room with his head held up high, a man who looked me in the eyes when he talked to me, and someone who knew what he wanted. Me. And since he wanted me so bad, I expected him to confidently grab me and kiss me until I was weak in the knees, and then make love to me on top of my desk, if that's what he desired.

I scooted my laptop to the side and knocked on my desk with my knuckles.

Oh, boy.

It was *very* hard.

Okay, maybe I needed to forget the part about making love on the desk. That didn't sound comfortable at all. Plus, I would probably kill him if he messed up my perfectly organized files.

Stick to the bed.

The bottom line was that as long as he was confident to know what I needed every day and knew my preferences, that should be good enough. If he were color-coordinated and could dress himself without my help, that would be a bonus.

I pulled my laptop closer and got back to my list.

2) Decisive: He should be able to make the right decision without my help. He should have the innate ability to know which night I preferred fish and which night I

preferred chicken and wouldn't bother asking if I had a preference because he'd know. He needed to be able to decide for himself, stick with his decision, and do it. Wishy-washy men need not apply.

3) Accountable: I wanted a man who would admit when he was wrong, because everyone knew that he would be the one who was wrong 99.99999999999 percent of the time. If he could get that through his thick, preferably non-bald head, we could have a bright future together.

4) Fiscally Responsible: He should know about finances, how to manage his money well, and have an impressive portfolio of growth stocks, treasury securities, municipal bonds, plus a high-yield savings account, and multiple real estate holdings. There was no way in hell I was going to be his sugar mama. He needed to hold his own. And speaking of holding his own, the man should know how to aim while going to the bathroom instead of splashing all over the place. Okay, this shouldn't go under fiscal responsibility, but I refused to have a separate trait for peeing and bathroom etiquette.

5) Open-minded: I wanted a man in my life who knew that my career was most important to me and wouldn't nag me because I was working late.

6) Not afraid to ask for directions: I knew this one would be hard to find in a man, but a woman could hope, right?

7) Kind and Generous: I wanted to meet a man who wouldn't hesitate to do things for others without expecting anything in return.

Someone like Nick Morris.

I'm not sure why my thoughts jumped to him, but he *was* kind enough to pick me up off the floor at the gym after I fell off the bike like an idiot. I eyed the light switch he had installed on the wall in front of me. I had to admit that was kind as well, and generous since he said he wasn't going to charge me for it.

Still, he's taken a huge risk by doing that without my permission.

Being a risk-taker was not a quality I wanted in a man and would never be on my list, even if he were as good-looking as Nick.

I scarfed down the rest of the second croissant and stood, knowing Dee would be arriving any second since it was 7:29 and she had never been late a day in her life.

At seven thirty on the nose, the doorbell rang.

"It's open!" I yelled and waited for her to come into the office. I was surprised as my eyes started to burn and I thought of what happened on the airplane again and the possibility of never seeing Dee again.

She entered the office without saying a word, set down a stack of folders and her laptop on my desk, and hugged me like it was her last chance to hug me in my life. "Thank God you're okay." She held me tight. "I don't know what I would've done without you."

Tears streamed down my face as I pushed her away to look her in the eyes. "You would have less stress in your life, we both know that for a fact."

She wiped her eyes and shook her head. "It wouldn't have been worth it. I would rather lose all my hair from stress and know that you were still my best friend and alive."

I hugged her again, sniffling. "You're probably the only woman I know who would look beautiful with a bald head. Well, you and Sinéad O'Connor. Okay, no more crying, we have work to do." I pulled away and pointed to the plate on the other end of the desk. "Your croissants, as requested."

"I only wanted one."

"I'm spoiling you today."

She smiled. "There is no reason for me to have a problem with that."

"Grab a cup of coffee. The pod is already in the machine. Just press start and you're good to go."

Dee set her laptop on my desk. "Thanks. Be back in a jiffy."

I wiped my eyes again and settled back behind the desk in my chair.

I forwarded my document to Dee, so she would have it when she came back from the kitchen with her cup of coffee.

A minute later, Dee returned to the office with her coffee, sat opposite me, and immediately took a bite of the first croissant. "Hmm. So good." She turned and glanced at the french doors. "Wow! Those are amazing. Why aren't they open?"

"I was about to open them to let in the fresh air, but you can do the honors, if you want."

"Of course." Dee stood and opened the doors all the way, admiring the view of the backyard before sitting back down. "Now, *that* is a great view of your roses."

I smiled, admiring them. "Sure is."

Grandma Meg had helped me plant the roses, so they would always have a special place in my heart. Every time I looked at them, I thought of her. She told me I needed to stop and smell them regularly. I admit I had been slacking in that department, but would make more of an effort to be outside when everything was finished.

There was so much space in my backyard that was not being utilized. It would still look spacious, even with the new fountain being installed.

Nick also incorporated feng shui in his backyard designs, the ancient Chinese art of using energy to harmonize individuals with their surrounding environment, bringing luck, health, and opportunity my way.

Dee squeezed my arm. "You must be excited."

I nodded, looking through the screen doors to the backyard. "I am." I pointed to the light switch. "Nick even installed a switch on this side so I can turn on the outside lights without having to go to the family room."

"What a great idea," Dee said with a mouthful of croissant. "That was a nice touch."

I nodded. "It wasn't part of the plan, but lucky for him I liked it. Hopefully, he won't take any other liberties or he's going to get it. Of course, who knows if Nick will ever take me seriously again after my impersonation of Marilyn Monroe last night."

Dee slapped the top of the desk with her hand. "What did you do? Did you add a fake mole above your lip and sing happy birthday to him in a sexy way?"

"It was much worse than that. I flashed him."

"I can't believe I missed it! Top or bottom? And were you drunk?"

"*Not* drunk. Honestly, I don't know how much he saw, but I was like Marilyn in the movie *The Seven Year Itch* in the scene on the subway grate. My dress flew up toward my head and it took everything I had to get it back down and cover myself until he could turn off the fan that was on the floor."

"I wish I could have been there. Were you also wearing a white halter dress?"

"I don't even own one."

"What about your undies?"

"Pink lace."

"I *love* those."

"Me, too."

"Well, maybe we should cancel the online dating. If you showed Nick your goods, he's going to be pursuing you like a maniac. I doubt any man can pass that up. Men stutter around your cleavage. They can't even form coherent sentences."

I laughed and pointed to her laptop. "Can we get on with this, please?"

"Of course, Marilyn." She rubbed her hands together. "Okay, let's find you your soulmate."

"I sent you something I worked on last night. Check your email."

"Okay." Dee opened up her laptop and clicked a few times. "Got it. Characteristics of the perfect man?" She looked up. "Okay, maybe I shouldn't read this since the perfect man doesn't exist."

I huffed. "Of course, he does."

"No. He. Doesn't. Now, there may be the perfect man for *you*, but that does not mean he's going to be perfect. Let's be honest here, he needs to have at least a few issues just to *consider* going out with you. Unless he's a masochist, of course."

I crossed my arms. "Did you forget that you're my friend? Give me back that second croissant."

Dee pulled it back out of my reach. "No. And I'm telling it like it is. You're not perfect, either. There's no such thing as a perfect man and you need to find someone that you like so much you're willing to put up with his flaws. Because he *will* have flaws. You do. I do. Everyone does."

"I disagree. I think you're perfect."

"Okay, you have a *really* good point there." Dee flipped her hair back proudly and smiled.

I laughed. "Are you going to open the document or not?"

She nodded. "I'm going to, but I have a feeling I'm not going to like it."

"Open it."

"Okay, okay . . ." She stared at her computer as she took a sip of her coffee. "Wow."

"What?"

She pointed to her computer. "I have to ask you—are you looking for a soulmate or a business partner? What kind of traits are these? Decisive? Fiscally responsible? Are you serious?"

"Of course, I'm serious. If he has decision-making capabilities and fiscal responsibility, that means he's got a good head on his shoulders. Should I put *smart* instead? Would that make you feel better? Or college educated?"

"The man of your dreams may not have gone to college. Have you even considered that?"

"Ha! Not even a little."

"Your soulmate could be a mechanic or a machine worker or a gardener or a—"

I held up my hand. "Stop right there! We are not on the same page."

Dee smirked. "We are not even on the same planet. Earth to Ruth, wake up. Hang on a second."

I heard the trash sound effect on her computer.

I pointed to her laptop. "You deleted my document, didn't you?"

"You bet I did. I told you we were doing this my way and the first rule is you are *not* allowed to choose his profession or the size of his portfolio. Size doesn't matter."

"What are we talking about here?"

"You *know* what I'm talking about." Dee sat forward in her chair. "I already opened an account in your name on this dating website and created your profile." She turned the laptop around so I could see. "Now these are realistic qualities that you want in a man."

"Oh, I can't wait to see this." I glanced at her list that she wrote for me on the website. "Honest, a sense of humor, compassionate, patient . . ." I laughed and glanced at Dee. "This is you! I should just marry you." I pushed the laptop back in her direction.

"Laugh all you want, but you already have thirty-three messages in your inbox since I posted your profile last night. Men want you."

"Let me see that." I pulled the laptop back in front of me and scrolled through the pictures of some of the men who had messaged me. "Hmmm. Some of these men are handsome, I'll give you that much, but we can get rid of this guy here. I'm not going out with a bus driver. Delete." I deleted his message and went to the next message. "This man is a fisherman? No way. He's going to smell when he comes home from work every single day. Delete." I deleted his message and scrolled to the next one. "A nuclear power reactor operator? Seriously? Who willingly, of sound mind, would want to do a job like that? No brain cells is not attractive. He's going to infect me with radiation and one of my eyeballs is going to fall out of its socket. *Not* attractive. Goodbye, radiation man." I deleted his message and pushed the computer back to Dee again. "Already, I can see your way is not going to work."

She sighed. "You're not even giving these guys a chance and they could be amazing people." She pointed to her screen. "And what about this guy? He's a hunk." She started to turn her laptop back in my direction.

I threw my hand up to stop her. "I'm not even going to look at his picture. Tell me what he does for a living."

"He's a plumber."

I made the sound of a gameshow buzzer. "I'm not going out with a plumber, regardless of how much he knows about pipes."

"Basically, I need to go through all these messages and ignore all blue-collar workers."

"Pretty much! Look, I agree that there's a chance that some of them may be decent people, okay? But I would like to meet someone who works in an office environment or is a business professional who understands business, at least. Then they will get what I'm trying to do with my career and support me. And I don't mean support me financially. I mean they will be on my team and root for me as I go for my dreams. A plumber is going to come home, show me his butt crack, and ask me what's for dinner."

Dee laughed. "He only shows his butt crack to his clients and *you* are being completely ridiculous."

I laughed. "Yes, I know I am, but I'm trying to get my point across. I will never have a thing for blue-collar workers!"

Nick appeared in the backyard on the other side of the screen doors, looking in our direction. "Good morning."

"Good morning!" I said with too much enthusiasm, trying to cover my gaff in case he heard me.

"Good morning," Dee said.

Nick continued toward the other side of the roses where the fountain was going to be installed today, dropping his tool bag on the ground.

I leaned in toward Dee and whispered. "Please tell me that landscaping is not a blue-collar job."

"Sorry, I just can't do that." She took a bite of her second croissant and shook her head.

Crap.

Now, I felt horrible.

Dee gestured toward the backyard. "And you would rule out a gorgeous man like Nick because of what he does for a living? The man is fine. Who cares what he does? Then again, Brandon is gorgeous too, and of course he is closer to my age. Brandon is H-O-T!"

Brandon appeared in the backyard on the other side of the screen doors, carrying a box and looking in our direction. "Good morning!" He was looking at Dee, not me.

"Good morning," Dee and I said at the same time.

Now it was Dee's turn to lean toward me with what I can only imagine is the same horrified look I had on my face a minute ago. "Please tell me he didn't hear that."

I smirked. "Sorry, I just can't do that."

Dee frowned. "Maybe he can't spell."

"I guarantee you he C-A-N."

"Who's more pathetic, you or me?"

"That's up for discussion."

Dee finished her croissant and gulped down the rest of her coffee. "Okay, anyway, I will go through and delete all blue-collar workers, even though I don't want to. That is still going to leave you with about twelve men, I think. And you're going on a date with one of them tonight."

"What?!" I leaned in again since Brandon and Nick both glanced toward the house after my outburst. "I have a date?"

"Seven thirty at Jake's."

Jake's was a tasty seafood restaurant right on the beach in Del Mar. It was one of my favorite places to eat, close enough for me to walk to. I couldn't believe she'd set me up on a blind date already.

"If I have a date with him, that means you've been talking to him and pretending you were me."

"Basically. I didn't want you to scare off the first potential man."

"How would I scare him off?"

"By opening your mouth." She laughed. "And I think you'll love what he does for a living."

I was scared, but I had to ask.

"What does he do?" I whispered.

She smiled. "He's a chef and a restaurateur."

"He owns the restaurant?"

Dee nodded. "He sure does! A businessman, plus he can cook for you anytime you want. What more could you ask for?"

Okay, I had to admit that sounded appealing.

He wasn't working in an office environment, but I think I could get used to the idea of going out with a chef. Chefs work hard, are career-driven, and only want to deliver the best product to their customers because their reputations are on the line with every single plate that leaves the kitchen. He could be another perfectionist, but I would be okay with that, because that meant he cared. And hopefully he would prepare me elaborate dishes since I rarely cooked.

"You're thinking too much," Dee said. "Stop that. You're going on the date."

"Okay—I'll go on the date, but it's not going to be dinner."

"Why not? Dinners are more romantic."

"That's *exactly* why I want to avoid it. I don't want something romantic with a man I've never met before and in this case, someone I've never talked to. Lunch dates have a ticking clock since people only have so much time before they need to get back to work. I have an out. If I don't like the guy, I have the perfect excuse to leave."

"That's not going into the date with a positive attitude. You need to *believe* that there is a chance he may be the one you've been searching for all your life."

"I'm being realistic. We both know that the odds are against him out of the chute because I'm not going to settle for just anyone. But, if the man gets past the first round, the first date, he will graduate to a dinner date and I may even wear a dress for that one! All first dates are lunch dates only. No exceptions and I won't budge on this."

She studied me for a moment and sighed. "You're already making this difficult and we haven't even started yet. And you're not going to wear a business suit on a first date, whether it's a lunch or dinner. *I* will not budge on this. Trust me, I know what I'm doing."

"Fine. Set up a lunch date. In fact, see if you can make it happen today since it's still early."

"It may be a possibility since it's his day off. I'll message him."

"That would work out great, then I could go straight to the tea with Judy afterwards. And we'll see how good you are at matchmaking. Don't get your hopes up, though."

"I want you to be happy and in love and have something in your life besides work and me. *Someone* special." She reached across the desk and squeezed my hand. "The only thing I have is hope for you."

"If you make me cry again, you're fired."

"Right . . ." She typed a few things on her computer and smiled. "Okay, I sent a message to try to change the date to lunch instead of dinner." She stood and walked toward the door. "I'll make myself another cup of coffee while we wait to see if Barney responds."

I took a sip of my coffee and almost spit it out. "Wait!"

Dee stopped and turned around.

"Barney?"

"Yeah, that's the chef's name."

"Barney? Really?"

Dee leaned against the doorframe. "What seems to be the problem?"

"Is the guy a hundred years old?"

"He's forty-two and I don't see an issue here."

"Well, I do. There's no way I will be able to look at a man named Barney with a straight face when all I'm thinking of is a purple dinosaur. Please tell me he has a nickname that I can use instead of Barney."

She took a step toward me and held up her index finger. "He does, actually! His friends call him B.J."

I winced. "That's even worse. Do you *know* what that stands for?"

"Barney Junior."

"Not even close. Wait, if he is Barney Junior that means there are two of them."

"Do you have a thing against BJs? Maybe I need to put that in your profile."

I pointed to the door. "Go get your coffee, would ya?"

Dee laughed. "Don't be quick to judge. Give him a chance."

Was I being too picky with the names? After what had happened to me on that plane, all I wanted was to meet a decent man. I knew that much. I also knew that if he did nothing for my mind and my libido, I was going to *adiós* him in a heartbeat.

CHAPTER EIGHT

RUTH

Barney and I were seated outside on the patio at Jake's restaurant under an umbrella just inches from the sand on Powerhouse Beach. We had already ordered lunch, the waiter had brought us our drinks, and we were ready to engage in a little getting-to-know-you conversation to see if we connected on some level.

It was a gorgeous day and the beach was alive with activity. There were sunbathers, surfers, people playing volleyball, and kids building sandcastles.

Even though I came into the date with a little trepidation, I had to admit that my attitude had changed when Barney walked into the restaurant, looking like a young Hugh Grant.

Okay, maybe I could figure out a way to like the name Barney after all, since the man was a chef, a restaurant owner, and looked good enough to eat. Hopefully, he had a personality to match because his good looks were only going to get him so far.

The waiter returned and placed an order of fried calamari on our table that we didn't order. "Compliments of the chef."

"Thank you." Barney winked at me. "It pays to know people. Then, if you work the system right, you butter them up, and ride the gravy train to free calamari on the house. Works like a charm every time."

If he thought a free appetizer was going to impress me, he was dreaming. Plus, he admitted that he kissed people's butts to get free things.

Don't be quick to judge. Give him a chance.

I would take Dee's advice for now, especially since my favorite item on the menu was being prepared at that very moment, but my bullshit detector had never failed me before and the meter already had some movement at the beginning stages of this date. Not good.

Trust your gut.

Barney snapped a photo of the dish and winked at me again. "It's for my Instagram page." He picked up a piece of the calamari and analyzed it, nodding his appreciation. "This restaurant is the cream of the crop and *this* macadamia panko crust is the greatest thing since sliced bread." He held it in the air between us like he was going to feed it to me.

It was a little bit presumptuous of him since we had just met, but oddly enough I found it romantic at the same time. I leaned forward to get my mouth closer, but then he pulled it back out of reach.

What the hell was that?

I was all for a little playful fun, but this was way too early in the dating game for such nonsense because I didn't even know the man yet. Plus, I was starving. I didn't like people teasing me with food when I was hungry. Did the man have a death wish?

Barney held the calamari close to his mouth like he was going to take a bite of it and then snapped a selfie with his phone.

Whatever.

I grabbed my own piece, dipped it in the sweet and sour sauce, and took a bite.

Divine.

Barney snapped another selfie with the beach behind him and then set his phone down on the table. "My job as chef and restaurateur brings home the bacon, but marketing plays a big part of my success. That's why you'll see me taking numerous photos. I make a lot of dough, but social media and my online presence are my bread and butter. It keeps me as busy as popcorn on a hot skillet. I've got two hundred thousand hungry followers who will eat up anything I dish out online, except for the rare few who are nuttier than a fruitcake. Like my last girlfriend, for example."

I waved off his comment. "Please, let's not talk about exes."

Barney ignored me. "She was prettier than a Georgia peach, but a few sandwiches short of a picnic. She didn't understand that social media was one of the most important things in my life and that I needed to stay on top of it or the competition would eat me alive. Social media is my meat and potatoes."

"I thought you said it was your bread and butter."

If he was going to bore me to death with food idioms, he should at least get them straight.

"Potato, potahto, tomato, tomahto. It's the same no matter how you slice it."

He continued to ramble on about his ex, without making eye contact with me, which was one of my biggest pet peeves.

I wonder if he realizes I'm still here. He must love the sound of his voice.

That made one of us.

I stuffed another piece of calamari in my mouth and wondered if this guy had any plans at all of shutting his pie hole.

I could play his food idiom game as well as he could.

He was still rambling on about leaving the toilet seat up or down.

Was he a natural-born talker?

Or was he going on and on because he was nervous?

No. He was another idiot.

This date was getting worse with every word that came out of his mouth and was going to end fast if he kept it up. They needed to hurry up and bring me my food.

Barney took a sip of his beer. "Anyway, I had another ex who I would compare to a spring salad with pine nuts and cranberries, you know what I mean?"

"I can't say that I—"

"She left a bitter taste in my mouth. I dropped her like a

hot potato because it was obvious that she wasn't going to cut the mustard. You know? Why would I want to hang out with someone who's boring?"

"Or me? Why would *I*?"

"Exactly! I always say that if you want to be with me, you get the whole enchilada. And if not, I am out the door like albacore."

The last time I checked, tuna live in the ocean and do not enter or exit through any door.

Thank God the waiter returned and placed our lunch orders on the table in front of us, grilled rainbow trout for Barney and Baja fish tacos for me.

The sooner I ate, the sooner I was out of there. Barney and I were not going to happen in this lifetime or any other lifetime. Normally, I would have already left by now, but I hated wasting food.

"Hey—how about a photo? Just the two of us?" Barney held up his phone.

"That's quite all right."

He would most likely have stuck it on social media and the last thing I wanted was there to be proof that I knew him or that the two of us ever went out on a date.

He shook his head. "No—I meant a picture of just the two of *us*." He gestured to his plate. "Me with my trout." He handed me the phone and held the plate of fish under his nose, a big smile on his face like he thought this was just as fun as Disneyland.

Already bored out of my mind with this doofus, I zoomed in on Barney's scalp to see if his hair was real. I snapped the picture, turned off his phone, and handed the phone back to him.

Barney glanced at his phone. "That's weird. My phone is dead."

"And your fish is cold. Eat." I wolfed down my first fish taco in four bites and then picked up the second one to begin work on it, while Barney ignored his trout and began talking about another ex as he tried powering his phone back up.

"She was as thin as an Italian breadstick and—"

I held up my hand. "Please . . . stop." I set the taco down, in desperate need of changing the subject to something more enlightening while I finished my food and got the hell out of there. "Tell me something about *you*. For instance, what's your specialty in the kitchen? I know you're a chef, but not much more than that."

"Ahhhh. My specialty?" Barney smiled proudly. "Bagels."

I waited for him to laugh and tell me he was joking, but the silence became awkward.

I jumped in to get some clarification. "Bagels? What do you mean?"

"I own a bagel shop. I told you I made a lot of dough. Ha!" He laughed and slapped the table, causing the trout on his plate to go airborne for a brief second.

I stared at him. "Bagels? Really?"

"Plain, asiago, blueberry, sesame, onion, garlic, egg, you get the idea. Over seventeen varieties and ten different spreads, everything homemade. With three locations to serve you." He grabbed his wallet, took out a business card, and handed it to me.

I read the big bright red letters printed on the front of the business card. "Barney's Bagels?"

He's not kidding.

"That's me! The king of bagels." He gestured to the card. "Turn it over!"

I flipped the business card over to the other side. It had a frequent bagel bingeing program with ten small boxes, one for each visit. All ten boxes had an X stamped in the middle of them.

"Ha! What do you think of that?" He pointed to the card. "Didn't I tell you that it pays to know people? You just got yourself a free bagel and you didn't even have to butter me up. Christmas came early. You're welcome!" He leaned back in his chair, proud.

I was about to leave, but then changed my mind, in the mood to call him on his bullshit. Men like Barney needed to be put in their place.

I pointed at him. "You said you were a chef."

"I *am* a chef! Well, okay, a *pastry* chef, but it's the same thing."

"Pastry chefs bake cakes and pies and *pastries,* hence the words *pastry* chef. A bagel is not a pastry. It's a bread. That makes you a baker."

"Do you have a problem with me being a chef?"

"No, I have a problem with you *saying* you're a chef when you're not. You purposely withheld information on your dating profile, which is essentially lying. You called yourself a chef because it sounds better than baker."

A couple of sips of my iced tea and I was out of there.

Barney stared at me, frowning. "I don't know if I'm imagining this or not, but I seem to be getting a very negative vibe at our table."

Nooooooo. You don't say.

"What gives?" He gestured to me and then back to himself. "I mean, we have so much in common and it's easy to talk to you."

I choked on my iced tea.

He shrugged. "What's your beef with me?"

I wiped my mouth and set down my napkin. "That! You're obsessed with relating everything you talk about to food."

"I'm a chef! Chefs talk about food!"

"But are you *really* a chef? Come on."

"A pastry chef *bakes*," he repeated. "Bagels are—"

"Baked. I know. And you said you were a restaurateur. Where did you get that from?"

"I *am* a restaurateur."

"You own a bagel shop, Barney. You even said so yourself."

"Potato, potahto—"

"I was very clear that I was looking for a man who was upfront with me. Did you even look at my dating profile? Or did you just look at the pictures?"

He considered the question, nodding. "Here's the thing . . . it's like when I go to the movies, I rarely watch the trailers ahead of time because it spoils the experience since they always show the best parts. It's the same thing with the online profiles. I would rather skip all the words and sentences and descriptions because people write whatever they want on those things anyway. I mean, I put long-term relationship, but I'm totally okay with something more casual, if you know what I mean."

"At least you're finally coming clean about your dishonesty. Is that what you want? Do you want *me*? Can you see us together?"

He leaned forward, like he thought I was asking seriously.

What a douchebag.

"Oh, yeah. I can picture us together. I'm *very* good at visualizing."

"Well then . . . picture me walking out of here without you and never seeing you again. Can you picture that?"

"I prefer not to."

"You don't have any other choice." I opened up my purse, pulled out a twenty-dollar bill and dropped it on the table. "Good luck, Barney." I stood and walked toward the door.

"You forgot your free bagel!" I heard him call out as I cut between a few tables and practically sprinted toward my car in the parking lot.

"What a waste of time," I mumbled to myself as I got in my car and put on the seatbelt.

I don't like wasting time.

When I wanted something, I made a plan.

I went for it.

And I always got it.

I wanted love, but I wasn't off to a good start.

Inside my car, I pulled my phone from my purse and

immediately sent Dee a text, tapping the letters of each word a little harder than I probably should have.

Ruth: We need to talk!

Dee: Why are you texting me when you should be getting to know Barney?

Ruth: He's a loser and that's all I need to know. I just left the restaurant.

Dee: Seriously? I don't think it was even thirty minutes.

Ruth: Twenty-five. On the bright side, I did get to enjoy one of my favorite meals, although I ate it a lot faster than I normally do. I hope I don't get gassy.

Dee: Feel free to take your time coming home, just in case.

Ruth: I'm not coming home until after my tea with Judy, so relax your nostrils. I'll see you this afternoon. We can regroup and plan my next move.

Dee: No planning will be necessary. You have 31 more men who sent you messages while you were gone. You need to choose the next victim. I mean, choose the next person to go out with. We can go through your choices when you get back. I'll be here and won't leave until you're satisfied. Trust me.

Ruth: I'll think about it. How are the guys doing out back? Making progress?

Dee: The fountain has been installed and they are adding the water. It's beautiful! It's been fun watching Nick and Brandon work with their shirts off. Those sweaty muscles glistening in the sun. Almost as hypnotizing as your cleavage.

Ruth: Are they really working with their shirts off?

Dee: I guess you'll find out when you get home, won't you?

Ruth: Tell me.

Dee: Nope. Gotta run. My boss doesn't like it when I'm messing around on my phone.

I laughed and stuffed my phone back in my purse.

Dee had a talent for distracting me when I needed it most. I suddenly didn't feel bad about the pathetic date with Barney. Maybe it was because I was thinking about two handsome, shirtless men working in my backyard.

Those sweaty muscles glistening in the sun.

Why did I have the urge to cut short my tea with Judy and get back home as soon as possible?

CHAPTER NINE

RUTH

Later that afternoon, I arrived back home and tossed my keys on the kitchen counter, glancing out the window to see the latest developments on the backyard project.

Okay, that wasn't true.

I have no shame.

I was looking to see if there were any shirtless men out back.

Unfortunately, there were not.

Nick and Brandon were laying a path of stepping-stones on the ground that led to the foundation where the gazebo would eventually go.

They were both fully clothed.

I shook my head, disappointed that Dee had lied, but at the same time feeling a little pathetic that I longed to see half-naked men from the comfort of my own home.

"Hey!" Dee said from behind. "How was the tea with Judy?"

I turned around and nodded. "Very nice. I like her, but she kind of bummed me out at the same time. Remember I told you that all her friends had moved away, and that she had outlived her husband and her daughter?"

"Yeah."

"Well, she sits at home most days and most nights, watching reruns of her favorite shows. She gets all her food delivered. She's not even motivated to leave the house anymore. And the last three times she did leave the house was to go to three memorials for friends who died. How sad is that?"

Dee nodded. "Very sad."

"I want to do something for her."

"Like what?"

I shrugged. "I haven't figured out that part yet. Maybe a weekly get-together over tea, unless I can think of something else. She seemed to enjoy the time with me and being out. I think the only thing stopping her from going out is that she has nobody in her life, really."

"Maybe she needs to find other ladies who get together regularly, like for a book club, a meetup, or something else. My mom is in a Bunco group and she has a blast. Well, I think they focus more on the food and drinks and chatting than the actual Bunco itself, but they do have fun."

"Not a bad idea at all."

"I know." Dee smiled and gestured to the backyard. "What do you think of the progress in the yard? I closed the sliding glass door, in case there was any dust."

"I haven't seen it yet." I flipped back around to take a look at the fountain. "Oh, wow."

It was already flowing with water. I knew what it was supposed to look like since I'd picked it out of a catalog, but it looked even more amazing in person. And Nick had already set up the two concrete benches I had picked out, one on each side of the fountain.

I opened up the sliding glass door to hear the water. "This I could get used to."

"How could you not have seen it when you came in? You were looking through the glass when I walked up behind you."

"Was I?" I could feel my face heating up, but I wasn't going to admit that I was gawking. "Hmmm. I'm not sure."

Dee leaned forward to get a look at my face and then laughed. "You were checking out the guys, weren't you?"

I turned to her, grabbing her arm and squeezing it. "It's all *your* fault. You put those thoughts of glistening muscles and all that in my head."

She was still laughing. "Yeah, but I didn't think you would believe me. Okay, I call dibs on Brandon. You get Nick."

"Shhhh! Keep it down or they'll hear you." I shook my head in disbelief. "And you're calling dibs on Brandon like he's the last piece of pie?"

"Piece of meat," Dee corrected. "Beef cake. And mama's hungry."

"Now, you're starting to sound like Barney."

She laughed. "I have no idea what that means, but let's take a closer look."

"No! I'm not going to go gawk at men."

"Of course not, you already did that." Dee slid open the screen door. "I'm talking about the fountain, silly." She grabbed me by the hand and dragged me outside.

"Oh . . . that. Right."

"Hey, guys!" Dee said, waving.

The guys turned around, both smiling and approaching us.

"The fountain looks amazing." Dee continued to pull, but I was able to yank my hand free, and did my best to look relaxed. "How about some lemonade? You haven't even taken a break in the last few hours and you must be thirsty."

"I'm good, but thank you," Nick said.

"I would love some," Brandon said. "Thank you."

Dee smiled. "Come inside and grab some while Nick shows Ruth the fountain."

I can't believe she is making a move on him right before my eyes!

I gave her a look to let her know I knew exactly what she was up to, but she gave me a knowing smile and led Brandon back to the house.

Nick pointed to the fountain. "What do you think?"

I nodded, sitting on the bench. "I love it. It's so peaceful."

He sat on the bench next to me. "Yeah, I've always had a thing for fountains since I was a kid, tossing coins in. You picked out a good one. And you have excellent feng shui and an auspicious backyard since I made sure the water is flowing toward the house."

"And what does that do again?"

"When the water flows toward the home it brings prosperity and abundance."

I smiled. "I like that."

"Plus, you get the additional health benefits of the fountain since the soothing sound increases your serotonin production, so you will feel happier, while helping relax the mind. Perfect for someone who needs to take a break from working too much."

I blinked. "Who told you I work too much?"

"Well . . ." He had a dazed look on his face, looking like he was caught off guard by the question. "I thought that was why you hired me. To create a zen garden, your own little spiritual retreat to disconnect from the stress of your job. Maybe I misunderstood Dee back in the planning stages. Are you saying you don't have stress?"

I scoffed. "No—I would never say that. I've got plenty."

"Well then, this will definitely help you, and we've only just started. We are going to kill your stress before *it* kills *you*."

"Dee says the same thing."

"Hey, I know all about stress."

I studied him for a moment. "You seem like the most relaxed man in the world."

He chuckled. "Now, maybe, but not before."

I looked up into the sky when I heard the sound of a plane flying overhead. My thoughts traveled back to my flight from hell and thoughts of dying.

I didn't like that feeling at all.

It was like I couldn't control my emotions.

Nick leaned closer. "Are you okay?"

I tried to shake the negative thoughts from my head. "Yeah. I'm fine." Maybe if I said it enough times it would be true.

"Close your eyes."

I turned to Nick. "What?"

"Close your eyes. I want to show you something."

"How am I going to see if my eyes are closed?"

Nick chuckled. "Believe me, you will. You will see *and* feel."

"That's okay. I'll pass. I should get back inside."

He crossed his arms, waiting. "Seriously?"

"Seriously." I stood to go back in and—

Nick stood as well. "Okay, let me show you something you can do to relax, then you can do it when I'm not here, if you're more comfortable with that. You're going to use your fountain for your health." He gestured around the yard. "I mean, that's why you have me doing all this, so you might as well learn how to let it benefit you, health-wise. Deal?"

I nodded. "Okay, make it quick."

"Great. Sit."

I huffed, letting him know I didn't appreciate being told what to do. "Are you always so pushy?"

"Only when I believe in something fiercely. Stress is like poison, but I'm going to help you."

"I still don't understand how you can know about stress when you work with plants and trees and fountains all day in the outdoors."

"I'll tell you one day *after* you try this exercise. I'll even close my eyes and show you how to do it."

Who was this man?

But the gauge on my bullshit meter wasn't even moving. I was confident he wanted to help me. Plus, his voice was deep and sexy as hell. I kind of wanted to hear him talk more. Still, I didn't feel comfortable closing my eyes in front of him since I barely knew the man.

I sat back down and crossed my arms.

"Great." He sat back down next to me. "Uncross your arms." He chuckled. "Yes, I'm being pushy, but crossing your arms is negative energy. You want to be open to positive energy."

I uncrossed my arms. "There. Happy?"

He nodded. "Not as happy as you'll be when you try this, but yes, I'm happy. Okay, here's what you're going to do when I'm not here. When you need to disconnect and clear the stress and negative energy out of your body, sit here in front of the fountain and close your eyes like this." He closed his eyes. "Then you'll take a few long, slow, deep breaths in and out while listening to the water."

Nick breathed in and out slowly, his shoulders and face completely relaxed.

I liked his confidence that he had no problem closing his eyes in front of me.

I was jealous of his eyelashes.

He was well-groomed, too. No unibrow or explosion of hair coming out of his nose and ears like some men I'd seen. He kept his hair on the shorter side, which accentuated his strong jawline. He had a small scar on the edge of his chin, but it didn't take away from his good looks.

I couldn't help wondering how he got the scar.

One thing was for sure—Nick was an attractive man.

"Now, I want you to *really* listen to the fountain," he said, his eyes still closed. "Don't identify what you hear as water. It's just a sound. Listen with curiosity, and then let the sound surround you, like it's giving you a hug."

Is he serious?

His eyes were still closed. His face was relaxed. Maybe he was.

"Any other sounds you notice around you, just let them be. The two doves on the fence, that motorcycle, the dog barking, my voice. Sounds will come and go, and that's okay. Let them be."

I eyed the two doves on the fence, not having noticed them until he had mentioned them.

"Focus on your breathing as you continue to listen to the water. Then, when you're ready, open your eyes and give thanks for your moment of *me*-time. And that's it! Promise me you'll try it some time."

I turned to him. "I'll promise if you tell me how you know about stress."

"In the interest of getting you to do this exercise, I'll tell you. But you first."

We sat there listening to the fountain for a few seconds longer.

"I had a near-death experience," I blurted out.

He pointed up to the sky with his index finger. "Involving an airplane, I presume?"

I nodded. "Yeah. Yesterday. The pilot had to do a belly landing without landing gear. We all thought we were going to die."

"That's horrible."

"It was. You probably saw it on the news."

Nick shook his head. "I don't watch the news."

I arched an eyebrow. "No?"

"Too much negativity and stress. I prefer reruns of *I Love Lucy*."

I whipped my head toward Nick. "I *love* that show. My favorite episode is the one where she's stomping grapes in Rome."

He grinned. "One of my favorites . . . I also like the episode where Lucy and Ethel are working at the chocolate factory and stuffing candy in their mouths and blouses."

I laughed. "That's a classic. Did you know Lucille Ball and Desi Arnaz had a summer home here in Del Mar? It's still there, right on the beach."

I nodded. "I *did* know that. And after they got divorced, Desi lived in the house full-time. But did *you* know that I designed the courtyard on their property?"

I stared at Nick, wondering if he was serious.

My bullshit detector was confused at the moment.

I could feel his sincerity, but I was pretty sure that would've been logistically impossible for him to have done any design work for them since they hadn't lived in that house in decades and Nick wasn't old.

There's only one way to find out. "How old are you?"

"Forty-five." Nick chuckled. "Okay—I know what you're thinking. I didn't say I designed the courtyard *while*

108

they were living there. The house has gone through a couple of owners and remodels since then."

"Now that makes sense."

"Anyway, just remember . . . you promised you would try this stress-buster exercise. And it sounds like you need it. Especially when you have thoughts of you-know-what." He pointed to the sky.

"Yeah . . . you can't imagine what it feels like to think you're going to die."

"Well, actually, I can imagine it very well, because it happened to me," Nick said.

I cocked my head to the side. "You thought you were going to die?"

"I almost *did* die. I guess you can say I was teetering on the edge of life and death." He pressed his hand to his heart. "My ticker wanted to stop ticking. Well, it actually did for a little bit."

"What happened?"

"Heart attack five years ago, at the age of forty."

"I didn't know people could have heart attacks at such a young age."

"It's not as common, but it can happen." He pointed to the scar on his chin. "I got *this* from hitting the floor after the heart attack." He patted his chest. "I have another scar here from the surgery. So, you were wondering how I know about stress, well, stress almost killed me. I'm okay now, and still have some work to do, but I don't want to see anyone go through what I went through. Not even my worst enemy."

The poor guy.

Without thinking, I instinctively placed my hand on top of his hand and patted it. "Wow. I'm so sorry, but I'm glad you're okay."

Nick glanced down at my hand on top of his, and I quickly pulled it away, and stood.

What am I doing?

Dee came back out of the house, Brandon trailing behind her, both with lemonade.

I pointed toward the house. "I should get back to work."

"Oh no, you don't," Dee said. "You have the day off and there will be *no* talk of work from you."

I flared my nostrils at her. "When I say *work*, I don't mean *work*, work. I mean *we* have things to do. Remember?"

Good save on my part.

"Right! We need to get back to finding you a man!"

She didn't just say that. Someone please tell me I'm hallucinating.

Dee must have been loopy from Brandon's presence because usually she was smarter than that. That was no excuse, but I would wait until we got inside to kill her with my bare hands.

Nick glanced back and forth between me and Dee.

I smiled at him. "A man to do my hair is what she means. I prefer male hair stylists. Girl stuff, you know?"

He nodded but didn't say anything.

I gestured to the house again. "Dee? I need your help." I turned to Nick. "If you change your mind about lemonade or anything else to drink, come inside and help yourself. No need to ask."

Brandon held up his cup of lemonade. "So tasty. Thanks, Dee."

Dee gave him a little bow of the head. "Of course. Let me know if you want more." Without another word, she followed me back inside the house to my office.

I sat in my chair and swiveled around to face her. "What was that out there?"

She placed her lemonade on my desk and took a seat. "Just a little slip of the tongue. Don't worry, he didn't catch on. And anyway, what's the big deal? We're on a mission to find you a man. It wasn't like I was lying."

"Yes, but the whole world doesn't need to know about my private life. I don't want Nick to think I'm desperate or something, and that I need your help to find a man."

Dee arched an eyebrow. "Since when have you *ever* cared what a man thought of you or of something you did?"

I stared at Dee, not knowing how to respond.

It was true.

When was the last time?

I usually didn't give a fig what they thought.

Why would I care what Nick thought?

Dee pointed at me. "You're not answering."

"I don't know why I care, but I do."

"I know why." She smiled. "You like him."

I huffed. "Please . . ."

"He's a nice guy."

"Of course, he's a nice guy. I never said he wasn't."

"And attractive."

111

"I see what you're doing here. Look—just because your girlie parts twitch when Brandon is around doesn't mean the same will happen with me and Nick."

"My girlie parts don't twitch. They do a happy dance and flutter like a—"

"Can we please move on? Otherwise, I'm going to open my email and start working."

Dee shook her finger at me. "No work." She opened her laptop. "Let's get back to your love life."

"Or lack thereof."

"Not for long, if I have anything to do with it. Okay, Barney was a no-go."

"Barney was a *hell* no. All the guy did was talk about himself the entire time. And he wasn't even a chef. He makes *bagels* for a living."

Dee nodded. "A baker. Nothing wrong with that."

"Nothing wrong with that if you tell me you're a baker. Plus, he was looking for a hookup and that wasn't going to happen. I would like to meet a man who doesn't lie, is that too much to ask for?"

"You have nothing to worry about since I already have you lined up for another lunch date tomorrow."

I crossed my arms. "I thought we decided that you weren't going to pretend to be me?"

"Not true. You expressed your concern and disapproval, but you never actually told me not to do it again."

I shook my head. "You're taking advantage of me because you're irreplaceable. It's blackmail, actually. How do you feel about yourself?"

She smirked. "I feel fantastic, thanks for asking."

112

I laughed and pointed to her laptop. "Tell me what he does for a living."

"He's director of sales for a solar company."

I nodded. "Okay, okay. Not bad at all."

A director of sales had a lot of responsibility, no matter the company. He would have to oversee and manage all aspects of the sales department, hire, train, and inspire a team of salespeople, maintain strong focus on overall customer satisfaction, plus collaborate with other high-level members of the leadership team. There was no doubt in my mind that a corporate man at this level was smart and would be able to appreciate and understand how important my career was to me. Now, hopefully I found him attractive.

"Photo, please."

"Feast your eyes on this." Dee flipped her laptop around to show me. "Ta-da!"

Surprisingly, he was another good-looking man.

Even more so than Barney.

"Not bad at all, I have to admit," I said. "Okay, what's the plan since you're the deceptive one and arranged everything?"

"You're meeting him in front of the amphitheater at Amici Park."

"In Little Italy?"

Dee nodded.

"Please don't tell me this is a picnic."

"No, not at all. He wants to show you something at the park, that's all. He said it would take a minute and then you'll walk around the corner for a bite to eat. He likes casual places to eat. That works well for you since you can get your food fast and make an escape, if you need to. Although I *do* want you to go into this date with an open mind. Visualize him being a match for you. Visualize you both having a lot in common and that it leads to a second date."

"Well, he does have a solid high-level job and he's handsome. Plus, he scores points for choosing Italian food. We are off to a very good start. I hope he picks a good restaurant."

"Have you ever eaten at a bad place in Little Italy?"

"Good point, even though I prefer to pick the restaurant. Wait, what's his name? If it's anything like Barney you can cancel the date immediately."

Dee hesitated. "His name is Elmer."

"Cancel the date."

"Mortimer."

"Cancel."

"Wilbur."

"Cancel."

Dee laughed. "I'm kidding. His name is Max."

I studied her for a moment. "Is it *really* Max?"

"Yup."

"I like Max, even though I know five dogs with the same name. As long as he isn't Mad Max. Were there any signs of him being unhinged, psychopathic, or someone who launched a personal vendetta against a gang in Australia because they killed his wife and only son?"

Dee laughed. "No, no, and no, mate. My first impression of him was a good one. And you'll be happy to know he's the opposite of Barney when it comes to talking. He doesn't dominate the conversation. He's direct and to the point."

"I like that." I let out a sigh of relief.

Oddly enough, I had a better feeling about this date than the one with Mr. Bagel Man. But everything would be null and void if he had the personality of a turnip.

CHAPTER TEN

RUTH

My first day off in years had come and gone and I was back to work early the next day in my home office, so early the sun had barely begun to peek into my backyard. I felt energetic and confident I was going to have a productive day.

I took a sip of my first cup of coffee and eyed my to-do list for the day, which included a conference call with my boss and a video conference with Dee since she wasn't working from my place today.

There was too much to do, which was why I never took a day off in the past, but I wasn't going to obsess about that now. I had a plan to meet a man and I was sticking to it. I just hoped things would get better after that disaster with Barney.

I decided the best thing to do would be to break up my

day into two parts. Things to do before my lunch with Max, and the things I would do after lunch. As long as there weren't any major interruptions or surprises, I was confident I could get everything done.

My phone vibrated and I checked the caller ID.

It was my boss, Gary Stansfeld, managing partner at Stansfeld Investments, and the man I would be replacing in the not-too-distant future.

I answered the call. "Good morning, Gary."

"Good morning, Ruth. Congrats again on the Amsterion deal."

"Thank you."

"You're having a banner year. Do you think you have one or two more deals in you this year?"

"I'm working on two at the moment and should have an update in the next couple of days."

"Great. Because I'm ready to retire, although you didn't hear that from me." Gary chuckled. "Anyway, we'll need to go over the details on restructuring Amsterion. We need to have everything in place and ready to go."

"Of course. Sorry, but did I get the time wrong today? I thought we were going to talk at two."

"There's been a change in the plans and that's why I'm calling now. I need you to come down to the office today."

"Is something wrong?"

Usually I only had to go into the office one day a week at the most and the last time Gary had arranged an impromptu meeting, there had been layoffs. I was confident my job was not in jeopardy, but this was unusual.

"Nothing's wrong," Gary said. "The board thought it would be a good idea for our most senior partners to be at the meeting. I agreed. You, Mason, and Steve will have a chance to see how we do things, plus provide input on how the organization is running. It will be a great way for you to get your feet wet."

Okay, well that was different. I loved working from home, but being able to attend my first board meeting was exciting and something I had been looking forward to.

"I'll be there. What time?"

"Nine."

"Sounds good. See you then."

"Oh, and uh, try to take it easy on Mason today. I know you two butt heads when you're in the office, but keep in mind he still has a huge stake in the company. You'll need to keep the peace until you're at the helm."

"Of course. Don't worry about a thing. See you at nine."

I disconnected the call and set my phone on the desk.

It was true Mason and I butted heads a lot, which I didn't like since we were working for the same company. It would definitely make it awkward once I took over, but that would be his problem, not mine. When I took over, the men would have to check their egos at the door.

We play as a team or you're out, it was as simple as that.

The thing I disliked the most about Mason was that he was friends with my archenemy, Stewart Peters. I certainly hoped he would never leak confidential company information. It wasn't something I needed to worry about, but it had crossed my mind. Hopefully, he was not that stupid.

I glanced at my to-do list, knowing I would probably be up until at least midnight with this hiccup in my plans of having to go to the office and attend the board meeting. I would have to rearrange some things, but I would keep the lunch in place since I had to eat, and the office wasn't far from Little Italy. I had never turned down an Italian meal in my life, so the thought of canceling the lunch hadn't even entered my mind for a second.

I love my carbs.

The first thing I had to do was let Dee know about the change of plans.

As usual, she was one step ahead of me when my phone vibrated with a text from her.

Dee: I canceled our video conference since you're coming to the board meeting.

Ruth: Good morning to you, too. Let's meet after lunch.

Dee: Got it. Speaking of which, I would totally be your best friend forever if you brought me some lasagna and garlic bread.

Ruth: You're already my best friend, so what else do you have to offer as a bribe?

Dee: I will CONTINUE to be your best friend.

Ruth: Sounds like you're blackmailing me again. When will the madness end?

Dee: When I see lasagna on my desk. Oh, and don't forget the garlic bread and parmesan cheese.

I laughed, but then stopped when my phone vibrated again with a call from Nick. He was supposed to be at my place any moment to start work. Hopefully, there wasn't a problem.

I answered the call. "Hello?"

"Good morning, Ruth. It's Nick."

"Good morning. What's going on?"

"Well, I'm kind of in a predicament and I'm trying to figure out what to do."

"Okay . . ." I said. "What seems to be the problem?"

"My neighbor's dog got loose and I'm not able to get a hold of them. I have her with me and I'm not sure what to do at this point."

"Can't you drop her off at one of those doggy daycare places?"

"I tried. The place said I needed to have proof that the dog was up to date on all shots and that they needed to do a temperament test, to make sure it got along with the other dogs. I don't have access to any of the dog's health records so it's not even an option."

Just great.

It was my second hiccup of the day. The last thing I wanted was my backyard project to get behind schedule or me thinking about it when I needed to focus on a hundred other things. Fortunately, I was a problem-solver and this wasn't rocket science.

"How well-behaved is she?"

"She's been professionally trained," Nick answered. "Very obedient. She's a good girl."

"If you keep her outside and you promise she won't tear my place apart, you can bring her with you to work."

"That's perfect! She can relax in the shade under your patio cover. Are you sure you don't mind?"

"If it's going to keep the job on schedule, I don't mind. As long as she doesn't poop and pee all over the place, I'm okay with it."

"Great! I'll make sure to take her for a walk and pick up after her. Thanks so much. I'll see you soon."

Thirty seconds later, my doorbell rang.

Swinging the front door open, I froze.

It was Nick.

With the dog.

"Seriously?" I pointed to the beautiful golden retriever with the tail banging against the wall.

Nick shrugged. "Sorry—I didn't know what else to do, so I called you from your driveway."

I crossed my arms. "Quite presumptuous of you to think I was going to offer for you to bring the dog with you."

"Well, actually, I was going to ask you, but you offered first."

"And what if I had said no?"

He grinned. "You're *way* too kind to say no."

"You obviously don't know me very well."

The dog lunged forward and began to lick my hand.

I loved dogs but have never had one because I hate hair on my work clothes.

"This is karma."

I snorted. "Right. Karma that I have a dog at my house. Not even close."

"No. Her *name* is Karma."

"Oh . . ." I scratched the dog on the top of the head. "Hello, Karma. Are you a smart girl?" I leaned down and held my hand out. "Shake."

Karma lifted her paw toward me.

I grabbed it and shook it, smiling. "You *are* a smart girl." I stood back up and turned to Nick. "I need to head out and will be gone most of the day. I have an unscheduled meeting at the office. I need you to assure me that she won't tear up the place."

"I promise," Nick said. "And thanks again."

I headed to the bedroom to change into my work clothes. One of the advantages of working from home was that I could work in my yoga pants or shorts or whatever I wanted. That would change once I became managing partner since I would be expected to be there regularly, but that was something I would have to deal with and adjust to.

A minute later, I heard Karma barking in the backyard.

Who knew what Nick and Karma were up to back there?

Maybe Karma saw one of the neighborhood rabbits and was freaking out.

I slipped out of my yoga pants and pulled my work clothes from the closet to change, choosing one of my favorite outfits.

Karma continued to bark, which was starting to annoy me. Nick said she was trained, but it sure didn't seem like it.

Why was she barking so much?

"No, Karma!" Nick yelled. "Stop that!"

"What is going on?" I mumbled to myself.

I looked out the bedroom window and screamed in horror.

Karma was tearing up my precious rose garden.

I banged on the window. "Stop that!"

I ran from the bedroom, down the hallway, and through the kitchen to the backyard.

I yanked the sliding glass door and stepped outside, marching toward the dog who had dug up part of my rose garden. The roots were exposed on two of the bushes.

My precious babies.

Both Nick and Karma stood there, frozen, both staring at me. It would be hard to determine which of them had a guiltier face at the moment.

It didn't matter.

This was all Nick's fault.

"I didn't see anything I wasn't supposed to see!" Nick blurted out, suddenly breaking eye contact with me and looking away.

I shook my head, confused. "What are you talking about?"

He pointed toward me, but still avoided looking in my direction. "You're not wearing any pants."

I jerked my head down, and to my horror, I was standing there in my panties.

Shocked, I screamed, causing Karma to bark again.

"Don't move, either of you!" I ran inside the house, back to the bedroom, and sure enough my business clothes were still on the bed where I had left them earlier.

"I flashed Nick again," I mumbled to myself, shaking my head in disbelief. "I can't believe this."

I slipped into my work clothes and went to the bathroom to double-check that I was fully clothed before heading back out to the backyard.

Nick and Karma hadn't budged an inch.

"Can I look now?" Nick asked.

"Yes. You can look now," I said. "I can't believe what you've done."

Karma lay down, putting her head on top of her paws.

"I'm sorry," Nick offered. "I ran out to the truck to get a few things. I wasn't even gone two minutes and she did this. I have no idea why."

I took a few steps and surveyed the damage. "You ruined my rose garden."

"No, no, no." Nick stepped toward me. "They're not ruined. You had some issues with these roses before Karma did this, if we're being honest here. They were already in bad shape."

"Excuse me? You tear my roses apart and then insult me and tell me that it didn't matter because I don't know how to take care of them?"

"Not at all. That came out wrong. Look, don't worry about this. I'll take care of it. You won't even know it happened. I'm going to fix it."

"No. You've done enough. I don't have time to deal with this crap right now. Just leave it be."

"Ruth, look, Brandon will be here any minute and we can just—"

I held up my hand. "Please. Focus on what I paid you to do, can you do that for me? I'll deal with this mess when I get home later."

I turned and headed back inside the house, not waiting for Nick to answer.

This wasn't how I envisioned the day starting out, but I wasn't going to let it bend me out of shape. I had encountered far worse disasters in my career.

This was far from over, though.

CHAPTER ELEVEN

RUTH

I had waited ten years to sit in on a company board meeting and now that I had finally done it, I could sum it up in one word.

Boring.

The two hours spent there could have easily been reduced to thirty or forty minutes. Sure, we talked about pending agendas left over from the previous meeting. We even discussed how the organization was running. But most of the time the men talked about their latest sports outing out at Torrey Pines golf course, a new car they had heard about or bought, or how much money they made in the stock market this week.

Boring, boring, boring.

I wanted to talk more about business and how to help the company grow.

I had almost fallen asleep until Mason glanced over at me.

He was grinning, like he wanted to say something.

I decided to call him on it. "Yes?"

Mason shrugged. "The men have been dominating the conversation. Is there anything you would like to discuss? I'm sure Gary wouldn't mind."

"Go for it," Gary said.

Mason smiled.

My bullshit meter was pegging in the red.

I wasn't going to fall into his trap.

Lucky for him, I wasn't in the mood to butt heads. "I'm good, thank you."

"No, really." He leaned forward on the table and folded his hands like he was eager to listen to what I had to say. "Feel free to talk about high heels or cupcakes or whatever floats your boat."

A couple of the guys chuckled.

"You don't ever learn, Mason. Ruth has got your number. This won't end well." Gary shook his head *no*, warning me to not take the bait.

I sat up in my chair contemplating my next move.

I respect people who treat me with respect.

Mason didn't fit in that category.

Even when someone and I had different opinions, I would always try to see things from their point of view if they were passionate and sincere about something.

Mason was just being a dick, as usual.

Keep in mind he still has a huge stake in the company and you will need to keep the peace until you're at the helm.

I'm grateful Gary reminded me of this because I was so close to telling Mason that I was impressed that he was flexible enough to have his foot in his mouth and his head up his butt at the same time.

I smiled, knowing the day would come when he would get what he deserved. "I'm good, thanks so much for asking."

Mason huffed and crossed his arms, looking disappointed that I hadn't taken the bait.

Gary winked at me, looking content that I hadn't played Mason's game.

Sometimes it's better to take the high road.

Not always, though.

In fact . . .

"Oh . . ." I couldn't help changing my mind. "I noticed you were the only one here who didn't talk about your round of golf at Torrey Pines. Why is that?"

A few of the guys laughed and one of them said, "That's because he shot a one-oh-two"

"I don't wanna talk about it," Mason said. "Are we done here?"

I wasn't ready to let this one go. "That's a par seventy-two course, am I right, fellas?"

"Sure as hell is," said Steve, one of the other partners.

"That would mean Mason shot thirty over par. Well, I guess you were just having an off day."

Mason glared at me. "Hey, I was driving the ball well off the tee, but just couldn't get a handle on the putting once I got it on the green."

I nodded. "Maybe you just need to grip it and stroke it harder. You know what that's like." I winked.

Laughter filled the conference room as Gary cleared his throat and stood. "Meeting adjourned. Remember, we need to come up with some fresh ideas for new revenue streams. I'll be sending an email to the entire staff later today." He walked around the large conference room table and leaned close to my ear. "I thought you said you were going to take it easy on him."

"Believe me, I *was* taking it easy."

After stopping by Dee's desk to say hello, I was out the door, driving the ten minutes to Little Italy. I parked on State Street near Amici Park, and walked past the bocce ball courts to the amphitheater inside.

Max was leaning casually against a pillar in his black pin-stripe suit, his hair slicked back, grinning, like he was posing for some men's magazine.

He was trying way too hard, but I wouldn't hold that against him.

Max pushed himself off the pillar and closed the distance between us. "Ruth. So good to meet you in person." He held out his hand.

"A pleasure." I shook his hand and then looked around the park. "I must have eaten in Little Italy a hundred times, but I've never been to this park before."

"It's small, but has lots of personality. Follow me. I'd like to show you something."

Max didn't feel the need to say anything as I followed him to an unspecified location. The man was short on words, but that was a thousand times better than Babbling Bagel Barney.

I was still curious why he wanted to meet at the park, but I would find out soon enough.

Hopefully it wouldn't take long because I was starving. And after having to listen to Mason and the other suits all morning, I needed a break.

Max led me past the adjacent dog park where I spotted a golden retriever chasing another dog and immediately thought of Nick and Karma.

Had I overreacted with him?

Maybe I'd been extra mad because I had flashed him again.

I definitely had a right to be upset, and decided I wasn't going to feel guilty about it.

Admittedly, it was sweet that Nick wanted to make sure nothing happened to the dog this morning, but not at the expense of my rose garden. I still didn't know what I was going to do with that disaster, but I wasn't going to worry about that just then.

"There." Max pointed to a group of trees past the dog park and stopped. "I like to watch and listen to the birds here. And lucky for us, it's mating season." He grinned and pulled out some folding binoculars from his suit jacket pocket, flipping them open and looking through the lenses.

Was he spying on the birds as they did the deed?

Did I have a sick pervert on my hands here?

A minute later, Max handed the binoculars to me and then pointed at the tree. "Look half way up, then a little bit over to the right."

I hesitated, but then grabbed the binoculars from Max, pressing them to my eyes.

I moved them around to try to see better, trying to find what he was looking at, and finally found it.

"Oh, wow." I zoomed in a little more to get a look at the bird's nest with three little baby finches. "That is the cutest thing."

"I usually like to head out into nature to bird watch, to one of the state parks, but I discovered that there are some brilliant examples of nature right here in the city, in our own backyard."

I watched as the mama bird fed food from her mouth to the baby birds.

I pulled the binoculars away from my eyes. "So cool. Thanks for sharing that with me."

Max nodded and took the binoculars from me, folding them and sticking them back in his pocket. "You're welcome. Let's get something to eat."

Now he was speaking my language.

Maybe I'd worried about Max and had been bent out of shape for nothing. He just wanted to show me a bird's nest and nothing more. It was sweet, actually, and a very good sign.

Now, hopefully the rest of the date would be just as nice.

We walked through the heart of Little Italy and right by Sogno di Vino, Sorrento Ristorante, Mona Lisa Deli, and Filipi's Pizza Grotto, the wonderful smell of each place practically stopping me in my tracks.

Any of these will do! Where are we going?

Then we rounded the corner and—

"Watch out." Max grabbed me and pulled me out of the way of a kid riding his scooter on the sidewalk.

"Thank you." I watched the boy disappear down the sidewalk, weaving in and out of the people like a maniac. "That was close."

A gentleman.

Max was scoring points rather quickly with me and we hadn't even made it to lunch yet.

I continued to walk down the sidewalk and—

"Can we stop in here for a minute? I need to pick up something for the birds in the park." Max pointed to an informal place with tables and chairs outside.

What could he possibly buy for birds at an Italian restaurant?

"Oh. Okay."

I was hungry, but he was doing something nice for the birds. How could I have a problem with that? I looked up to see the name of the restaurant, but we were directly under the overhang and I couldn't see a thing.

It didn't matter because like Dee said, there wasn't a bad place to eat in Little Italy.

I glanced down at one of the tables to see what people were eating as I followed Max inside, then stopped, confused, when I noticed sandwiches.

Not just any sandwiches.

Bagel sandwiches.

"Ruth!" Barney came from around the register at the counter and approaching me with way too much enthusiasm. "I thought I'd never see *you* again! Hey, spill the beans. You couldn't resist the temptation of one of my bagels. Or maybe it's me. Did you come in to chew the fat?" He gestured to himself. "I know it sounds cheesy, but I am the creme de la creme of the single men. Okay, maybe not cheesy, more like creamy. Ha! Did I say that?"

This had to be a joke.

I stared at him.

Max was staring at Barncy, too, most likely wondering who the hell he was and why he was looking at me with googly eyes.

I knew Barney said he had three locations, but I had never seen a bagel place in Little Italy.

And of all the places, Max chose this place to stop in?

"We opened this *restaurant* a month ago and look at this place." Barney winked.

Thanks for clarifying. I don't care.

"Packed like sardines. That's why they call me the king of bagels." Barney held out his hand. "Sorry, where are my manners? I'm Barney, head chef, the big cheese, and restauranteur."

Somebody gag me.

"I'm Max." He shook Barney's hand. "How do you two know each other?"

Barney smiled. "Ruth and I are dating."

"What?" I yelled, startling some of the customers at the table next to us. I lowered my voice. "We are *not* dating. We went on one date and that was it."

"Okay, you got me there, but you came back for more of the Barney. Am I right or am I right?" He turned to Max

133

and sized him up from head to toe. "What about you? How do you know Ruth?"

This can't be happening.

Max grinned. "Well, technically we just met. This is our first date."

And our last if I decide to make a run for it.

"Really?" Barney's gaze popped back and forth between me and Max. "And what do you bring to the table?"

Max looked confused, looking around the bagel shop. "Which table are you talking about?"

"You know? What do you have to offer Ruth? I mean, what do you do for a living?"

Who was he? My father?

"I'm director of sales for a solar company."

Barney lit up. "Seriously? I've been thinking about getting solar! Give me your card."

Max glanced over at me, hesitated, then pulled out his wallet, giving Barney a card.

"Great! And I have something for you!" Barney pulled out his business card and handed it to Max.

Those big bright red letters printed on the front of the business card almost blinded me again.

"That's me!" Barney gestured to the card. "The king of bagels. Plain, asiago, blueberry, sesame, onion, garlic, egg, you get the idea. Over seventeen varieties and ten different spreads, everything homemade. With three locations to serve you. Turn the card over!"

Here we go. The free bagel show.

Max flipped the business card over to the other side and nodded his approval of the frequent bagel bingeing program and the ten boxes that had an X stamped in the middle of them. "Thank you."

Barney smiled. "Christmas came early. You're welcome!"

Like a broken record.

"I'll give you a call later after work to chat about the solar. Does five or six work for you?"

Max winced. "Oooh, can you make it tomorrow? I have bowling league with the boys tonight. First night of the new season. I can't miss that."

"Seriously? Lucky you. I used to bowl way back in the day. I had a pretty high average. Man, I miss those days."

"What was your average?"

"Two hundred."

Great.

Talking about bowling would rank up there with the boredom of the board meeting mixed with the pain of a root canal and a couple of slaps to the face.

I glanced back at the door, wondering if I should walk out right now.

Max nodded. "One of our guys had to drop off the team. You're welcome to join us. We could use someone with your average."

This can't be happening.

Barney's eyes lit up. "I would *love* to! I've got a lot on my plate, but I can always make time for bowling. Hey, let me give you a dozen free bagels to show my appreciation. Maybe we can meet up for an early dinner before bowling, if you're open."

Max nodded. "I'd love to."

I smirked. "You're like two peas in a pod."

"Good one!" Barney said, turning back to Max. "Let me show you what I've got, my friend."

My friend? Just like that?

It looked like it was a match made in heaven.

Why am I even here?

There was no reason to be. Because it looked as if Max and Barney were going to be best buds. Which meant I would be seeing Barney again in the future on a regular basis if Max and I dated.

No freaking way in hell.

I would rather shave my legs with a cactus and then dip them in jalapeño juice.

Barney put his arm around Max and led him toward the display case like they were old friends who hadn't seen each other in a while.

While Barney bragged about the bagel recipes in detail and how he would take them with him to the grave, I used the opportunity to sneak out the front door and dart down the sidewalk.

"There she goes again!" Barney called out from behind me. "She's a runner and a tough nut to crack. You forgot your free bagel again!"

I ignored him and raced around the corner, slipping inside the front door of a restaurant.

I didn't even know which restaurant it was, but it didn't matter.

I was starving and would have eaten cardboard at that point.

I would have to have lunch with Dee in the office, and then get back to my massive to-do list. I placed my order for Italian food. As I waited for the food, I sent a text to Dee.

Ruth: Another bust.

Dee: What? How is that possible? The date started ten minutes ago. You already left?

Ruth: I left skid marks in the driveway, which is not easy since I was on foot. Maybe I should wear my running shoes to the next date, just to be prepared.

Dee: What happened this time?

Ruth: Barney happened.

Dee: Barney? I don't get it. You were supposed to meet Max.

Ruth: I did and then we ran into Barney.

Dee: Sounds like fate.

Ruth: More like a nightmare. But hey, Barney is going to buy solar panels for his house from Max and Max received a dozen free bagels and a new bowling partner. Sounds like they were meant to be.

Dee: And what do you get out of the deal?

Ruth: Freedom from not seeing either one of them again. The only thing I want at this point is some food in my system before I kill somebody. I already ordered and will be there shortly to eat with you. And by the way, this online dating thing is not working at all.

Dee: Don't worry because Dr. Dee is here to prescribe just what you need. Another 25 men who want you! You're in demand! And I have you scheduled for another lunch date tomorrow. And yes, I'm still pretending to be you. Sue me.

Ruth: Do you secretly want to be me when you grow up?

Dee: Who said I was ever going to grow up?

I laughed and tucked the phone back in my purse. Even with two bad dates in a row, I was still adamant about finding my soulmate. I didn't know what I had to do, but I did know that I wasn't going to give up.

I was going to find love, even if it killed me.

CHAPTER TWELVE

NICK

I had to admit that I was a little nervous, waiting for Ruth to come back home after that debacle this morning. She told me not to touch anything, to leave everything the way it was, but the guilt I had carried in my shoulders and neck wouldn't let me leave it like that. Ruth had made her thoughts very clear to me and that's why I needed to make it right. Actually, I made it better.

Yes, I was stubborn sometimes, but I also wanted to always make things right. I'd spent all day with Brandon making sure Ruth's backyard was in better shape than when she had left it and gone to work this morning. I'd even brought in a couple of extra guys for a few hours to help.

Ten hours working, nonstop, no breaks except for the bathroom, and no food.

The only time I left the backyard was to take Karma down the street for a quick pee.

Brandon had gone to buy dog food, a leash, and poop bags for me since I still hadn't been able to get a hold of Karma's owners. The dog had been a good girl all day long, like she knew she had gotten in trouble this morning and was trying to make up for it.

I was dead-tired and starving, but I wasn't looking for sympathy from Ruth or anyone else because I was the one who had gotten myself into this mess, along with the help of a beautiful dog who was just being a dog.

I wanted Ruth to be happy.

At first, I was tempted to go home after we had finished the job and let Ruth be surprised when she came home and found the place put back together. But then I thought I needed to explain some things, especially why I felt the need to disobey her direct orders. I had three surprises for her, and hopefully they would be enough to smooth out any friction between us.

"I hear a car out front," Brandon said, moving some of the loose dirt around the rose bushes with his hands one more time.

I grabbed the empty bags of fertilizer, bunched them into a ball, and stuck them in the recycle bin on the side of the house. Then I returned to the backyard and sat on the bench by the fountain, waiting for Ruth.

Sure enough, a minute later, Ruth peeked through the kitchen window out to the backyard.

Her jaw dropping open could have been perceived as a good sign or a bad sign, depending on what was going on in her mind. I wasn't a mind reader. I would have to wait to find out.

Please let her be happy when she sees what I did.

Ruth came outside and took a few steps toward the roses, pointing at them. "I told you not to touch anything."

I nodded. "You did." I turned to Brandon. "Why don't you go ahead and take off. I'll talk to you later."

He creased his brow. "Are you sure?"

I almost wanted to laugh.

He was probably thinking of staying around to protect me from Ruth.

I can handle her.

He'd obviously forgotten that I had been married to someone a lot like her.

"I'm sure." I shooed him away toward the side yard with my hand. "Seriously. You can go."

He hesitated. "Okay, but make sure you eat something. You've been working almost ten hours without a break or food and that's not good for your heart."

"What?" Ruth said. "Are you crazy? Why would you do something like that?"

"He's exaggerating," I lied. "Talk to you later, Brandon. Thanks again for everything."

"You're welcome. Good night." He smiled at Ruth and walked by the both of us.

"Good night," Ruth said, which was a good sign.

The silent treatment would've been a lot worse.

We both watched Brandon disappear through the side gate.

Ruth turned back to me. "Please explain yourself." She took a few steps closer to the roses and inspected them. "I told you not to touch these. You don't know the significance of these roses and what they mean to me."

"Actually, I do."

"Is that right?" She placed her hands on her hips in an all-too familiar move I had seen before, letting me know that she was confident I had no idea what the hell I was talking about and that she was looking forward to setting me straight. "You know that my grandmother planted them with me before she passed and that they're *very* special to me?"

What did I tell you? I saw that coming a mile away. And she did set me straight because I was wrong in my assumption. I thought she just loved her roses. I had no idea they were connected to someone in her past who brought her special memories.

I winced. "No, I didn't know that part about your grandma. My condolences."

"Thank you, but she lived a good life. Died at ninety-five, happy and satisfied."

I forced a smile at Ruth, trying to calm the waters. "That's good to know."

"Yes, but that's beside the point." Karma walked over to Ruth and licked her leg below the dress. "Not now, Karma. *You're* the one who started this. Why did you dig up my roses?" She scratched the dog under her chin. "You can't go doing things like that, even though we know it was someone else's fault, not yours."

Ruth lifted her head and glared at me.

I thought it was sweet that she was talking with Karma and petting her, even if it did include the little dig at the end. Ruth had a soft side my ex rarely showed. Crystal hadn't liked dogs. Hadn't liked any animals, for that matter.

"Some dogs dig out of curiosity," I said, hoping to explain what had happened. "But I know what caused this and it's actually *your* fault."

Oops. That came out wrong and a little too strong.

"Excuse me?" Ruth crossed her arms, another famous move that showed me she had put her guard up and was ready to fight to the death. She wanted to distance herself from me and let me know that what had come from my mouth was complete nonsense.

In other words, I was an idiot.

I happened to agree with her.

My bad.

Now, it was time to recover from my mistake.

"Sorry," I said to start. "What I'm trying to say is that your roses are dying."

"Of course they are. Your dog killed them!"

"Okay, first of all, Karma is not my dog, although if I *do* get a dog one day, I would love to have one just like her because she's adorable." I reached over and stroked her golden coat along her back. "Second, nobody *killed* your roses, although they were not in the best of shape before Karma went digging. You haven't been taking care of them properly. That's why the leaves have been turning brown and look scorched. We have already discussed that stress kills. Well, your roses are seriously stressed out right now. You've been over-fertilizing them." I pulled one of the leaves off and handed it to her.

She inspected the leaf. "Over-fertilizing them?"

I nodded. "Yes. And third, you have most likely been over-fertilizing them with chicken manure or blood meal."

She nodded. "Blood meal. How did you know?"

"It doesn't matter. It isn't such a bad idea, unless you overdo it. Ammonia is good for healthy plant growth, but too much of a good thing can result in death. Plus, dogs are attracted to the smell of blood meal. They think there's something dead below the surface, and *that* is why they try to dig it up."

She looked at me, then the leaf, and glanced at Karma, speechless.

Ruth being speechless left *me* speechless.

I wasn't expecting it at all.

I cleared my throat, ready to share the three surprises that hopefully would put this all behind us, in order to move on. "I brought in a soil expert today who diagnosed the rose problem and told me exactly what I needed to do. We were able to clear out most of the old compost without damaging the roots and add something that had less ammonia to balance out the pH level. And you've been giving them too much water as well, especially since they aren't getting enough sun." I pointed to the neighbor's tree that had been growing over her fence. "I trimmed back that tree to give the roses more sun in the afternoon. I also added a drip irrigation since you had been watering them by hand, obviously, and getting too much of the foliage wet. Not good when it doesn't get enough sun. No charge, by the way."

Ruth was still speechless.

I gestured behind us. "And your waist-high planter boxes are done."

"What?" She flipped around, her mouth dropping open as she approached the planter boxes against the other fence. "Oh, I love this."

"That makes me happy. As you can see, it also has a drip-irrigation that is ready to go. You can start planting those organic vegetables whenever you're ready."

I'm pretty sure I heard her sigh.

"And one more thing . . ." I walked over to my toolbox and bent down to grab the small folded red towel sitting on top, handing it to Ruth.

She looked down at the towel and then glanced up at me. "What is this?"

"Look inside. It's something I found. Well, I need to give credit where credit is due." I chuckled. "Karma dug it up. Not sure if it's yours, but . . ."

Ruth unfolded the towel slowly and looked inside. "My . . . locket." It only took a few seconds before her eyes teared up. "You found it."

A good sign because I hoped I had found something special that she had lost. It indeed was a locket, most likely sterling silver, considering how well it held up after being buried in the dirt for who knew how long.

She rubbed the outside of the locket, trying to remove some of the caked-on dirt. "I can't believe you found this. My grandmother gave it to me. Now it's all starting to make sense because I lost it right around the time she helped me plant the roses. I thought it was gone for good." She held it in her palms, close to her heart.

Then something happened that caught me off guard.

Ruth lunged toward me and hugged me tightly. "Thank you."

Not wanting to feel like a stiff, I wrapped my arms around her and hugged her back. "You're welcome."

"Seriously. Thank you from the bottom of my heart." I could feel the heat from her words against my neck. Then she suddenly pushed away, as if she realized how long we'd been hugging.

I cleared my throat. "Hey, don't thank me. It was Karma." I laughed, wiped my hands on my pants, and bent down to close my toolbox. "Okay, I'm going to get out of your hair. I'll see you in the morning. Good night."

She stood there, a dazed look on her face, rubbing the locket again with her thumb and index finger, deep in thought.

I decided to leave, since it appeared that Karma and I were no longer in the doghouse.

I grabbed my toolbox and walked toward the side yard.

"You lied to me, by the way," Ruth said from behind me.

I stopped in my tracks, not expecting that at all.

I guess I needed to turn back around.

And here I thought I had made the perfect escape.

CHAPTER THIRTEEN

RUTH

I couldn't in good conscience let Nick walk away without a word or without offering him a bite to eat after what he had done today. I wasn't happy with him for not listening to me after Karma had dug up my roses this morning, but I appreciated that he'd tried to make things right, and the way things turned out. His heart seemed to be in the right place.

Nick more than made up for the rose disaster with the miracle of finding my precious locket that I thought I'd never see again. I guess one could argue that if the dog hadn't dug up my roses, I would have never found my locket.

Still, I wasn't happy that he had worked all day without taking a break or eating. Sure, I had done the exact same thing numerous times in my career, but my work wasn't labor intensive out in the sun. Plus, who knew how that affected his heart condition?

I would still find a way to feed the man. It was the least I could do.

Nick stopped and flipped around to face me. "What did I lie to you about?"

"You told me Brandon was exaggerating when he said you hadn't eaten or taken a break in over ten hours."

Nick shook his head. "When I said he was exaggerating, I was referring to the part where he said it wasn't good for my heart. He's not a doctor. He's not allowed to make that statement."

"What if he's right?"

"What if he's wrong?"

"Have you eaten today? Yes or no."

Nick hesitated. "No, but—"

I let out a frustrated breath. "Inside. Now."

Nick chuckled. "And you call *me* pushy?"

"Look—I went to an Italian restaurant today for lunch and—"

"For your date."

I stared at him. "How did you know I had a date? Did Dee tell you?"

"No—you told me."

"When?"

"Just now." He chuckled. "But before that, yesterday, Dee said she needed to get back to finding you a man, but then I'm pretty sure you lied when you said it was for a hair appointment."

I stared at him.

Now he was accusing me of lying?

Yes, I did lie, but that had nothing to do with it.

Nick shrugged. "Hey, it's nothing to be embarrassed about. Having someone in your life is a good thing." He twisted toward the fountain. "I love the sound of the water. Have you tried my breathing exercise yet?"

"No."

"Well, you should."

"I can't. I'm trying to be mad at you."

He took a deep breath in through his nose and let it out slowly through his mouth. "Of course. Please continue. Go ahead and yell if it makes you feel better."

He closed his eyes and inhaled again.

Did anything ever ruffle Nick's feathers?

The way he exuded peace and tranquility was impressive and annoying at the same time.

Did he even have a pulse?

What kind of life was that, going around and pretending that he didn't have a care in the world? He was exactly like Judy in the airport, except he was better looking and didn't have a pukey-green suitcase. At least, I didn't think he had one. It didn't matter. The only difference I could see between the two of them was that Nick looked happy and Judy did not.

I sighed. "Can I get back to my point?"

"By all means . . ."

"Then open your eyes and pay attention."

He opened his eyes and turned to me, not saying anything.

"Thank you. Now, where was I?"

"You went to an Italian restaurant today for lunch."

"Right. Anyway, I went to an Italian restaurant today for lunch, *by myself,* and ordered some food to go for me and Dee, not knowing that the meals I had ordered were family-style that served four to six people. I love Italian food, I love my carbs, and I definitely love leftovers just as much as the next person, but it was way too much food for me and Dee. *You* haven't eaten. You'll be doing me a favor by making sure the food doesn't go to waste. You must be starving."

Nick nodded. "You didn't have a date then?"

"Why are we back on that? What does that have to do with anything?"

"Well, because you accused me of lying, and it would be perfect if you lied, too. Then the score would be even, that's all."

"The score? Is this a game to you?"

He grinned. "It could be. You're not having fun?"

I couldn't believe I was hearing this.

And I would never admit I was enjoying it.

All I wanted to do was put some food in the man's system because I felt guilty that he hadn't eaten all day. Why was this so difficult?

"Are. You. Hungry?" I asked. "Yes or no."

"I am, but you're already paying me. I don't need you to include meals."

"I'm not running an all-inclusive resort here. It's just tonight. One meal. It's the least I can do, considering all you did today. And you found my locket. Plus, you'll be doing me a favor since I don't like to waste food."

Nick stood there, staring at me, arching an eyebrow.

It was like he didn't trust me.

I let out a frustrated breath. "Please eat. You're killing me."

He looked down at his clothes. "I'm a mess."

"I don't care. If it makes you feel better, we can eat out here on the patio with Karma. And feel free to wash up in the bathroom while I warm up the food."

Surprisingly, Nick finally agreed.

He gave Karma some food and took her out to the front for a pee. Then he grabbed a clean shirt from his truck and went to use the guest bathroom to wash up.

I scooped the container of lasagna and pasta into a large serving bowl and stuck it in the microwave to heat up. I poured myself a glass of wine from the bottle I had opened yesterday, taking a sip, and checking my phone for messages after I heard it vibrate.

Dee: Did you kill Nick? Don't answer that! I don't want to know. Make sure you hide the body well and delete this message.

Ruth: I decided to spare him this time. Remember that locket I lost?

Dee: Of course. The silver one your grandma gave you.

Ruth: Nick found it.

Dee: That's wonderful! Where did he find it?

Ruth: Under the rose bushes that Karma dug up.

Dee: That's amazing. I know how much it meant to you. See? Everything happens for a reason. It's a good thing I was smart enough to hire Nick for you. Make sure you do something nice for him.

Ruth: You sound like my mother. We're getting ready to eat. I need to run. Talk later.

Dee: We? What do you mean WE?????? You and Nick are having dinner together?

I laughed and set the phone down without answering her, satisfied that I had gotten her back for telling me Nick and Brandon were working in the backyard, shirtless, with glistening muscles.

As I was pulling the food from the beeping microwave, I considered that Dee would be asking a thousand questions later, but that was par for the course. I also knew we would be talking after dinner since we needed to discuss my lunch date for tomorrow.

Nick entered the kitchen wearing the fresh T-shirt he had gotten from his truck. "Thanks again for this. It wasn't necessary, but I do appreciate it."

"You're welcome. Like I said, they're leftovers. I have way too much. I had a bottle of red wine already open and poured myself a glass. Would you like some?"

He arched an eyebrow again.

What was it with this guy? If I didn't know any better, I would think he didn't trust me at all.

Unless he thought I was trying to seduce him.

Could that be it?

He needed to get over himself.

"I'm not trying to get you drunk if that's what you're worried about. It's dinner wine. I mean, who ever heard of Italian food without wine? Nobody is twisting your arm. Either you want to have some with your dinner, or you don't."

He nodded. "I do. Thank you."

I poured him some wine, and then raised my glass. "To lost and found lockets."

"Cheers." Nick clinked my glass. "And to grandmothers." He winked and clinked my glass again.

That was sweet.

We took the food and the wine to the patio table and sat to eat.

Karma came over and lay underneath the table by my feet.

I leaned against the table to pull the food a little closer to us and noticed something odd. I grabbed the edge of the table and wiggled it.

"What?" Nick said.

"Nothing. This table usually annoys the hell out of me because it shakes so much, but now it's not shaking."

"Oh—I fixed it. Two of the legs were loose."

I looked under the table where Karma was lying down and then back up to Nick. "When did you do that?"

"Yesterday."

"Why didn't you say anything?"

"Because it was no big deal."

Maybe not to him, but I liked his initiative. "Wow . . . thank you."

"My pleasure."

"Just remember I'm paying you for all the work you do here."

"I'm not going to charge you for that."

"Yes. You are."

He chuckled. "Hmmm. Okay, let's see then. Ninety

seconds to fix two table legs . . ." He thought about it. "Got it. That will be one scoop of pasta."

"I was already going to give you a scoop of pasta."

"I guess I'll have two scoops then."

I shook my head. "Oh . . ." I looked back toward the kitchen. "I forgot the parmesan cheese. Very important. I'll be right back."

"I'll grab it for you."

Before I could object, Nick was already up and heading back to the house.

"On the refrigerator door, right side," I called out to him. "Oh, grab some napkins, too. Next to the toaster."

"Got it."

I watched Nick through the kitchen window as he went to the refrigerator, opening it for the parmesan cheese. Then he grabbed the napkins, pausing for a few seconds to look at something on the kitchen counter.

Wait a minute . . .

Had he looked at my phone?

Hopefully he didn't see a text message pop up from Dee.

I tried to get a read on Nick's face as he came back to the patio table and sat down across from me, wondering if he had seen something.

He handed me a napkin and the parmesan cheese, a suspicious smirk on his face.

"What?" I asked, almost certain he'd seen a text on my phone.

"Nothing. This looks amazing. Lasagna and . . . what is this?" He pointed to the pasta.

"Penne Bisanzio. It's penne pasta with fresh tomatoes, diced eggplant, mozzarella cheese, and fresh basil. Help yourself."

"Don't mind if I do." He scooped a spoonful of the pasta onto his plate. "Is this a regular thing for you, eating Italian food twice a day?"

"Not regular, but I would never complain about it."

"But it's your favorite food?"

"I like everything. Italian, Chinese, Greek, burgers, hot dogs, sushi, you name it."

"Me, too."

We were both quiet for a minute as we served ourselves.

Nick and I both looked up at each other when we moaned at the same time with our first bites, but I quickly glanced back down at my lasagna, taking another forkful.

Then we both lifted our wine glasses at the same time, each of us taking a sip.

That was weird.

It was like we were mimicking each other. Or heaven forbid, of one mind.

Why was my brain scrambled around him? We were two adults eating food at my house, nothing more, nothing less.

I took another sip of my wine, glancing across the table at Nick.

I could tell he was inside his head with thoughts, biting his lower lip. There was something on his mind and he wanted to say it, I was sure of it.

Taking a sip of wine, he grinned, and set the glass on

the table. "Oh . . . Dee wants you to call her when you're done eating with sexy Nick."

I blinked.

"Oh wait, was she talking about *me*?" His bottom lip quivered as he took another bite of food, avoiding eye contact like what he'd said was completely normal. "Do you know another Nick?"

I set my fork down. "I can't believe you read the text message on my phone."

He threw up his hands in defense. "Hey, the phone vibrated and lit up like a Christmas tree when I was standing by the kitchen counter. What am I supposed to do? It was impossible to ignore it. It wasn't like I was waiting there, praying for a text to appear on your phone."

"Right . . ."

"Oh—and Dee needs to know where you want to eat for your next date." Nick laughed.

Scoffing, I balled up my napkin and threw it at him. It bounced off his forehead.

Nick grabbed the napkin from his lap, handing it back to me. "You dropped something."

I shook my head and poured myself more wine. For some reason I gave him more, even though he didn't ask for it or deserve it.

I fought hard to hold back a smile, even though I was embarrassed. Maybe it was because that was the third or fourth time I'd embarrassed myself with the man, and it was starting to become a regular thing.

I pointed my fork at him. "Say you're sorry."

"For what?"

"I can give you a list."

He chuckled. "I'm a big fan of lists, but I didn't do anything wrong."

"That was a private message from Dee to me. You read it."

"A private message in public view. You're dating . . . what's the big deal? Everybody dates at one point or another because they want someone in their lives. And those who say they don't need anybody are lying. Personally, I *love* being in a relationship, although there's nobody in my life at the moment."

"Probably because people don't appreciate you invading their privacy."

"I can assure you, that's not it."

"Yeah, then why are you single?" I took a sip, waiting for his answer.

Nick chuckled. "You mean, what's *wrong* with me? Hey, you're single. I could ask you the exact same thing." He took another sip of his wine. "Although I already know the answer. We don't need to go there." He grinned. "This lasagna is fantastic."

I stopped chewing. "Please. Enlighten me. Tell me why I'm single."

This oughta be good.

"You're a stunning woman, I'll tell you that much."

I blinked.

What?

That sounded like a compliment.

Okay, it was *definitely* a compliment.

Why was he complimenting me when he was supposed

to be telling me why I was single?

I felt the patio heating up.

I took another sip of wine, waiting for him to continue because I didn't know if he was being serious or yanking my chain. My bullshit detector was not even moving at this point. I could only assume it was faulty and needed a tune-up because why would he compliment me when he was supposed to be giving me a list of my faults?

I waited for him to continue.

"Some people might say that your beauty is off the charts," Nick continued.

I don't get what's happening here. Nick was not my type at all, but why did I like that he thought I was beautiful?

"Most men would never have the confidence to approach someone like you because they think you're out of their league."

I nodded. "You're saying I'm single because I'm attractive. Is that it?"

He shook his head. "No—that has nothing to do with it."

I let out a frustrated breath and took another sip of wine.

This guy was going to drive me crazy.

"Other people might say that you're single because of the attitude that you exude."

"What attitude?"

"It's like you have a sign on your forehead that says *Back Off*. Or maybe *back* is not the correct first word." He laughed.

I crossed my arms. "You're saying I'm single because I don't want men to waste my time and I let them know it?"

"Nope. That's not it, either. Some men are courageous or just plain dumb and will still try to ask you out anyway." He held up his wine glass. "I love the wine, by the way." He took another sip. "Delicious. Here. Have more." He topped off my wine, even though I didn't ask for it.

Nick was going to make me scream.

Why was he stalling?

Was he going to tell me why I was single?

What on earth was taking him so long?

I swear this man is part sloth.

Finally, he glanced at me again. "You're single because you put your job first, above everything else in your life. You're a workaholic." He held up his hand, like he thought I might object. "And before you get all bent out of shape, I'm not saying that there's anything wrong with that. You get to choose exactly how you want to live your life. If that's what makes you happy, then more power to you. You're happy, right?"

I opened my mouth and closed it.

Happy? Me?

I wouldn't necessarily say that I was *happy*.

But I wasn't depressed, either, so there was that.

Nick continued to stare at me, waiting for an answer.

Now, I just needed to decide if I was going to lie or not.

CHAPTER FOURTEEN

RUTH

I had read somewhere that female dragonflies fake their deaths to avoid males. I was trying to decide if I wanted to do just that, because I wasn't in the mood to answer Nick's question.

He was still staring at me. "It's not a difficult question. Either you're happy or you're not."

"And if I am and I know it, do I need to clap my hands?"

He chuckled. "Sure. Why not?"

I sighed. "I don't feel the need to analyze my emotions minute-by-minute and day-to-day as I bust my butt working toward my goal. If it makes you feel any better, I know I'll be *over the moon* with happiness once I take over the company as managing partner."

He nodded. "Okay. Fine. Basically, you're saying that

you'll enjoy the destination when you get there, but not the journey."

"In essence, yes."

"Once again, I'm not judging, just observing and commenting, but it does bring up another interesting question."

"Interesting for whom?"

Nick ignored me. "Why can't you enjoy the journey as much as the destination? Sounds like double the fun to me unless you don't like your job."

Who was this guy? My non-appointed, annoying career counselor and spiritual guru?

He cocked his head to the side. "You don't like your job, do you?"

"Whether or not I like my job does not determine how good I am," I said. "I'm the best in my field. How many people can say that?"

"Congratulations, but I didn't ask you if you were good at your job, I asked you if you *liked* what you did for a living and if it makes you happy. I already know you're successful. This house is amazing, you wear nice clothes, and drive a fancy car."

I glared at him.

"Okay, forget about that. Forget I even asked."

Thank God the interrogation was over.

I took another sip of my wine, wondering why he was analyzing me in the first place.

How much have I had? I was starting to feel tipsy.

Nick put more pasta onto his plate. "This second scoop is for fixing your table. Your account is now paid in full."

He winked. "What do you do, by the way? I know you said you wanted to be managing partner, but what are you doing now? If you don't mind me asking."

Finally, something I don't mind talking about. "I'm partner at a consulting firm, a corporate takeover specialist."

"Oh, that sounds intriguing. And what does that entail?"

"I find undervalued companies with superior products, but inferior business or marketing skills. Because they're having issues, we buy them at a fraction of what they're worth."

He nodded. "And after you find these companies and buy them, what do you do with them?"

"We gut them and sell them for a profit."

"Like a hostile takeover?"

I lifted my wine glass to my lips, but then paused. "No. A hostile takeover happens when an entity attempts to take control of another company *without* the consent or cooperation of the target company's board of directors. During *our* process, the board of directors *agree* to sell to us. It's one hundred percent consent and cooperation. It's more like a friendly acquisition."

"And do people lose their jobs in the process?"

"Yes. Always."

He took a sip of his wine, nodding. "Doesn't seem very friendly to me."

"We aren't the ones who put the company in that position in the first place. If they don't sell to us, most of them will go bankrupt or die a slow death, unless someone else comes along to snatch them up."

"Okay, but let me ask you this . . . why don't you go in there and help them turn the company around instead of gutting it?"

I crossed my arms. "Because that's not my job. It's not what my company does. That's like asking a professional tennis player why she doesn't kick the fuzzy green ball with her foot instead of hitting it with a racket."

He chuckled. "Fair enough." He took a sip of his wine, deep in thought, eyes on me. "Boy, there's one thing for sure, you and I are like surf and turf."

I had no idea what he was talking about. "Come again?"

"I am the land and you are the sea."

"If you're trying to be philosophical, you've completely lost me."

"You. Me." He gestured to me and then to himself. "We're complete opposites. I build things. And *you* tear them apart." He shrugged and grabbed the serving spoon. "I think I'll help myself to more of this delicious pasta."

What the hell?

Why was Nick criticizing what I did for a living? And why did I suddenly feel like crap? Normally by now I would have been putting a guy in his place if he'd said something like this to me. Was it because what he said was partially true? I was confusing myself at the moment, but one thing I could clearly see: Nick didn't like what I did for a living and had no problem telling me.

And where does he get off asking me all these questions?

You're happy, right?

Is everyone supposed to be happy and love their jobs?

For most people, a job is something that's necessary to pay the bills.

Nothing more.

You don't have to love it.

But you sure as hell do love that you can pay the bills every month with that paycheck.

Suddenly, the patio was hot again, but this time because of an infuriating man, not because of any compliment that he'd sent my way.

I needed to vent.

And there was one person who always had my back.

I took another sip of wine and then stood. "Excuse me for a moment."

"Of course."

In the kitchen, I grabbed my phone to send a text to Dee.

Ruth: Nick said my job is to tear things apart. Can you believe that?

Dee: An accurate analysis on his part. Are you really having dinner with him? You didn't answer my 1000 text messages.

Ruth: Never mind that! You're taking his side?

Dee: There are no sides here. It's either the truth or it's not the truth. Nick happened to nail it on the head. You DO tear companies apart.

Ruth: And that's it?

Dee: No, you need to find the company first after countless hours of research, and then you tear it apart. We don't discount the fact that you bust your ass to make it happen. What's the problem? You just figured out what you did for a living after all these years?

I stared at the phone.

I can't believe this.

Yes, I knew what I did for a living, but I didn't look at it from that point of view.

Why would I?

Companies survived by making money and Stansfeld Investments had been doing very well since I had arrived. It wasn't like I was doing something illegal or immoral. I was working for a legitimate company and my job was to look for investments. And when I found opportunities with lots of potential, I turned them into a financial gain for Stansfeld.

That was my job.

And it wasn't like the owners of those companies were complaining when we wrote them that big fat check. Yes, people lost jobs in the process, but was that my fault?

Honestly, my job had changed over the years since I had first started with the firm. And maybe I had enjoyed it more at the beginning when my role was more on the research end and not the strategic planning and implementation side.

I certainly had a lot less stress back then.

Still, the way Nick and Dee described my job, it sounded so negative.

Almost cruel.

Dee: Are you still there? I hope you're not in the process of killing Nick right now.

Ruth: I'm still on the fence.

Dee: You can't punish him because he told you the truth. He's the best in the business and it will take a long time to find a replacement. Plus, if he leaves, he takes Brandon with him and I want to have that man's babies!

Ruth: Relax. I'm not going to fire him.

Dee: My ovaries are very happy to hear that.

Ruth: Nick said he and I were surf and turf.

Dee: Opposites?

Ruth: Yes! How did you figure that out?

Dee: I am the almighty wise one. Opposites attract.

Ruth: You think you know everything.

Dee: I do. Feel free to ask me for advice. Just $1.99 per minute. Yes, you appear to be opposites, but you do have at least one thing in common.

Ruth: I doubt that.

Dee: You both like to tell the truth even if it hurts. Don't fault him for that because you do the exact same thing.

Ruth: You're taking his side again. I'm not listening.

Dee: Yes, you are.

Ruth: I should get back. I'll talk to you after he leaves.

Dee: Does this mean Nick isn't getting a goodnight kiss from you?

I turned my phone over so there was no chance of Nick seeing that ridiculous text.

There was zero possibility of Nick and me kissing.

Ever.

It was like he said, we were total opposites.

And even if I did think he was attractive and even a little charming when he wasn't completely annoying me, nothing would ever happen between us because he didn't believe in what I did for a living. He didn't think it was okay for me to put all my focus into my work. I wanted a man who would let me be myself, and who would support my decisions.

I headed back outside to the patio and sat back down across from Nick, picking up my fork and taking another bite of my lasagna.

"Everything okay?" He had a concerned look on his face.

"Everything is fine."

"Good. I was worried that I had upset you or annoyed you."

"Upset me, no. Annoyed me, yes."

He nodded. "Sorry. I tend to speak my mind, which gets me in trouble."

I sighed. "Believe me, I know exactly how that is. I'm one of the few women working in a male-dominated industry. If I don't speak up or defend myself or my position, they'll walk all over me. I will *never* allow that to happen."

"Good. You shouldn't. You're obviously a smart woman who knows what she's doing. And I must say I'm impressed with your drive and determination."

He was back to compliments now?

I wished this man would make up his mind.

He held out his hand across the table. "Once again, I apologize."

I glanced at his hand and then took it, shaking it. "Apology accepted."

He smiled. "Good. And thank you for this delicious dinner. I was starving."

"You're welcome. And you need to promise me that you won't skip another lunch while you're working for me. Take regular breaks whether you need them or not. That's the law, plus it's the right thing to do."

"I promise. And honestly, I'm usually good about taking breaks. Today was a little different though, after what happened with this girl here, and I wanted to get everything done before you got back." He leaned down and petted Karma on the head. "I promise tomorrow I'll be back to my normal schedule of taking twenty to thirty breaks per day."

I pointed my finger at him. "Don't push your luck."

He chuckled.

I smiled and gestured to Karma. "What are you going to do with her?"

"Honestly, I have no idea. I've left voicemails for the owners and sent them text messages, but I haven't heard back from them yet. I even had Brandon drive by their home, but it's like they just disappeared. It doesn't make any sense, but I guess she'll be sleeping with me tonight."

Lucky dog.

I can't believe my thoughts went there. Was it the wine?

I picked up the bottle and then looked inside with my right eye.

It was empty.

"I don't remember drinking that much wine."

He chuckled. "I do."

I laughed. "You're not supposed to notice things like

that." I took the last sip of my wine. "I'm going to need to get back to work soon."

Nick checked his watch. "At this hour? Oh, I forgot. You're a workaholic."

"Don't start."

He stood and started grabbing plates. "I'll help you with these and then I'll let you go."

"Leave that stuff right where it is. I'll take care of it later."

Nick shook his head. "No can do. I wouldn't think of it. You provided me with one of the best meals I've had in a long time. The least I can do is help you clean up."

Inside the kitchen, Nick began rinsing off the plates and silverware.

I grabbed a plate from him and stuck it in the dishwasher. "You don't do well with following directions, do you?"

He scraped pasta off one of the plates before rinsing it. "You're very observant, but can you get mad at a person because they're being nice?" He gave me a pouty face. "I think not."

I tried to ignore that he was being cute. "Nice or not—you don't want to get on my bad side."

He smirked. "Hey—let's get one thing straight; I've seen you come, and I've seen you go, and I can confidently say you *don't* have a bad side."

Did he really say that?

Nick turned to me, holding a dish in his hand, watching me.

We locked gazes.

The water continued to run in the sink.

The air between us seemed to be filled with attraction.

Or maybe it was my drunken, desperate imagination.

How could I trust my gut when it appeared to be on vacation?

I finally had to break the silence between us. "Are you flirting with me?"

"Me? No way!"

"Good, because that would be weird."

"Weird, indeed."

I pointed at him. "*You're* the one who said we were complete opposites, and I agree with you. Even if I try hard to picture us together—"

Nick stopped rinsing the dish and looked at me. "You're trying to picture us together?"

"No!" I yanked the dish out of his hands and stuck it in the dishwasher. "Why? Have you?"

Nick shook his head. "Of course not. Why would I do that?"

"I don't know. Why would I?"

"I don't know!"

We stared at each other like we were in a standoff, waiting for the other person to make a move. What type of move, I had no idea.

This was getting weirder by the minute.

I grabbed the wine glass from his hand and stuck it in the dishwasher. "Can we change the subject, please?"

"We weren't talking."

"Is it hot in here?" I loosened my blouse, but then wondered if I flashed him again.

Nick glanced down at my cleavage and swallowed hard. *Yup. Looks like I did.*

He jerked his eyes back up to mine. "Yes. Hot. Very hot. I think it would be a good idea if I left now."

"Okay . . ."

He glanced over at my phone on the counter.

"I saw that."

Nick laughed. "I don't know what you're talking about."

"Right . . ."

"But if you still need a recommendation for a great restaurant for your date—"

"That's quite all right."

"You said you like sushi, right?"

I hesitated and sighed. "Yes. I love it."

He stopped the water from the faucet and turned to me. "You have to try Sushi Ota. It's right off the freeway near Mission Bay."

I nodded. "It's good?"

"*Very* good."

"I'll keep it in mind then."

"Well, also keep in mind that it's located in a strip mall, but don't let the casual nature of the place deter you from checking it out."

"Casual is one of my favorite words."

"Mine, too."

How could it be that we had another thing in common?

"I eat there all the time. You'll love it." Nick stuck the last piece of silverware in the dishwasher and closed the door.

I handed him a towel to dry his hands. "Here you go."

"Thanks." He dried his hands and set the towel on the counter next to my phone. Then he eyed the phone again. "I think I'll wait here and see if any interesting messages pop up from Dee."

I playfully pushed Nick on the arm. "You can go now." Why did it feel like I was flirting then? Was I crazy? Time to end these shenanigans. "I really do need to get to work. I may be up all night."

"If you get overwhelmed, go sit by the fountain and close your eyes. Don't feel guilty for taking time for yourself. Trust me."

For some odd reason, with all that had happened with me and Nick today, I did trust him.

It didn't make sense considering how frustrating and emotional the day had been.

The drama with the roses.

Nick finding the locket.

Butting heads with Mason again.

The ridiculous date I had with Max.

The countless times I wanted to kill Nick during dinner.

And what happened to us while we were putting things in the dishwasher?

I've seen you come, and I've seen you go, and I can confidently say you don't have a bad side.

I would be lying if I said my heart rate hadn't picked up speed after he said that.

He'd denied flirting with me, but it sure felt like that was exactly what he was doing.

Nick packed up his things, along with Karma, said goodbye, and went home.

Back in my office, I sent a text to Dee.

Ruth: Nick is still alive. And before you ask, no, we didn't kiss.

Dee: I guess that makes heavy petting a long shot.

Ruth: I'll pretend you didn't say that. But I'm curious how a man can frustrate me and intrigue me at the same time.

Dee: You mean turn you on?

Ruth: I didn't say that.

Dee: You like him.

Ruth: Are you even listening to me? He frustrates me!

Dee: Have you ever met a man who didn't frustrate you at one time or another?

Ruth: No.

Dee: Good, then that part cancels out and the only thing that is left is a man who intrigues you. Looks like you and Nick need to go out on a date.

Ruth: Tomorrow, you and I are going to do a video conference. I want to make sure you're not hitting the crack pipe while you're working. Now, on to more important things. Tomorrow is also the last chance I'm giving you to try things your way. Then I'll have to take matters into my own hands. This will be date #3 and that is plenty to evaluate and determine if it's a complete waste of time. Good luck. What's his name and what does he do for a living?

Dee: This guy is a sure thing. His name is Edward and he is a very successful entrepreneur. He owns the Bathroom Remodel Warehouse right across the street from the Marine Corps Air Station in Miramar. You know that big toilet-shaped glass building with all the palm trees around it?

Ruth: That's his?

Dee: Yup. He's worth millions and knows plenty about business. He'll be able to appreciate your climb to the top and all the work you're putting into it. He's looking forward to lunch with you tomorrow. All he needs is the time and the place.

Ruth: Tell him to meet me at Sushi Ota in Mission Bay at noon. I've never been there, but Nick says it's the best. Make sure you tell him it's a casual place.

Dee: Got it. Talk to you tomorrow.

Ruth. Wait a minute! I almost forgot. Where's the picture?

Dee: Hang on.

A minute later, Dee texted me a picture of Edward and I liked what I saw.

Ruth: Just like Barney, Max, and Nick, he's good-looking.

Dee: HOT is more like it.

Ruth: Let's hope this one has a personality.

Dee: But why are you including Nick as a comparison? You've never gone out with him and claim you have no interest in him.

Ruth: Forget about it.

Dee: I know why.

Ruth: I don't want to hear it. Gotta run.

Dee: You like him.

Ruth. How could I like Nick? That man is impossible.

Dee: Yes, but with a little bit of work he'll be easy.

Ruth: Pretend we're talking and now I'm hanging up on you.

Dee: Ha! You can't hang up on a text!

Ruth: Watch me!

I laughed and set my phone on the desk. I opened up my email and jerked my head back when I saw the insane amount of unread messages waiting for me. The only thing I could do was to start going through them one-by-one, replying, deleting, or saving for later.

Two hours later, I still hadn't gotten through all of them.

My shoulders tensed up again just thinking about how much work I still had to do. The pleasurable wine buzz that I had gotten with Nick was long gone.

Nick.

What was the deal with that guy? And why was I thinking about him again? He was like one of those paintings in the museum that every time you looked at it, you saw something different.

I couldn't figure that man out.

There was much more to him than I could have ever imagined. I hadn't even scratched the surface yet. He was a smart man, no doubt about that. But I had a feeling he got most of his knowledge from life experiences, and not a textbook or a school. He had this raw energy and confidence that usually came from street-smarts. That was the only way he could have known about me without knowing me so well.

As hard as it was for me to admit it, Dee was right when

she said Nick hit the nail on the head about what I did for a living.

I did tear things apart.

Nick told me what he saw, but he was also clear that he wasn't being judgmental, just stating the facts. How could I get mad at him for that?

You're a workaholic. You get to choose exactly how you want to live your life and if that's your preference, if that's what makes you happy, more power to you. You're happy, right?

If I would have answered him honestly, I would have told him *no*, I'm not happy.

Sometimes it does feel like life is passing me by.

Like I need to stick my hand out to grab it and slow it down.

That flight from Phoenix taught me something: I had all my eggs in one basket and that I didn't want to die alone.

At least I was doing something about it, but I did have a lot of things going on.

My shoulders tensed up even more, just thinking about it.

If you get overwhelmed, go sit by the fountain, and close your eyes. Trust me.

I glanced out the open french doors toward the fountain and listened to the soothing sound of the water. Maybe that's what I needed just then. I needed to get out of my comfort zone and do something I wouldn't normally do.

I closed my laptop and stood, willing to finally give it a shot without Nick watching me.

Once outside, I sat on the bench in front of the fountain and closed my eyes.

Now, I needed to remember Nick's instructions.

Any sounds you notice around you, just let them be.

It was late, and there wasn't much noise outside anyway.

I could hear the water, a few crickets, and that was about it.

Nick told me I needed to take a deep breath and let it out slowly as I continued to listen to the water. Then do it again three times, no hurry. I did as he instructed, breathing in and out three times, as I focused on the water. Then I did it again. And again.

Then something magical happened a few minutes later as I sat there in silence.

My heart rate slowed.

My body relaxed.

My shoulders didn't feel so tense.

I didn't have a thousand thoughts fighting for my attention.

I felt peace.

I opened my eyes and stared into the cascading water, still relaxed.

I continued to listen to the fountain, feeling more relaxed than I have felt in years.

It was like I'd had a glass of wine or two.

My buzz had come back.

All that in a few minutes?

"This crap really works," I whispered to myself.

I nodded and stood, glancing over at the light in my office, not feeling motivated to do anything, which was new for me.

Then I did something I hadn't done in years.

I decided to go to bed without finishing everything on my to-do list.

I was tempted to start feeling guilty, but then Nick's words popped into my head.

Don't feel guilty for taking time for yourself.

I would try to take his advice, but I couldn't help feeling that I was going to pay for this the next day.

CHAPTER FIFTEEN

RUTH

Surprisingly, last night was the best night of sleep I'd had in a long time. Was it the pasta or the wine or the quiet time I had spent by the fountain before I went to bed? I had no idea, but it was amazing and perfect. Well, except for one little problem.

The dream I'd had about Nick.

Okay, maybe "dream" wasn't the correct word.

Fantasy.

Much more accurate.

It started with me flashing him again, and everything spiraled out of control from there.

I did everything I could to not let my thoughts drift back to Nick as I lay in the dark last night. Every time he popped into my head I would try to focus on something else. I even tried counting sheep, but the sheep suddenly turned into deer who were eating grapes, which reminded me of wine, which led my thoughts right back to the dinner with Nick.

It was a complete failure.

That's why I'd come up with the plan to avoid Nick all morning. How could I look him in the eyes after I had let him do all those things to me in my dream?

Impossible.

Little did I know it would also be impossible to avoid him since I had to go to the kitchen to get my four cups of morning coffee. He would be able to see me very clearly through the kitchen window each time I did so. And keeping the french doors closed on such a beautiful day would've been conspicuous. The only thing I could do was try to maintain a low profile and keep any type of conversation with him short and to the point.

And avoid eye contact, if possible.

I had to admit I was very excited that today would be the day that they would begin installing my gazebo. According to Nick, the gazebo had already been customized and fabricated offsite. All they had to do was put the custom pieces together, almost like a puzzle.

In a couple of days, my gazebo would be ready to use and all I would have to do was add the furniture that I had already purchased and that was in my garage. I couldn't wait to use it for the first time and could even envision myself occasionally working with my laptop out there.

After my morning croissant and coffee, I was busy at work.

"Knock, knock." Nick peeked through the open french doors of my office.

Startled, I banged my knee on the desk. "Ouch, ouch, ouch, ouch! Come in!"

Nick opened the screen door and closed it behind him. "You okay?"

I nodded, rubbing my knee, avoiding eye contact as planned. "Yeah. Fine. I jammed my knee into the desk. No big deal. What's a little collision with a solid wood desk that weighs three hundred pounds?"

"How long have you been accident prone?"

"How long have I known you?"

He grinned. "That was my fault?"

"You're the easy blame—let's go with that." I stuck my head under the desk like I had dropped something and was looking for it.

"And I suppose it was my fault when you fell off the bike in the—"

"No, no, no, no, no." From below the desk, I shook my finger at him. "The first rule about the gym is never talk about the gym. Ever."

"Of course. Well, can you at least tell me how your wrist is? I noticed you haven't been wearing the brace the last couple of days. I hope that's a good sign."

"It is, thank you for asking. How can I help you?" I pretended to organize files in my file cabinet with my back to him, so I didn't have to look at him.

"Well, I feel kind of funny asking, but . . ."

Silence.

Why didn't Nick finish his sentence?

Don't turn around. Wait it out.

More silence.

What the heck was going on with Nick behind me?

The silence was too awkward.

I had to speak. "Did you pass out?"

"I'm here."

I kept my head down. "And why haven't you finished your sentence?" I pretended to shuffle more things around in the cabinet.

"Why are you avoiding me?"

"I'm not!"

Okay, I didn't have to be so adamant. I think I overdid it there.

"Then look at me," Nick said.

This man was too smart for his own good and it was pissing me off.

I stopped fidgeting with the files and slowly turned around, locking gazes with him, but trying not to think of the dream. "See? I'm looking at you. You were saying?"

He arched an eyebrow. "Why are you acting weird? Is this about last night?"

"What happened last night?"

"I don't know. You tell me."

I flipped my hair back, laughing, trying to play it off. "I don't know *what* you're talking about, and I do need to get back to work. What did you need?"

Nick hesitated. "As I was saying, I feel kind of funny asking, but I promised Brandon I would since I owe him more than a few favors."

I nodded. "He wants to know if Dee is single?"

Nick's eyes widened. "How did you do that? Did you get that from your women's intuition?"

"Yes."

"Tell me what I'm thinking right now."

I shook my head. "I have intuition, not ESP."

"Well, *I* have ESPN, but that's a whole different ball game." He gave a cheesy smile. "See what I did there?"

"I do."

"And you don't think it's funny?"

"I do not."

"Not even a little."

"Nope."

"Hmmm. Tough crowd. By the way, how did you sleep last night? Did you have any weird dreams?"

Oh, no.

How did he do that?

I needed to Google "men's intuition" and see if there was such a thing and if we ladies had some competition. What's next? Spa and shopping days for the guys?

Nick snapped his fingers in front of my face. "Are you okay?"

"I'm fine."

"Well, the reason I asked is because I had a dream and you were in it."

I wanted badly to know what the dream was about, but what if it was hot and steamy like mine? Nick was the only man who had ever made me blush and I didn't want it to happen again.

I have no willpower with this man.

Maybe if he told me just a little.

"What happened in the dream?" I finally asked.

"We were in the water at the beach. Out of nowhere, you grabbed me and kissed me—"

I held up my hand, already feeling my face heating up and feeling the urge to hide my head under the desk again. "That's enough."

"What? You said you wanted to know."

"I thought it was going to be something innocent, like we were at the farmers' market or at the movies. I didn't know you were going to launch into fifty shades of Nick."

He chuckled. "It was just a kiss."

I wasn't going to talk to Nick about kissing. "I'm going to change the subject. Brandon wants to know if Dee is single and she is. And she's interested in him. I'll ask her if she wants me to pass along her phone number. Go." I pointed to the door. "Now."

"You're bossy."

"I know."

"Do you always get your way?"

"Always."

"Okay, but for the record, you don't intimidate me."

"Believe me, that is painstakingly obvious."

He laughed, not saying another word, and finally left my office.

I slumped back into my chair, watching him walk away.

What was with that man?

Why did he make me nervous? And why did I always act like a bumbling fool around him? And more importantly, why had he dreamed about me kissing him?

This was not a good time to have Nick's lips on my mind.

"Focus," I said to myself, getting back to my laptop. "You have a lot of work to do."

Three hours later, I had caught up on the work I hadn't finished yesterday and even tackled a good portion of today's to-do list. Luckily, I didn't have to deal with Nick the last hour since he and Brandon had left to go run errands and pick up materials for the gazebo installation.

Now, on to more important things. I was starving and ready for lunch.

I arrived at Sushi Ota right at noon and pulled into the first parking spot I could find. Nick wasn't kidding when he said the place was located in a strip mall, but it must have been good because it looked crowded inside.

Hopefully, we wouldn't have to wait long because I was ready to eat.

I swung open the front door, stepped inside, and recognized Edward immediately from his photo. He wore jeans with a white polo shirt and a navy-blue blazer.

He was taller than I expected and even better looking.

I liked that he knew it was me and held my gaze with a smile as he approached me.

Head up. Shoulders back.

Confident. Smooth stride. Good.

"Ruth. A pleasure to meet you." Edward pulled a bouquet of flowers from behind his back and handed them to me. "Pretty flowers for a pretty lady."

"You're very kind. Thank you." I smelled the flowers, noting the fresh scent of roses and tulips. I was pretty sure I even smelled eucalyptus in there, even though I couldn't see it.

"You're welcome."

"Your table is ready," the host said, asking us to follow him.

After sitting, I placed the flowers on the chair next to me and hung my purse there.

We ordered food and drinks and just when I was sure we were ready to get to know each other, Edward excused himself to go use the restroom.

No big deal.

The main thing was that there were no immediate red flags.

So far, so good.

I took a sip of my tea and—

"You took my advice," Nick said from behind me.

I sprayed my tea across the table. "Son of a nutcracker!" I stood and slammed my knee into the table, reaching for the napkins and wiping up the tea. "Look what you did!"

"Look what *I* did? Hey, I consider myself to be talented in many ways, but I assure you it would be impossible for me to spit something out of *your* mouth."

"You know what I mean. You scared the crap out of me." I walked around to Edward's chair and wiped it dry. "And *what* are you doing here?"

"Eating."

"I can see that, but—" I glanced toward the bathroom to make sure Edward wasn't coming back, and then tried to keep my voice down. "Why are you here *now*? You planned this?"

"Of course."

"You admit it!"

"Yes. I admit to being hungry and then deciding to come to one of my favorite places to eat, especially since I was warned yesterday by a brutal dictator that I shouldn't skip lunch."

"You recommended this place for my date and then showed up to spy on me."

Nick looked calm and cool like the most annoying, good-looking cucumber I've ever seen. "And why would I show my face if I were spying on you? That defeats the purpose of *spying*, don't you think?"

I didn't know how to respond to that.

"You never told me when your date was. Dee said nothing about it in her text. It could have been next week or next month for all I knew. Do you think I planned on eating here every day until you showed up?"

"Maybe!"

He pointed toward the bathroom. "Here comes your date. Good luck."

"Oh!" I quickly sat back down and waited for Edward.

Luckily, he was distracted as he stopped to say hello to one of the sushi chefs. I was relieved he hadn't seen me talking to Nick. But how was I supposed to act natural and be myself knowing that Nick was seated directly behind me, listening to every word?

It's no big deal. Pretend Nick isn't here.

I forced a smile at Edward as he returned and took a seat across from me.

I took a sip of my tea, ready for small talk.

He gestured back over his shoulder with his thumb. "You wouldn't *believe* the bathrooms here. Top of the line and modern with the perfect balance of porcelain and tile, well-lit, and a urinal so clean you could drink your tea out of it."

Ewww!

I almost sprayed the tea out of my mouth again.

Nick snorted behind me.

Edward folded his hands on the table. "According to your profile, you do corporate takeovers?"

I nodded, glad we weren't going to talk about urinals anymore. "I do."

"Very admirable. I have a lot of respect for women who are go-getters like yourself." He paused, like he wanted me to respond.

"Thank you. That's what I do. I go and I . . . get."

Another snort from behind.

Why had I said that?

I couldn't think straight with Nick close by.

Edward took a sip of his tea. "I'm curious—what's the hardest part of your job?"

I thought about it for a moment. "Oh, I don't know. Probably having to rely on other people to get things done. Most of the time it's easier to do it myself."

"I know exactly what you mean. Too bad we couldn't clone ourselves. Wouldn't that make life much easier?"

I smiled, completely agreeing with him. "It certainly would. Until that day, I will continue to work fourteen to seventeen-hour days."

"Your dedication is amazing. You're a take-charge kind of woman."

"Thank you."

"Where did you get your education?"

"USD and UCLA."

"I'm impressed, you've got brains *and* beauty. You're a real powerhouse."

"Well, I don't know about that, but I've got big goals and I'm working my butt off to achieve them."

"Determination is good. You're an eager beaver."

Another snort from behind.

Ignore Nick. He can't handle that Edward can see all my positive attributes and that he appreciates them.

Edward downed the rest of his tea and poured himself another cup from the pot on the table. "Would you like more?"

Kind and considerate. Appreciates what I'm doing.

"Not at the moment, thank you." I pointed to my tea cup. "I drink pretty slowly."

Another snort from behind. "Unless it's wine."

Edward glanced over my shoulder. "Did that man behind you say something?"

I shook my head. "I didn't hear anything."

I was close to swinging around in my seat and strangling Nick.

Edward drank his tea in one gulp and poured himself another cup.

How was he not burning his mouth?

I could still see the steam coming off the tea as he drank it.

"Oops." Edward stood all of a sudden. "Looks like I need to return to the bathroom for an encore. Be right back in a jiffy." He took off his blazer and hung it on the back of his chair.

"Oh . . . okay." I watched him walk toward the bathroom, expecting Nick to say something snarky, but I was wrong.

Nick didn't come over and didn't say a word.

Good. Let's hope it stays that way.

I was going to ignore him.

I needed to focus on my date and not let Nick get to me.

Fortunately, he was completely quiet, which was a nice change of pace.

Too quiet, actually.

What was he up to?

Had he left?

Maybe I got lucky.

I pulled my compact from my purse and flipped it open, angling it to see behind me in the mirror. I jumped when I saw Nick grinning back at me.

I swung around. "Spying on me again?"

"Says the woman looking for me in her mirror. And what's this guy's deal with all his visits to the bathroom?"

"If you're that concerned, why don't you go see for yourself?"

"My guess is an enlarged prostate, unless he's in the early stages of pregnancy." Nick snorted.

I crossed my arms. "What's with all the snorting? You sound like a pig."

"Your date was contemplating drinking tea out of a urinal. Who's the pig here?" Nick jumped up and came around to sit in Edward's seat. "And worst of all, he's the biggest butt-kisser west of the Mississippi."

"What are you talking about?"

"He's planting seeds in your head to make your ego happy right before he moves in for the kill."

"My ego? You can't be serious."

"Oh, I am. I've seen guys like this before. He pretends that he cares about every word coming out of your mouth, in the hope that you'll think he's kind and a good listener. He tells you everything you want to hear about yourself, to give you this warm fuzzy feeling of being accomplished and loved. And then he's going to try to get you into his bed."

I had one of the best BS detectors and I didn't believe it for a moment. "That is absurd. Have you ever thought that maybe he's a good person and is being sincere?"

"It's not sincerity when the words used are for personal gain. You're a go-getter, a take-charge kind of woman, you don't mess around, you're an eager-beaver." He chuckled. "I bet he'll ask you back to his place before lunch even ends."

"You're delirious. Can you go now?"

"Tell me what he does for a living and I'll leave you alone."

I kept my mouth shut.

"Ruth?"

"Fine, he owns the Bathroom Remodel Warehouse over on Miramar Road. Now go."

"The big toilet-shaped glass building with all the palm trees around it?"

"The very one."

He swung around back toward the bathroom and then

glanced back at me. "That explains it. The guy is sick and twisted. He's probably lying naked on the bathroom floor right now. Ten bucks says he goes back to the bathroom again before you leave."

"No bet. Get back to your table before he sees you."

"I'm going." He closed his hand into a fist and raised it. "Be strong, you powerhouse go-getter."

"I've already started ignoring you."

"I'm okay with that as long as you pay attention to your date and the con job he's pulling over on you."

Con job? Right. I wasn't born yesterday.

I flipped back around and glanced over toward the sushi prep area, hoping the food would be coming soon.

Edward returned and sat, gesturing back to the bathroom like he had done before. "They have the best soap here. You *have to* smell my hands." He held his hands in my direction.

I waved Edward off. "That's quite all right. I believe you. You own the Bathroom Remodel Warehouse on Miramar Road?"

"Going on fifteen years now. I sell toilets, but business is nowhere close to being in the crapper." He laughed. "I never get tired of that one. How long have you been doing corporate takeovers?"

"Ten years."

He shook his head in amazement. "You're really a dynamo."

Nick snorted from behind. "And an eager beaver."

"Not funny, Nick!" I threw my hand over my mouth.

Crap. I said that out loud. Not good.

"Nick?" Edward asked, leaning to the side to glance over my shoulder. "Who's Nick?"

I moved my head to block his view. "That's a good question. If we're talking about Christmas, well then, Saint Nick is probably the answer you're looking for. If you love boybands, there's Nick Carter from the Backstreet Boys and Nick Lachey from Ninety-Eight Degrees."

Edward stared at me.

"I kind of prefer Justin Timberlake, although he's a *Justin* and not a *Nick*, obviously."

It didn't look like my load of bull was working, which was not a surprise. You can't cover up crap with more crap and hope it smells like roses.

Edward stood and looked past me. "Are you Nick?"

"That would be me," Nick said from behind.

I covered my face with my hands.

This can't be happening.

Nick was ruining my date.

Edward's gaze popped back and forth between me and Nick. "Are you on two dates at the same time?"

"What? No!"

"It certainly seems that way. What kind of sick game are you playing with me?"

"I'm sorry, Edward. I . . . uh . . . it's not what it seems."

"You could have at least had the decency of being a little more discreet and eating with him another time."

Nick chuckled. "Believe me, we had dinner last night and she assured me it was a one-time thing."

"Nick!"

"I don't need this crap." Edward stood and yanked his jacket from his chair, practically knocking it over.

A couple of things fell from his jacket pocket onto the floor.

Nick jumped up and picked them up, handing them to Edward. "You dropped these ultra-ribbed condoms."

Condoms? Seriously?

Edward eyed Nick up and down. "Don't be ridiculous. Those aren't mine."

"Sure, they are. They fell out of your jacket pocket with this business card." Nick held it closer to his eyes, analyzing it. "You're not Edward Butts, President and CEO of Bathroom Remodel Warehouse?" Nick chuckled. "Wait, you sell toilets and your last name is Butts? That is classic. Do you mind if I keep the card? I want to show my friends. Good thing for you that your parents didn't name you Harry or Seymour."

"Give me that." Edward yanked the business card from Nick's hands. He walked behind me and grabbed the flowers from the chair next to me. "And *you* don't deserve these. Enjoy the sushi and the bill." He turned and walked out the door without another word.

My pulse pounded in my temples.

I was going to kill Nick.

I just needed to figure out how I was going to dispose of his body.

CHAPTER SIXTEEN

RUTH

A few seconds later, the waiter arrived with the giant sushi platter, placing it in the center of the table, then glancing back toward the door. "Your gentleman friend left?"

I nodded. "There's been a change of plans."

He gestured to Nick. "He will join you?"

I shook my head and flared my nostrils. "*He* is going back to his own table."

"Yes, I am." Nick walked behind me and sat down.

I pointed to the sushi. "Could you do me a big favor and wrap this up to go?"

The waiter bowed. "Of course, ma'am."

"Oh . . . one second." I opened my purse, pulling out a credit card and handing it to the waiter. "Here you go."

"Not a problem at all." The waiter walked away with the platter of sushi and my credit card.

I sat there, shaking my head in disbelief, still thinking about what had happened.

Luckily, Nick was smart and being quiet.

I pulled my phone from my purse and sent Dee a text.

Ruth: Did you eat yet?

Dee: Please don't tell me your date is over.

Ruth: It is. And let it be known that this is the day that Nick is going to die. I have sushi I'm taking to go. Do you want to eat with me?

Dee: Whoa. Backup. What did Nick do this time? And why are you talking about him when you should be talking about Edward?

Ruth: Edward and Nick met at the restaurant.

Dee: Huh? Why do all your men run into each other?

Ruth: Because obviously my dating life is cursed.

Dee: Or it's a sign. But remember, you can't kill Nick, because if you do, you will effectively kill my love life! Hey, I have an idea and it's something you're good at. What about giving Nick a wedgie?

Ruth: Not funny.

Dee: Then why am I dying of laughter over here? Anyway, don't worry about Edward because you're going to meet the man of your dreams this evening.

Ruth: I told you, no dinner dates. It's lunch first, and then if they're worth my time, they can have a second date over dinner.

Dee: It's not a date with a specific man. It's speed dating.

Ruth: No, no, no, no. I've heard about speed dating and

I'm not interested. Besides, I told you Edward was your last shot and now I'm going to find a man my way.

Dee: You said TODAY was my last shot and the day isn't over yet. The speed dating is happening TODAY! And this is not your usual speed dating. The men have been prescreened, are all over 40 years old, and all are successful business professionals. You can meet up to 20 guys. That's 20 dates in less than an hour!"

Ruth: Whoop-di-doo.

Dee: I prefer whoop-di-DEE, thank you very much. Anyway, the way you're going about it now, 20 dates would take 20 days. I thought this would be much more productive. One of those guys has got to be a keeper. Plus, it's being held downtown, and you need to go over there to meet the CEO of Caltonic Industries at four thirty.

Ruth: I'll think about it.

Dee: You're going. I already paid the $150.00.

Ruth: $150.00 for one hour? Are you crazy?

Dee: That is debatable, but this is a high-end event. They get rid of the riffraff, so you don't have to. I told you, this is way better than the average speed dating event.

Ruth: I said I'll think about it.

Dee: You need to think A LOT about it. By the way, YES to the sushi. Are you coming by the office or should I meet you at home?

Ruth: Home. I'll be there in 20 minutes.

I took a sip of my cold tea and set the cup down. It wasn't worth topping off with hot tea because I would be leaving any minute.

The waiter returned with my check and the sushi in a bag.

"Thank you." I signed the credit card slip and took my copy.

I stood and took two steps toward the door, but then paused in front of Nick's table, wanting to say something. He hadn't apologized for his behavior and I would give him the opportunity now.

He casually took a sip of his tea, looking calm, as usual.

Was it possible that he'd really eliminated stress from his life or was he on Valium all the time? How could he be relaxed after what had happened? Where was the guilt? Where was the groveling?

I glanced down at his plate and froze.

To my surprise, he was eating one of my favorite things on the menu at any sushi restaurant, the Dragon Roll. Although some sushi places added their own creative touches, most Dragon Rolls had sticky rice, shrimp tempura, cucumber, and thinly sliced avocado on top resembling the scales of a dragon. And of course, it wouldn't be complete without the spicy mayo.

I had actually ordered some myself and had it in my bag to go but would now have to wait to get home to eat it. Also Nick's fault.

"The sushi here is out of this world." Nick grabbed a piece of the Dragon Roll off his plate and dipped it in the soy sauce with wasabi and ginger.

I glared at him. "I wouldn't know."

"Well, here's something you *should* know . . . I was only trying to help. I didn't want to see you get hurt."

"If that was helping, I'd hate to see what happens when you try to cause problems." I eyed the chair across from him, wondering if we should talk this out and clear the air. I didn't want any awkward moments at the house when he got back to work.

"Have a seat," he said, like the mind reader that he apparently was.

I hesitated, but then pulled out the chair across from him and sat. I placed the bag and my purse on the chair next to me, not sure where to start.

Nick didn't look like he was in any hurry to talk about things. He popped the whole piece of the Dragon Roll into his mouth. It shouldn't have been a surprise that he could fit the whole thing in there, since there was already sufficient evidence to prove Nick had the biggest mouth in town.

Okay, that wasn't fair.

Honestly, I felt bad for even thinking it.

Because Nick was right when it came to the intentions of Edward.

The truth was, I was mad because I could normally see men like Edward coming from a mile away. Most likely I would have caught it at some point, but what also disappointed me was that Nick saw what type of man Edward was before I did. I was smart enough to know that my ego didn't like that, but it was more than that.

I was also worried.

I was off my game.

It felt like maybe I was losing control.

And *that* part I could blame on Nick.

The man frustrated me and distracted me like no other.

I felt vulnerable around him for some reason, and that caused me to make mistakes.

It was like I had my head in the clouds.

Nick ate another piece of his Dragon Roll, chewing slowly, not even worried that I was sitting there starving to death and was going to pass out at any moment.

"Don't you have *anything* to say for yourself?" I eyed the last two pieces of sushi he had left on his plate.

Nick shrugged. "I should be asking you the same thing. Where's your gratitude?"

"Gratitude? You can't be serious."

"I am. Was I right about Edward or not?"

"Yes, but—"

"I was protecting you."

I crossed my arms. "I don't need protection. I'm a big girl and have never had problems handling men."

"I have no doubt about that whatsoever, but I wanted to make sure, in case you were off your game."

Off my game?

That's my line!

I stared at him.

"You seemed a little distracted," Nick said.

"Because of you! *You* distract me."

"Do you mean today or always?"

"Always."

He nodded and grinned. "Is it my charm or my good looks?"

"Both!" I threw my hand over my mouth, because it was evident my mouth was much bigger than Nick's. I removed my hand. "Neither. That's what I meant."

He shook his finger at me. "You already put it out there. You can't take it back now." He chuckled. "Anyway, my point is that I've got your back. That's what friends are for."

"Friends?"

"Of course. We're friends, right?"

"I . . ."

"I mean, I know I drive you crazy, but is that really *all* my fault? And come on, this is the second meal we're sharing in two days. This is getting pretty serious." He laughed.

"First of all, we're not *sharing* a meal."

Nick looked up, studying me. "Look, you don't have to be my friend. Nobody is twisting your arm. I'm just telling you I would like to be friends."

He flashed that grin again that seemed to always debilitate my brain.

I huffed. "Fine. We're friends."

Nick shook his head. "You're wound up so tight you're going to snap. Did you ever do the exercises in front of the fountain?"

I sat up in my chair. "Yes. I can't believe I didn't tell you, but it was *amazing*. And afterwards, it felt like I had a buzz."

Nick nodded, smiling. "I love that feeling. It's like the *Savasana* position at the end of a yoga class. Pure bliss. How long did you do it?"

"Honestly, it was only for a few minutes."

"Hey, that's all it takes. Even two or three minutes is better than nothing. You can gradually increase your time and benefit even more."

"I will. And thanks for sharing it with me."

"My pleasure. And now that we're best friends, I don't mind sharing something else with you."

"Best friends . . ." I laughed, but then stopped myself because it felt weird.

I honestly couldn't remember the last time I laughed with a man. With Dee, yes, all the time, but with the opposite sex? I was drawing a blank.

Nick gestured to my face. "Laughing looks good on you."

I didn't know how to respond to that.

"Okay, here we go." Nick grabbed one of the two remaining pieces of the Dragon Roll on his plate, dipped it in the soy sauce, and held it in the air toward my mouth, carefully keeping his other hand underneath just in case something dripped or fell. "Open up."

I stared at the piece of sushi. "What makes you think I want that?"

He raised an eyebrow. "I *know* you want it."

I was seriously starting to think that my hunch of him having some form of male intuition was true. Because I did want it. Badly.

But then I thought of Bagel Barney and how he held that piece of calamari in front of my mouth at Jack's restaurant, only to pull it away.

Nick wouldn't do that.

It was odd that my gut was confident of what Nick would or wouldn't do, even after his surprising behavior today. I did trust the man completely.

"Come on." Nick moved the piece of sushi closer to me, his grin even wider.

I hesitated, but then moved forward, opening my mouth.

He delicately slid the piece of sushi into my mouth with the chopsticks. "There you go. Now, I dare you to tell me you don't love it."

He watched me chew.

I felt goosebumps form on the back of my neck.

He really seemed to be enjoying my reaction.

I chewed slowly to my heart's delight, not wanting to finish it too quickly, emphatically nodding my appreciation. "Wonderful. Absolutely wonderful."

"Told you." He chuckled and grabbed the last piece of sushi from his plate to eat for himself, dipped it in the soy sauce, and surprisingly held it in my direction again.

"Uh-uh. One is enough, thank you."

Nick shook his head *no*.

"I'm not eating your last piece."

He shrugged. "I guess I can throw it away then."

"What?!"

I didn't mean to yell.

A few of the other diners looked in our direction.

"I said I'm going to throw it away. Too bad." Nick frowned. "All those starving kids in—"

"Okay!" I grabbed his wrist and pulled it in my direction, taking the whole piece from his chopsticks and chewing the divine creation.

He was watching me again.

His eyes on my mouth.

Grinning.

More goosebumps formed on the back of my neck.

He chuckled.

I wiped my mouth, now realizing I had been set up.

My BS detector was dead, obviously.

I shook my head. "You weren't going to throw that away, were you?"

"Are you serious? I was going to give you one more chance to eat it before I ate it myself."

I couldn't help smiling. "You're crazy."

"Maybe, but at least I'm not out of my mind like *some* people I know." He pointed his chopsticks at me.

We shared a laugh together.

Once again, it was the oddest sensation.

Especially since I'd been frustrated and angry ten minutes ago.

This was a true emotional rollercoaster, courtesy of Mr. Nick Morris.

I stared down at his empty plate, curious of something that I had just thought of. "Why did you give me your last two pieces of sushi?"

"Why not? Life is more enjoyable when you share it with someone, don't you think?"

I believed that to be true.

That was the reason I had started this whole dating campaign in the first place.

"Yes. I do believe that," I said. "But did you do it because you felt guilty about what happened with Edward?"

"I won't ever feel guilty for doing what I believe is right. My actions may not always have the best outcome, but as long as I have good intentions, that's what matters most. Plus, imagine marrying that guy. Could you see yourself with the last name of Butts?"

I laughed. "No."

"Ruth Butts. It kind of has a nice ring to it. Can I get you anything else, Mrs. Butts? Butts, party of two! At your wedding, the guests will say, 'Wow, I've never seen so many Butts in one place!'"

I laughed again. "Please . . . I don't even want to imagine what kind of a nickname they would come up for me at work if that was my last name. No, thank you."

"Do they have a nickname for you now?"

I nodded. "Ruthless."

He chuckled. "Why am I not surprised?"

"What can I say, I guess I earned it. What about you? Do you have a nickname?"

"Does Nick have a *nick*name?" He grinned. "See what I did there?"

"Yes, corny and maybe a little cute."

"A little? Anyway, in college, some of the girls called me Nick-fil-A."

I laughed. "I should have seen that one coming. Any others?"

He smiled. "When I was younger, I had two nicknames, actually. One was Knick-knack-paddywhack."

I laughed. "That's cute."

"The other one was *not* so cute."

"What was it?"

"Well, I had a weight problem as a child and some of the other kids called me Moby Nick."

My jaw dropped open. "That's horrible! Kids can be so cruel."

"They can be, yes. What about you? Any nicknames as a child?"

"No comment."

"Okay, now you have to tell me or I'm going on strike. Do you want the gazebo installed or not?"

"Speaking of which, don't you need to get back to work?"

"Says the workaholic who's hanging out at sushi restaurants like she has absolutely nothing to do. Which I have to say is quite surprising and refreshing, actually. But back to the topic at hand, I gave you two of my nicknames as a child. I'm only asking for *one* from you."

I sighed. "Think candy bars . . ."

Nick shook his head. "I've got nothing."

I winced. "Baby Ruth."

Nick erupted in laughter, a deep, hearty laugh. It was so infectious, I started laughing myself, even though I hated that nickname with a passion.

He wiped his eyes. "Good stuff. By the way, where did you find Edward?"

"Online dating, where else?"

He nodded. "It looks like you're not having much luck. It's the second day in a row that you've had a date with someone at a restaurant but didn't actually eat with the person."

"You think that's bad? Then there was the first date of the week where I wolfed down the food as fast as I could and practically ran toward the exit."

"Sounds like you're looking for the wrong type of guy."

"Sounds like *I* need to get back home if you're going to start giving me dating advice."

He threw up his hands in defense. "Fair enough, but I have the perfect solution for your dating woes."

"Thanks, but no thanks."

"Well, if you change your mind . . ."

I smiled. "Thanks for the sushi."

"My pleasure. I'm going to pay, and I'll be right behind you."

I walked out of the restaurant, placed the food in the back seat of my car, and got in.

I started the engine and sat there thinking while the car idled.

What happened in there? I felt relaxed.

For a moment or two or even ten before I walked out of the restaurant, it almost felt like Nick and I were having a completely normal conversation.

And I enjoyed it.

There wasn't any frustration.

I wasn't on edge.

And I actually laughed.

I glanced back toward the front door of the restaurant, my mind on Nick.

What the hell was going on?

CHAPTER SEVENTEEN

RUTH

Dee and I were still eating sushi in the kitchen, one of us occasionally glancing outside toward Nick and Brandon as they worked in the backyard. I had no doubts that the guys were talking about us, but that would make us even, since we were also talking about them.

"What's going on with you today?" Dee asked in a low voice. "Why do you keep looking into the yard?"

"I could ask you the same thing."

"Who's more pathetic, me or you?"

"It's a tie, for sure."

We laughed.

Dee pointed outside. "Let's go talk to them. Maybe, if we sneak up on them, we can hear something juicy."

"How old are you?"

I thought about it for a moment. "Mentally or physically?"

We both laughed again and then stepped outside, walking quietly toward them.

Nick pointed to part of the gazebo. "Tighten up that bolt there."

"Got it." Brandon grabbed the drill and tightened the bolt. "So, let me get this straight, you like her now?"

Like who? Like me?

"Hey, guys!" Dee said, even though she was only looking at Brandon.

I wished she had waited a little longer so I could have heard more and found out if Nick was talking about me. I guess I'll never know.

"How are you two doing?" I asked. "Wow, this is coming along nicely. Not bad for someone who takes extended lunches."

"I can skip my lunch tomorrow to make up for it." He winked at me.

"You're asking for trouble."

"I'll take your warning into consideration."

I tucked some hair behind one ear and smiled. "You'd better. And thanks again for the sushi recommendation. We loved it."

"We did." Dee smiled at Brandon. "Have you tried it?"

Brandon shook his head. "No."

"Oh—we should go some time, if you want."

"I would love to."

"Did you have questions about the project?" Nick asked.

I waved off his question. "No, no. I trust you with that."

"We were wondering what happened to Karma," Dee said.

"I was going to ask you earlier and forgot. I assumed she was back with the owners since you didn't bring her with you today."

Nick nodded. "Yes, she's back with them. She spent the night with me last night, which I admit I quite enjoyed, but the owners finally called me back this morning. Their daughter went into labor early yesterday and they all rushed to the hospital, leaving the dog in the backyard. They ended up being at the hospital for almost twenty-four hours because of complications."

"I hope everything turned out okay."

"They had a little bit of a scare with the birth, but it looks like mom and baby are going to be fine after some recovery time. As for what happened to Karma, someone was supposed to stop by the house a few times to check on her while they were at the hospital, but there was miscommunication, the gate was left open, and then the dog escaped. Luckily, I found her, and nothing happened."

"I agree, and the good thing is that she's back with her owners, safe and sound."

"Although she may not be with them for long. Because of the complications, the mom and newborn are going to stay with her parents for a while after they release her from the hospital. The problem is, the new mom is allergic to dogs. Anyway, I offered to take Karma."

"That was sweet of you." I squeezed Nick's arm. He glanced down at it and then locked gazes with me before I slowly pulled away.

I glanced over at Dee to see her reaction on the matter, but to my surprise, she and Brandon had moved away from us and were talking over by the planters.

When had they moved over there? Was I so transfixed by Nick that I hadn't even noticed they weren't next to us anymore? Was there a moment when I had blacked-out?

Nick cleared his throat. "I can't remember what I was talking about . . ."

That makes two of us.

"Anyway, I love dogs and haven't had one in such a long time," he added. "Karma's owners seemed to like the idea and said they would call me later to let me know. Well, we should get back to work. I'd like to finish most of the gazebo today. Are you okay if we work late?"

"As long as you take breaks every now and then, I have no problem with that."

"Great." Nick clapped his hands one time. "Brandon! Let's get back to work."

"Of course." Brandon turned to Dee. "Talk to you later."

She smiled. "You have my number."

I pointed to the roof panel on the ground. "I'll let you get back then."

"Sounds good," Nick said.

We walked back to the house, acutely aware that the guys were watching us.

After closing the screen door behind me, I walked toward my office.

Dee trailed right behind me.

I sat in my chair and swiveled around to face her as she sat down across the desk from me.

Both of us were quiet.

She stared at me.

I stared right back.

We were trying to read each other's minds, I suspected.

I had no doubts we were thinking about two particular men who were currently working in my backyard, but I had to ask. "What's with that big grin on your face?"

Her grin got wider, then she glanced out to the backyard. "I'm going to marry that man."

I shook my head in disbelief. "Oh, come on. They only say that in the movies."

"I'm serious. I feel it. And before you even mention it, it's not lust. It's the weirdest thing, but when we look at each other, it's like we're talking without the words. It's like we understand each other, without having been on a single date. I believe love at first sight exists. I know it sounds crazy, but I feel relaxed and at peace with Brandon when I see him, almost as if I've had a glass of wine."

I nodded, pretty sure it was the same feeling I felt when I sat in front of the fountain listening to the water with my eyes closed. Also, the same feeling when Nick fed me the sushi at the restaurant. How could someone feeding me sushi be so euphoric?

Still, there was a difference; I didn't think I was going to marry the man.

There were a few moments where I got the feeling that Nick wasn't such a bad guy after all.

I wanted to be friends with him.

I glanced through the screen doors as Nick and Brandon lifted one of the pieces of the gazebo roof over their heads to attach it.

Dee smiled. "And *you* have the hots for Nick."

"I do not. I admit that he's a fascinating man and—"

"Hot."

"Fine, he's hot, but it's possible for him to be hot without me having the hots for him. Those are two completely different things."

"If you say so."

I didn't think I had the hots for him. Really.

Dee leaned back in her chair. "In fact, why don't you prove you don't have the hots for him?"

I crossed my arms. "How am I going to do that?"

"By going to the speed dating event this evening. I think the reason you're resisting going is because you have feelings for Nick."

"That makes no sense. How could I have feelings for him? We haven't even gone on a date."

"Neither have Brandon and I. Yet . . ."

I blew out a frustrated breath. "Maybe I don't feel like going to speed dating because I know it's going to be a waste of my time."

"You have the chance to meet up to twenty men in an hour."

"I have the chance to meet twenty *losers* in an hour."

"The men have been prescreened, are all over forty years old, and *all* are successful business professionals."

"Blah, blah, blah, you've already told me that. Repeating information does not make it more appealing the second or third time around. It just becomes annoying."

Dee crossed her arms and glared at me.

She was the one person in the world who knew me better than I knew myself.

I couldn't take it anymore. "Fine. I'll go."

Dee studied me. "I don't believe you."

"Since when have I lied to you?"

"You mean *today*?"

I laughed and glanced over at my vibrating phone to check the caller ID. "It's Gary."

"He probably wants to know the latest on Caltonic," Dee said.

I nodded and answered the call. "Hi, Gary. What's going on?"

"Hey, Ruth. Just wanted to get the latest on Caltonic. Have you heard back from Byron?"

"Not yet."

"We need to push this one through. The board is getting antsy that we're not going to hit our numbers this quarter. How close are you to closing the deal?"

"I was hoping it was already going to be closed by now, but I'm guessing that it's still tied up with their legal department. I'm going to see Byron this afternoon. I can give you an update after I meet with him."

"Sounds great. Why don't you stop by the office after you meet with him? How's six o'clock?"

"Well, uh . . ."

I glanced at Dee.

"What?" she whispered.

"Hang on a second, Gary."

"Okay . . ."

I stuck the phone in my desk drawer and closed it, then leaned toward Dee, whispering, "He wants me to stop by the office after meeting Byron."

"No! No! No!" Dee said in a low voice, wagging her finger at me. "Don't you dare. That's your excuse for skipping the speed dating. You're going. I'll handle whatever Gary needs."

I stared at Dee, torn about what to do, and knowing I had to make a snap decision because Gary was still on the phone waiting. I had never said no to Gary since I had started working for the company ten years ago. Anything he wanted, he got it. If he wanted me to jump, I asked how high. He was going to suspect something if I said no, but part of me wanted to.

Dee shook her head emphatically. "Don't. You. Dare."

Don't feel guilty for taking time for yourself.

Why am I not surprised that Nick's advice popped into my head again?

I sighed and fell back into my chair, pulling the phone from the drawer and raising it back up to my face. "Hey, Gary. Yeah, unfortunately I can't make six o'clock. I've got things I've got to take care of this evening. I can give you a call with an update, though."

"Oh . . . Work related?"

Wonderful.

Why would he ask me that?

Now, I had to decide if I was going to lie to my boss or not.

I opted for the truth.

"No. Personal things." I winced, waiting for his response.

"Okay, okay . . . I must say that this isn't like you, Ruth. I hope it's important."

I nodded, even though he couldn't see me. "It is. *Very* important."

"Very well then. I expect an update ASAP."

"You got it."

I disconnected the call, set my phone on the desk, and sat back in my chair.

"What?" Dee asked.

I shook my head. "I don't know . . . I got the weirdest feeling in my gut."

"Your gut has always been right. What kind of feeling?"

I shrugged. "I've been busting my ass for ten years and have gone above and beyond what was expected of me, and this was the first time ever that I . . ." I sighed.

"You did this to yourself."

"Thanks for your support," I said.

"But it's true. Hear me out . . ."

"The stage is yours."

"Here's the deal . . . You let them know years ago, before your first day, during your interview, actually, that you were willing to have no life to get to the top. And you didn't say that to get the job. You backed up those words with actions. You've been clearing the exact path you wanted your career to take. You knew the company well when you started working for Stansfeld. They hire people who have no problem giving up everything for their careers."

"Yeah, but—"

"It's not wrong, because you signed up for this life. But the truth is, it's only going to get worse. When you become managing partner, you're going to have to account for yourself, plus *everyone* under you. That's a lot of people. And it's *a lot* of pressure and a lot of responsibility that the average person wouldn't come close to being able to handle. I have no doubt in my mind that *you* can do it, because you're the toughest, hardest-working, take-no-prisoners, kick-ass woman I have ever met in my entire life. The question is, are you going to be happy? Because that's what it comes down to. Will you be happy?"

"Now, you sound like Nick."

She smiled. "See that? Nick's on your mind again."

"I'm serious. He says I'm a workaholic."

"You are."

"He also said I get to choose exactly how I want to live my life and if that's my preference, if that's what makes me happy, more power to me."

"He's right again. The question is, will you be happy?"

I shrugged.

"Well, only you can answer that. And you need to be honest with yourself. Now, back to the most important topic at hand, the speed dating event."

"Yeah, that."

"You can skip the speed dating—"

"Make up your mind!"

"You didn't let me finish. You can skip the speed dating *if* you have a thing for Nick. It's nothing to be ashamed about. You keep telling me he's not your type, but I see something happening between you. Something changed. It's in your physiology when you talk about him. And the bottom line is, you can't choose love. Love chooses you."

I laughed. "Love? Seriously? Give me a break. Like it's that easy and I'm just going to find love in my own backyard."

"Sometimes *it is* that easy."

"I think you're confused. Just because I may think a man is attractive, or because I enjoyed a few laughs with him at the sushi restaurant does not mean it is *anywhere* close to love."

"You *laughed* with a man?" She sat back in her chair. "You didn't tell me this. That's amazing. It's unprecedented."

"I'll give you that much and it could've been a fluke. It doesn't *mean* anything. And to prove it. I'm going to the speed dating event."

"Seriously?"

"Seriously."

Dee stared at me again, but I forced a smile right back, letting her know I was making the right decision and would prove to her that I wasn't interested in Nick.

But if I were being completely honest, I needed to prove it to myself first.

CHAPTER EIGHTEEN

RUTH

After visiting Byron at Caltonic and confirming that everything was a done deal, I called Gary to update him, and then I walked into the Mexican restaurant where the speed dating event was being held. I had no idea what to expect. I was surprised that women were already seated in their places, ready to go, while the majority of the men were hanging out in the bar.

I had the sudden urge to eat chips and guacamole but decided against it for fear of having something stuck in my teeth during the dates and not finding out until I got home.

Luckily, the women stayed seated in the same place while the men would rotate around the room to each of the tables when the buzzer or whatever they used sounded to signify the date was over. Dee told me that each date lasted only three minutes.

I checked in and the host gave me my name tag that said RETH.

Seriously?

I mentioned the mistake and she let me know that the name tags were pre-printed since the event was sold-out, but that they would try to get me another one.

Until then, my name was Reth.

I squeezed through the men at the bar, grabbed a Heineken from the bartender, and waded back through the sea of testosterone, noticing that there were easily ten to twelve sets of eyes watching me as I made my way to my assigned table.

Could they be anymore obvious? What a bunch of horn dogs.

I sat and took a swig of my beer, waiting.

Lively Latin music was playing, and I couldn't help tapping my toes to the beat, waiting for the event to start.

A man grabbed a microphone from the sound booth and walked to the center of the dance floor, smiling. "Welcome to our speed dating event this evening. Are you happy?"

Cheers and applause filled the bar.

Oh, joy. I'm ecstatic.

Okay, maybe I needed to change my attitude because I paid a lot of money for this event. I didn't want to come off as a snobby bitch who thought she was too good to be there because we were all in the same boat.

We were all looking for love.

"We're glad you could make it!" the man continued. "Odds are, you're going to meet someone tonight. Will they be your soulmate? Only time will tell. Just a few quick rules. You get three minutes per date. When you hear the bell, your date is over and then the men will move to their right to start a new date at the next table. Mark your scorecards in between dates, so we know if you would like to see that person again. We'll send you an email tomorrow with contact details of the other person, if you both expressed the same interest. You're all business professionals here. *Do not* talk about your jobs. Talk about your interests outside of work, your hobbies, favorite foods, places you'd like to travel to, you get the idea. No business talk, got it?"

"Got it," everyone answered together.

"Are you ready? Let's do this! Your first date starts now!" He smiled and rang the bell.

I could see my first date approaching me and my BS detector was already pegging in the red.

It was the way he walked.

Was he going for a swagger like Mick Jagger or a drunk pimp limp? It was kind of a mix of the two. Or maybe he had an injured leg or a bad case of hemorrhoids.

No, that wasn't it.

Now, I could see it plain and clear.

His ego was showing.

The man was full of himself.

Not a good first impression.

I eyed his name tag.

Julian.

You don't see that name too often.

Please impress me, Julian. You're not off to a good start.

Julian took a seat, leaned back in the chair with his legs

spread wide, like he was trying to air out his junk. He glanced at my name tag. "Interesting name. How do you pronounce that? Wreath? Like a Christmas wreath? Or is that Reth like Seth Meyers?"

"It's Ruth, actually. It's a typo."

"Ah, I get it. Well, tell me something good, Reth."

"Pardon me?"

Was he not listening? I looked around, wondering if this was a joke. This guy was supposed to be a business professional. He didn't exhibit any type of behavior to suggest he knew a thing about business or sitting etiquette, for that matter.

"You know, tell me something about *you*. Anything." He checked his watch.

What was he doing?

Was he bored already on a three-minute date? Did he even want to be here?

"Do you like to swim?" Julian obviously wasn't patient enough to wait for me to respond.

"Love it," I answered, even though it was an odd question to start off with.

"One piece or bikini?"

I blinked, wondering if this guy was a pervert.

Maybe he carried women's underwear in his pockets.

"You know, do you have any preference on swimwear?" he added.

Another ridiculous question, but I wanted to see where this was going. "Bikini."

"Excellent choice." He checked his watch again, but this time he pressed a sticky electrode pad to the side of his neck where he'd had his fingers earlier. It was connected to a wire that he plugged into his phone.

What the heck is that and what the heck is he doing?

He looked up and saw me watching him. "Please continue. You were talking about your bikini. What color and how skimpy are we talking here?" He eyed my cleavage.

"What exactly are you doing?"

He kept his fingers glued to his neck where he stuck the electrode pad. "I know we're not supposed to talk about work, but I'm a *very* successful app developer. Made over a million last year, after taxes." He grinned. "Ever heard of the Diggity Dog app?"

"No."

"What about Diggity Dang?"

"No."

"Dag Diggity Dapitty Doo?"

"No."

"Hot Digitty Daggity Doggity Dogone Doo Bop De Doo?"

"No."

"Dang Dong Dung—"

I held up my hand. "I'm obviously not the target market for your apps and you still haven't answered my question. What exactly are you doing? What's with the contraption on your neck?"

"I'm monitoring my heartbeat for arousal."

I stared at him.

"It's the ultimate sign of a connection between a man and a woman. If you can get my heart rate up to a hundred and thirty beats per minutes, we've got a good thing going on here. For instance, when you were talking about your bikini, my app showed that my heart rate went up dramatically. Great sign! That means I am attracted to you and want to hear more of what you have to say. But when you were telling me that you hadn't heard of any of my award-winning apps, my heart rate dropped. Bad sign, but it's early. Go ahead, keep talking. I can't test my app if you don't talk."

Julian opened his legs even wider, like he was a construction crane wanting to pick up something.

"Please close your legs."

He shook his head. "What's your problem?"

"I'm the one with the problem?"

"Do you have PMS or something?"

"It's not PMS, it's you." It was time for me to end this charade. "Can you sing?"

Julian hesitated. "I've been known to carry a note or two."

"Yeah? Can you hit the high notes like Mariah Carey?"

"Of course not. That would be impossible for a man."

I eyed his zipper. "Not if I kick you in the nuts real hard. Care to test out my theory?"

He finally closed his legs. "You're a freak, you know that?"

"Of course. *I'm* the one who's a freak."

Julian stood. "I'm outta here."

"Hot diggity dog, I was hoping you were going to say that."

He walked toward the bar and, thankfully, out of my life forever.

Like clockwork, my bad luck with dating continued.

I sighed, wondering why I couldn't meet a man like Nick.

I froze, a little freaked out that I'd had that thought.

I took a big swig of my Heineken, trying to get him out of my head.

Fortunately, the bell rang.

"All right! Mark your score cards!" the host said.

I wrote negative one hundred points next to Julian's number and left the box blank where I was supposed to say if I wanted to get his contact info.

Hell, no.

"Okay, men, listen up! Please move to the next table on your right and good luck with your next date! I hope you're all having fun already!"

"The time of my life," I mumbled to myself.

The next man approached my table, wearing what appeared to be a fancy Italian suit and carrying a thin black leather portfolio.

He sat down and held out his hand across the table. "I'm Gustav. A pleasure to make your acquaintance, Reth."

I shook his hand and smiled. "Thank you. You, too. It's Ruth, by the way. It's a typo."

I guessed I was going to have to repeat that twenty times today unless the host got me a new name tag with my name spelled correctly.

Gustav shook his head in disgust. "Typos drive me insane."

"Me, too."

Okay, it was a small victory, but we already had

something in common. As long as he didn't check his heart rate and let me know if he was aroused, we were off to a good start.

Gustav pointed to the table he had just came from. "That last date didn't go well, unfortunately, but it was my own fault. I arrived late because my GPS stopped functioning as I was driving here. I took it for granted and it failed me, but I take full responsibility because I was supposed to update the software a couple of weeks ago. Luckily, I stopped and asked for directions and didn't miss too much. And here I am!"

I just stared at him.

Sitting in front of me was a man who admitted when he was wrong *and* actually asked for directions. Two of the qualities I was hoping to find in a man, even though I knew the odds were better that I would spot the Loch Ness Monster.

I needed to take a picture of Gustav.

He was a rare man and he now had my full attention.

Maybe I was finally going to get lucky and meet a decent guy.

He squeezed the black portfolio in his hands. "Sometimes the small chit-chat of a date can get in the way of what's most important to successful business people like ourselves." He opened his portfolio, pulled out a slip of paper, and handed it to me. "Here are my qualifications, as well as my investment portfolio. This can help you make a quick decision as to whether or not I'm worth your time." He winked. "I think my investments and net-worth speak for themselves. Let me know if you have any questions or need me to expand on anything that you see there."

Wow. This guy was well-prepared.

Smart, well-dressed, and right to the point.

I always appreciated a man who didn't beat around the bush.

Although I had to admit this was a little weird as I eyed the document that told me he was worth over twenty million dollars and had a house overlooking San Diego Bay.

Yes, another item on of my list of traits when I started on this dating journey was to find a man who was fiscally responsible. Someone who knew how to manage his money well, and had an impressive portfolio of growth stocks, treasury securities, municipal bonds, plus a high-yield savings account, and multiple real estate holdings.

Gustav had all of these things and more.

I nodded, reading the information. "Harvard, huh?"

Gustav nodded. "Graduated top of my class." He pointed to the document. "I'm sorry I ran out of space and I'm not a fan of two-page documents. I thought I would tell you verbally that I do have eleven other investment properties not listed under my real estate holdings. Palm Springs, Las Vegas, New York, Miami, Costa Rica, just to name a few. I have a team working for me at the moment to acquire more international properties. I'm open to investing in any part of the world. The goal has always been to be well-diversified."

I nodded. "You can't have a much better goal than that."

Gustav had almost all of the things I was looking for on the list I had created. He was confident, kind, smart, successful, fiscally responsible, open-minded, good looking, and had good decision-making capabilities.

On paper, he was perfect and matched everything on my list.

Why wasn't I doing backflips over him?

I should be leaning forward in my seat, eager to get to know as much as possible about him before the three minutes were up. I should be visualizing us on a real date and looking forward to it. The truth was, that was the furthest thing from my mind.

Are you looking for a soulmate or a business partner?

Dee's question popped into my head, front and center.

According to her, the traits I wanted in a man were ridiculous.

I was beginning to see her point.

She said I needed someone with a sense of humor.

A man who was compassionate, honest, and down-to-earth.

Someone like Nick.

Oops, I did it again.

I brought Nick back into the equation and I really needed to stop doing that.

The bell rang and snapped me out of my thoughts. "Wow, that was fast."

Gustav nodded. "Time flies when you're having fun." He stood and held out his hand. "It was a pleasure to meet you."

I shook his hand. "You, too."

I agreed that time flew when you were having fun, but there was nothing fun about the time I had spent with

Gustav. He was kind and a gentleman, there was no doubt about that. He was also well-organized and probably the sanest man of all my dates by far. But what had happened between us didn't feel like a three-minute date.

We met.

I reviewed his document.

And then he left.

It felt more like I was working.

And what was fun about that?

Nothing at all, that's what.

"Mark your score cards!" the host said. "Guys, it's time to move to your next date!"

I stared at the blank box where I was supposed to say if I wanted to get Gustav's contact information, contemplating what to do.

In the end, I had to be honest with myself.

I left it blank.

"Okay, men!" the host added. "Same thing as last time, please move to the next table on your right and enjoy your next date! I hope you're all getting the hang of this now!"

Here we go.

Date number three.

Just seventeen more to go.

That is, if I made it through all of them.

I was feeling less motivated about this event, plus I was starving. I was pretty sure I was going to bail on this if I didn't meet a candidate with a lot of potential soon. Especially if I kept smelling the fajitas on the sizzling platters.

I took another swig of my beer and set the bottle down, glancing over as the next man approached my table.

"Looks like I hit the proverbial jackpot," he said, his eyes wide as he sat down in front of me. "I'm Boyd and *you* are Reth. I love your name. It's just like Macbeth, only completely different."

"You lost me there."

He slapped the table. "Good! Just trying to keep you on your toes. That's a man's job. Anyway, I'm a certified alligator handler whose passions include foraging for wild mushrooms, collecting original comic book art from the Silver Age of Marvel fandom, and most importantly and most recently, I'm a *big* fan of William Shakespeare. What a wordsmith that man is."

"Was."

"Right. Was. The guy's dead. I love words myself in case you're wondering."

I'm not.

"I'm proud of my impeccable locution, do you know what I mean?"

"I don't."

"I'm still keeping you guessing! That's a man's job, to extrapolate, to satiate, and to—"

"Vacate? Now's the time. Make a run for it."

He slapped the table again and laughed. "Good one! You're hilarious."

I was serious.

"And what's the woman's job?" I asked.

Boyd sat back in his chair. "That's easy. A woman's job is to radiate and exfoliate."

He had either been sniffing glue or was high on the mushrooms he was foraging.

Either way, this guy was already gone. He didn't even know it.

I would have to wait out the time left on the clock and then hope the next date would be better.

Boyd looked around the bar. "Not a bad establishment, but it's not the place to cogitate or delve into the annals of possibilities. Hey, did you ever notice how the words annals and anal are so much alike?"

I shook my head. "Not even a little."

One minute left. Hang in there.

"Have you ever pondered the meaning of life and then come to the conclusion that you're existentially insufficient without a feasible way to elucidate a concept and that you might suffer the malaise that kept you from being one with who you are and who you are not?"

I sighed, ready to put yet another man in his place. "Look—I appreciate your ebullient and convivial attempt at communication, but it's nothing more than sesquipedalian loquaciousness. Furthermore, your disheveled and brusque articulation and verbiage might be considered avant-garde to the neophyte, but as someone who has been compared to a lexicographer, I consider it a blatant faux pas and boondoggle that comes off as more of a cacophony of informal confab that is the complete opposite of perspicacious."

His eyes went wide. "Holy cow. You're much better than I am."

"No shit, Sherlock."

Thank God the bell rang.

Boyd stood and studied me. "I'm guessing you're not going to want my contact info at the end."

"You're a smart man, Boyd."

He smiled. "Thanks! Maybe I'll see you at the bar later."

"There's a zero percent chance of that happening."

"Great. See you then."

I tried to wake myself up from this nightmare. Slamming the rest of my beer, I decided to give it one more shot. One more man. There were many other men in lineup, but there was only so much idiocy one person could take.

One more.

"Mark your score cards!" the host said. "Men! You know what to do, don't get lazy now! Same thing as before, please move to the next table on your right! Ladies, are we having fun yet?"

Only three or four ladies answered, giving me the impression that they were all suffering as much as I was.

I turned to my right to glance at the next man coming my way and—

No way. It can't be.

CHAPTER NINETEEN

RUTH

Dating after forty was like trying to find the least damaged item at a thrift store that didn't smell like someone had left it in their trunk for a year.

Why was being single so hard?

And why was Bagel Barney at the speed dating event?

"Ruth!" He danced his way toward me, doing one of the worst versions of the conga line I had seen in my entire life, lifting his legs in time with the rhythm of the Latin music playing from the bar music system. I watched his uncoordinated legs in horror, wondering if he was double or triple jointed, if there was such a thing.

One-two-three-kick. One-two-three-kick.

Why am I being tortured like this? What have I done to deserve this?

"What are the chances?" Barney said, out of breath from

his full body Latin convulsion that made me want to do shots of tequila so I could forget I ever witnessed it.

I pinched the bridge of my nose. "Considering my luck, I'd say that the odds were pretty good I was going to run into you again."

Barney nodded. "Yeah, I'm lucky, too." He glanced around the bar. "This place is packed like sardines, but you still couldn't hide from my free bagels, could you? One of these days you're going to try one." He laughed and sat down. "Didn't I tell you this was a sign? The stars have aligned, and nothing can keep us apart. The proof is in the pudding."

I stood up. "Sorry, Barney. I can't do this."

"Ahhh, come on, Ruth. Give me a shot. Most guys are all sizzle and no steak."

"I can't argue with you there."

"But with me, I'm one hundred percent USDA Prime Angus beef with—" He stared at my name tag. "Hey, did you change your name?"

"Yes, my name is Reth now."

"I *love* it. Hey—let's explore the possibilities of this thing called love."

"I'd rather not."

"It's not a half-baked idea."

"Yes. It is."

"You need to get to know me a little better and you'll see I'm not a bad egg at all. I admit that I'm an acquired taste, like anchovies or gorgonzola. Just ask Max." He pointed three tables down from us. "Hey, Max! Look who's here!"

This can't be happening.

I cranked my head to the side and sure enough . . .

"Hi, Ruth!" Max waved enthusiastically.

"It's Reth now!" Barney corrected Max, yelling across the bar. "She changed her name!"

"Great! Three more tables and I'll be with you to catch up!"

Because *so much* has happened since I had seen him yesterday.

What were we going to talk about?

That he and Barney were now best buds?

Time to make my escape.

I walked around my table to leave. "Good luck, Barney. I have to go." I continued toward the door without looking back.

"Looks like we're out of luck again, Max!" Barney called out from behind. "What did I tell you? She's a runner and a tough nut to crack!"

Back in my car, I ripped the name tag off my blouse, pulled my phone from my purse, and sent a text to Dee.

Ruth: Call the Vatican to see if they have any vacancies for nuns.

Dee: How many men did you make it through?

Ruth: Only five. And Bagel Barney made another surprise appearance. So did Max. Like a rash that I can't get rid of. I'm on my way home.

Dee: I'm still at your place but won't be here when you get back. Brandon and I are going out to dinner!

Ruth: Lucky you. Have fun. Let me know how it goes later.

Dee: Will do. Oh, and Nick has a surprise for you.

Ruth: What kind of surprise?

Dee: It's a surprise.

Ruth: Tell me.

Dee: No. But I promise, you're going to love it.

Ruth: Tell me.

Dee: No.

Ruth: You're fired.

Dee: I quit.

Ruth: Well played. You can keep your job.

Dee: I know.

I hated when she teased me like that. Now, I couldn't wait to find out what it was.

I needed something positive to change my mindset and I needed it now.

Maybe I would even do another breathing exercise in front of the fountain.

I caught myself going over the speed limit twice on the way home.

Slow down. You don't need a ticket.

I entered the house, set my purse on the kitchen counter, and opened the screen door to head outside to the backyard, stopping in my tracks when I saw such an amazing sight for sore eyes.

My gazebo was finished.

Nick was sitting inside of it, looking relaxed, of course.

Karma was by his side.

All my new furniture from the garage was set up inside the gazebo. Nick had even strung up the white lights around the border above his head.

I approached slowly, in awe, noticing the new wisteria planted near the ground of each post. I would have to be patient for it to grow and cover the gazebo, but I couldn't wait. A wisteria in full bloom was one of the loveliest sights.

"Wow!" I stepped inside the gazebo, did a spin, and then sat down on the red, thick-cushioned wicker chair across from him. "I love it."

Nick grinned. "I was hoping you would." He gestured to the dog. "Karma was hoping so, too."

I smiled, leaned over, and scratched her on the head. "Does this mean you get to keep her for a while then?"

"If you mean keeping her for the rest of her life, then yes."

"That's wonderful! I thought you were talking about something temporary."

"Honestly, I wasn't sure. I was willing to pitch in if they needed help. They said since they now had their first grandchild, and since the mom was going back to work in a couple of months, they wanted to be the ones to take care of the baby. That works for me!"

"So, Karma is officially yours."

Nick nodded. "She's mine. And I hope you don't mind me bringing her here without asking this time. I was banking on the fact that you would probably understand, plus since you and I are almost best friends now."

I laughed. "Yes. Almost." I glanced around the backyard. "I don't understand how you were able to do this so quickly. You're amazing."

"Well, I would love to take all the credit, but you have to remember that the gazebo was custom-built like a puzzle.

It was a matter of connecting the pieces. Brandon is the best worker a man like me could have and I couldn't have done it without him. Plus, I did bring in another worker for a few hours to run the electricity and connect the ceiling fan and the lights."

"Who planted the wisteria?"

"*That* would be me. Getting my hands dirty in the garden is one of the most pleasurable things to do, so there was no way I was going to let someone else do it. The good news is, we're way ahead of schedule."

"I don't think I've ever heard those words from a worker at my house."

He laughed. "Mark this date down in history."

"I appreciate that you're ahead of schedule, but there's no need to rush. I don't want you to hurt yourself."

Also, I don't want to see you go.

"You don't have to worry about that, since Brandon does most of the heavy lifting. And I *did* have an ulterior motive if I'm being honest."

"What is it?"

"I have a family reunion tomorrow afternoon that I'm going to and I didn't want to get behind schedule."

I nodded. "Is there a special milestone the family is celebrating?"

"No. It's something we do every year. Everyone looks forward to it."

"Do you have a big family?"

"I guess it depends on who we're comparing it to, but I think it's pretty big. We should have around fifty people there."

"Wow. I was expecting you to say twenty people or maybe twenty-five at the most. I guess we shouldn't compare your family to mine. I'm an only child and so are my parents. It's pretty much just us and my grandparents who live in Palm Springs."

Nick leaned forward and nodded. "I'm an only child too, but the difference is my dad had eight brothers and sisters, and most of them have had multiple children. It adds up quickly."

"It sure does."

"My mom came up with the idea of the yearly family reunion that wasn't connected to any holiday. There was a better chance of everyone not being away on vacation or too busy. For her, it was more important and easier to get together on our reunion day than Christmas, the Fourth of July, Thanksgiving, Easter, or any other day that families usually got together."

"That's such a great idea."

"She expects everyone to be there because, according to her, we all have had enough advance notice to make it happen. She made it very clear that she didn't want to be disappointed with no-shows."

I smiled. "She sounds like the matriarch of the family."

"She is. A strong, confident woman who doesn't take crap from anyone."

"I like her already."

Nick grinned. "Not a surprise."

Karma got up and moved closer to me, lying back down, and placing her head on top of my feet.

Nick pointed at her. "She likes you."

"Such a sweet girl." I petted her. "And has anyone disappointed your mom by not showing up to the reunion?"

"Not yet. The last four years in a row we've had a hundred percent of the family in attendance. And as soon as one family reunion ends, the date for next year's reunion is sent out by email."

We sat there for a few moments, silent, enjoying the sound of the fountain and the crickets.

It was a beautiful evening, and I was starving, although I wasn't going to say anything since I was enjoying sitting there in my new gazebo.

"You should come with me," Nick blurted out.

I blinked twice. "Where?"

"To the reunion."

Honestly, if I'd had to guess what Nick was going to say next in our conversation, I would've guessed a thousand other things before that.

Go with him?

To his family reunion?

Why would I go to the reunion with him?

And why would he *want* me to go?

"You look paralyzed," Nick finally said. "Should I call a doctor? Did you have an aneurism or is it another wedgie? Are you going to fall off the chair?"

I laughed. "*What* was my rule about the gym?"

"Never talk about the gym."

"And what did you do?"

"I talked about the gym."

"And how do you think I feel about that?"

"Hmm. I'm guessing that you're torn because I'm such a daring man who deserves kudos for defying a woman like yourself?"

I stared at him, trying to keep a straight face, which wasn't easy because he was cute when he was being silly.

"No?" He chuckled. "What's the problem? Why not come to the reunion with me?"

"Because I'm not family?"

"Brandon will be there and he's not family either. We have a great time, and there's no doubt you can use some fun in your life. Especially after your speed dating catastrophe today."

I froze. "I'm going to kill Dee."

He laughed. "If it makes you feel any better, she told Brandon, and then Brandon told me. I'm not sure if that means you need to kill two people, but I wanted you to know before you chose the weapon."

I stared at him.

"Look, you think too much and you need to loosen up. You're uptight."

"I'm not uptight. I'm focused on my goals and my concentration can sometimes come off as me being too serious."

"I thought girls just want to have fun? That's how the song goes. Or is it girls just want to work and work and work and then drop dead? When was the last time you had fun, anyway?"

I crinkled my nose. "Is this a rhetorical question or do you want the exact year or decade?"

"See? That's *exactly* my point. You can't even remember, and you need to get a life."

I would have argued with him just then if it weren't the truth. I had made a decision after the incident on the plane that I had to make changes, but what had I done that was fun lately?

Nothing.

I shouldn't have been too hard on myself because I had been making a concerted effort to find someone special in my life, even though I hadn't been having much luck yet. Why wasn't I meeting a man when I was putting myself out there? I wished I knew the answer.

"I have the answer," Nick said, as if he had read my mind.

That was weird.

"Answer to what?"

"To your dating woes, I mean. I can help."

This I had to hear.

I crossed my arms. "I really wouldn't call them dating woes, but—"

"That's exactly what they are. There will be at least five *very* eligible bachelors at the reunion. My cousins, so I can vouch for them. They're all considered catches."

"If they are catches, why are they single?"

"Why are *you* single?"

"Why are *you*?"

"I asked you first."

We stared each other down for a few seconds and then both laughed.

I shook my head. "Who's being more ridiculous right now, you or me?"

"I think it's a tie." He gave me a knowing smile.

It was like we were both attracted to each other, but neither of us was going to do a damn thing about it. Who was going to hold out the longest? This felt like a game of chicken.

"Come on," Nick said. "Spread your wings. Enjoy being with people who are the salt of the earth. Good people, great food, fun games on the beach."

I hesitated. "Why do you want me to go?"

Nick shrugged. "Because I know you'll have fun."

"Yes, but why do you *want* me to have fun?"

He opened his mouth and closed it.

"Nick?"

He hesitated. "Seeing other people sad makes me sad."

I crossed my arms and pouted. "I'm not sad."

"Okay then, let me rephrase that. Seeing other people happy makes me happy. Is there anything wrong with that?"

I shook my head. "No. Not at all."

"Good. Because I would like to see you happy."

I thought about it for another moment. "Before I say yes, do you have *anyone* in your family named Barney?"

He stared at me like I was crazy.

Maybe I was.

"No," Nick answered.

I nodded, satisfied. "Good."

He opened his wallet and pulled out a card. "But I did meet a guy named Barney who has a couple of bagel shops. He gave me this card for a free bagel."

I pointed to the card. "Tear that card up *now* and never step foot in his shop ever, if you appreciate our friendship."

Nick chuckled, then tore up the business card, sticking the broken little pieces back inside his wallet.

He slipped the wallet back in his pocket. "Done."

"You didn't even ask me why I wanted you to tear it up."

"It doesn't matter. It seemed important to you, so I did it. Remember what I said earlier? I want you to be happy."

"Thank you. Count me in. I'll go to your reunion with you."

"Good." He studied me for a moment. "You're a rare bird, Ruth."

"You are, too."

We shared another laugh.

Nick stood. "Karma and I should get going." He grinned. "Our family reunions are always the best. I'm glad you're coming. Three o'clock tomorrow and we always stay to watch the sunset. And who knows, maybe you'll meet someone special." He winked.

I already had.

His name was Nick Morris.

And what Nick didn't know was that I had agreed to go to the reunion so I could spend more time with *him*.

CHAPTER TWENTY

NICK

As I unfolded chairs on the beach at La Jolla Shores for our family reunion, my thoughts were on Ruth again and why she had been occupying space in my brain recently. I had come to the most obvious conclusion.

There was nothing sexier in the world than a confident woman.

Sure, she had issues, but who didn't?

And even though I had told myself and Brandon countless times that I would not be traveling down that road again, there I was, bewitched by a woman who I couldn't stop thinking about.

I had told Ruth that there would be eligible bachelors at the family reunion and that was true. But what she didn't know was that I used that as an excuse to get her there. I was the one who wanted to spend time with her, away from her house, where I was working for her.

I honestly couldn't see how something could work out between us, considering what she did for a living and her work schedule, but for some reason that didn't stop me from trying.

It was a beautiful day at La Jolla Shores beach, eighty degrees, and the sky bright blue and clear. I had grown up in the area and used to walk to this beach almost every day as a kid. It always brought back special memories when we got together there.

I already helped set up the canopies and tables for the reunion. Other family members set up the food and drink stations, while I unfolded the last few chairs.

We were ready for fun and just about everyone was there, except for Ruth. She told me it might be better for her to meet me here instead of picking her up, in case something came up with her work that she had to take care of at the last minute.

I gave her a hard time about it because I didn't want her to use work as an excuse for not coming, but she wouldn't budge on it. She assured me she *would* be here, and I had felt better after I had received her text letting me know she was on her way.

And there she is.

Ruth waved from the beach entrance, about forty yards away.

She stepped onto the sand, and immediately kicked off her sandals, letting them dangle from the fingers on one hand as she walked toward me. She carried a very large bag in her other hand, plus a beach bag hanging from one shoulder.

"Who is that *lovely* woman, Nicky?" my mom asked.

My daughter, Lindsey, was also watching Ruth. "Dad, do you have a date?"

I shook my head. "You can both relax. She's *a friend*."

My mom watched Ruth. "A friend? With a look like *that* on her face? I seriously doubt that she's *just* a friend."

What *look* was she talking about?

I didn't see a look.

The only thing I saw was Ruth looking relaxed, which was a refreshing change.

"I agree, Grandma." Lindsey turned to try to get a read on my face. "Something's going on. She's glowing."

"*Nothing* is going on."

What was with these two?

Ruth dropped a sandal and stopped to pick it up.

She peeked inside the big bag she was carrying and then stuck her hand inside.

"Dad, if you're worried I'm going to disown you because you're going out with a woman that isn't Mom, get over it. I'm twenty-one, not five. And most marriages end in divorce anyway, so it's expected that you find someone else to hook-up with."

"Hook up with? Seriously? You do not have a dad who hooks up."

"You need to get with the times. Hooking up can mean getting together or forming a relationship, and there's nothing wrong or bad about it. What I'm trying to say is I'm glad you're putting yourself out there again. It's about time."

I huffed. "I'm not putting myself out there. I'm right here. And I told you, she's a friend."

"Whatever. We'll get the dirt from her since you're no help."

"You two take it easy on her. And don't tell her any embarrassing stories about me."

My mom placed her hands on her hips. "That's half the fun of being a parent! I get to pay you back for all the years you drove me crazy. Now, tell me the truth. What's going on between you two?"

"Hey, look at me!" I waved goodbye to Lindsey and my mom. "I can't hear either of you talking."

"Nicky!"

"Dad!"

I chuckled and decided to meet Ruth halfway, so she wasn't immediately bombarded and overwhelmed by my mom, my daughter, and the rest of my family.

I had completely forgotten to tell everyone that I was bringing someone. I was not surprised by the sudden interrogation. This was going to be a shock for many people in my family since it would be the first time they had seen me with a woman since my divorce.

Ruth stopped in front of me and dropped her sandals in the sand. "Hey."

She wore a flower-patterned summer dress that hung above her knees. I could see the string from her black bikini tied around her neck.

"Hey. Glad you could make it. You look beautiful."

A smile slowly formed on her face. "Thank you." She

glanced around the beach. "Did you bring Karma with you?"

"No. This beach doesn't allow dogs. But since I am now her official owner, I have all her papers and medical documents. I was able to leave her with the doggy daycare not too far from my house."

"That's great."

I nodded. "I sent out an email to the family with a picture to let them know about Karma and had five replies with offers to watch her whenever I needed someone."

"You can add me to that list, as long as she doesn't dig anything else up in my yard."

"I'm pretty sure that was a one-time thing because your soil smelled like bones and dead things." I chuckled and pointed to the flowers on her dress. "Black-eyed Susans."

She glanced down at her dress. "What do you mean?"

"The flowers on your dress."

"Really? I had no idea they were called Black-eyed Susans. How do you know that? You're a man."

I crossed my arms.

"Oh, right. You're that whatchamacallit, professional backyard designer flower guy, plant man."

I laughed. "What a coincidence. That's *exactly* what my business card says. Nick Morris, the whatchamacallit, professional backyard designer flower guy, plant man. It wasn't easy fitting all that on the card. I had to pay extra for printing."

She laughed and playfully pushed me on the arm. "Okay, give me a break, I'm trying not to think too much today."

"You're off to a good start." I chuckled. "By the way, we still need to talk about the flowers and plants for your backyard. I know you wanted to attract butterflies and hummingbirds." I motioned to her dress. "Anyway, *those* flowers attract butterflies. You might want to keep that in mind."

"I will. And I am loving the yard more every day. It's amazing how much personality the rocks added today."

Brandon and I had spent almost all morning moving the rocks from the delivery this morning. From the street to the backyard, wheelbarrow after wheelbarrow, exactly eight thousand pounds of rocks were transferred from the front to the back. Brandon did the wheelbarrowing and I moved the rocks into place in the backyard once he dumped each huge pile in front of me. It was like Ruth said, the yard was shaping up well and in record time.

"Now, we just have to plant the palm trees, succulents, and flowers. There are a few other things to take care of, but most of the big stuff has already been finished. Most likely we have a few days left on the job and we'll be out of your hair."

Ruth lost her smile.

She probably was thinking what I was thinking.

When the job was over, we wouldn't be seeing each other anymore.

"Nicky!" my mom called out. "You get over here right now and introduce me to your date!"

Ruth turned toward me and crossed her arms. "Do you want to explain *that*?"

I pointed to my mom. "I did *not* tell her this was a date. I told her you were a friend. That's all. I promise."

"That's not what I'm talking about." She waved me off. "I don't care about *that*."

Ruth didn't care if my family thought we were on a date?

"I'm talking about the part where she called you *Nicky*. You didn't tell me that was one of your nicknames. Explain that, Mr. Knick-knack-paddywhack."

"Nicky is not a nickname, *Ruthless*. It's short for Nicholas, like Nick. But there are only a few people who call me that."

"How come only a few? I think it's cute."

I couldn't tell if she was kidding.

"In fact, I may start calling you that now . . . *Nicky*." She smiled.

Ruth's voice was sultry, the way she said my name that way.

And that smile . . .

Breathtaking.

My heart beat faster.

We locked gazes for a moment.

Holy crap, something's happening between us right now at this very moment.

I had the sudden urge to kiss her.

That wasn't going to happen.

There was no way she could have the same urge.

And yet . . . why was she staring at my lips?

Maybe I had imagined it.

"You look like you want to say something," Ruth said.

"Me?" I replied, trying to get that thought of my lips pressed to her lips out of my head. "No. Nothing." I gestured back to the canopies and tables and my family already gathering around the food and nibbling. "We should probably get over there. I can make some introductions. My mom is waiting impatiently."

"We'd better go then."

"I want to apologize ahead of time for what you're about to endure."

Ruth laughed. "I can handle your family."

There was that confidence that I loved.

Loved?

Where the heck had that come from?

We walked toward my relatives, all of them hovering around in a bunch, watching us approach, no doubt wondering who the lovely lady was by my side.

They were ready to pounce on her like vultures. They had so much love and affection to give. That was the way my family was. They loved everyone. We had no black sheep. We saw the best in people and welcomed them with open arms.

Still, I couldn't help wondering if Ruth would be overwhelmed or a little uncomfortable by it.

My mom shook her finger at me. "It's about time, Nicky."

Ruth held out her hand. "Hi, I'm Ruth."

My mom pointed at Ruth's hand. "You can put that thing away. We're huggers in this family."

She smiled. "That's quite all right with me. I am, too."

She was? What happened to my hug? I got robbed.

"I'm Jan, Nicky's mom." My mom extended her arms around Ruth and pulled her in for an embrace like she'd known her forever. Maybe she was getting carried away because Ruth dropped the bag she was carrying.

That's my mom. She loves everyone.

"It's a pleasure to meet you." Ruth eyed the food area and then picked up the bag from the sand, handing it to my mom. "I can see you have a lot of food over there, but I never like to arrive to a party empty-handed. I hope you don't mind my bringing a couple of Bundt cakes."

My mom glanced at the logo on the side of the bag. "Nothing Bundt Cakes? They're my absolute favorite."

Ruth pointed to the bag. "Red velvet and lemon."

"You're a doll." My mom turned to me. "Your girlfriend's a keeper."

I sighed. "Mom. She's not my—"

"Nicky's dad, Ralph, is in the water, but this is my granddaughter, Lindsey. Nick's daughter."

"Nice to meet you." Ruth gave Lindsey a big hug and then turned back to me, keeping her hand on Lindsey's back. "You never told me you had such a beautiful daughter."

Lindsey creased her eyebrows. "Dad!"

I shrugged. "What? It hasn't come up in conversation yet. It's not like she knows *everything* about me."

Lindsey hooked an arm around Ruth's arm and pulled her away from me, smiling. "Don't you worry, she's going to know everything when I get through with her."

"What a *wonderful* idea!" My mom grabbed Ruth's free

arm. "Let's start from the beginning when Nicky was in diapers."

"Don't believe a word they say!" I shouted, as if that was going to do me any good.

Ruth looked back over her shoulder, laughing. "Are you trying to tell me you never wore diapers when you were a baby?"

"Most of the time he ran around naked," my mom said.

"Mom . . ."

"I couldn't keep clothes on that boy! Running around with his little ding dong—"

"Mom! Don't listen to her, Ruth. They're all lies."

Ruth laughed again. "I have the best BS detector around and right now the lies all seem to be coming from you, *Nicky.*"

"Oh, I love her already!" my mom said, the three of them laughing and making a rapid getaway.

I chuckled, happy that Ruth looked like she was already having a good time. The truth was, I wasn't worried at all about what she could find out from Lindsey and my mom. Anything they told Ruth would be harmless, plus it would be the truth, and how could I have a problem with that?

Well, as long as they didn't tell her that I still had the same teddy bear my grandfather had given me on my fourth birthday. I had named him the incredibly original name of Teddy and he sat on the shelf in my office.

Lindsey and my mom took Ruth around and introduced her to my other family members, my uncles, aunts, cousins, nieces, and nephews. They gave her the red-carpet treatment, smiling, laughing, hugging, staring in awe, like she was some hotshot Hollywood celebrity.

Ruth made it look effortless the way she worked her way through my family, practically fitting in from the very start. Like she was meant to be there. It was a stark contrast to the serious, stressed-out, uptight Ruth I had seen on more than a few occasions. She didn't look overwhelmed at all. In fact, it looked like she was eating it up.

Was it just the case of taking her out of a negative environment and sticking her in a positive one? Was I witnessing Ruth changing permanently right before my very eyes? Or was this a one-off where most likely she'd revert back to her serious side after she got home and settled back into her office?

I had no idea.

But I liked what I saw.

Every now and then, Ruth would look back in my direction, like she was checking in with me, giving me a knowing smile, before returning to being adored again.

It may sound silly, but it did something to my heart.

I truly did want to see her happy.

Now, if I could only spend some time with her, since that was the reason I had brought her here in the first place.

Ruth glanced back over at me again and smiled.

Lovely. Just lovely.

Brandon approached. "Better close your mouth before you choke on a sand fly."

I played it off, taking a sip of my root beer. "My mouth was open to take in some cool liquid refreshment. It's completely necessary unless I want the drink to dribble down my chin and stain my shirt."

Brandon looked toward Ruth. "You like her a lot."

I decided to come clean. "I do."

"There's nothing wrong with that."

"Unless I have a problem with what she does for a living."

"It's not like she's an assassin or a drug dealer." Brandon put his hand on my shoulder. "I think it's great you've been trying to eliminate negativity and stress from your life since the heart attack, but you can't make the entire world turn into sparkly unicorns who poop marshmallows and cupcakes."

"Where the heck did you get that from?"

Brandon laughed. "I have no idea. I was trying to be eloquent and failed miserably, but I do have another point."

"Let's hear it."

"Love lasts forever. Jobs don't."

"Okay, now you're back on track."

"I must admit that was a good one. Anyway, why don't you just have a good time and see what happens?" He glanced over at Ruth, who was playing beach paddle ball with my daughter. "Looks like Ruth is enjoying herself. She's a completely different person."

"I was thinking the same thing." I moved a few chairs under the canopy, so they were in the shade. "I thought you were going to invite Dee."

Brandon had let me know in between one of the many wheelbarrow hauls this morning that he and Dee had the most amazing dinner last night. Then he asked if he could bring her to the reunion. Every single person in my family, including my parents, thought of Brandon as a family member. He didn't even have to ask.

"I did invite her." Brandon pointed to Dee at the beach entrance. "In fact, there she is now. I'll be right back. I need to go kiss somebody."

"Seriously?"

"Hey—I don't ever joke about kissing."

Brandon walked over to Dee and, sure enough, he kissed her.

I walked toward Ruth, planning on kidnapping her back from my family.

Ruth smashed another ball way over Lindsey's head with the paddle. "Sorry!"

"No worries!" Lindsey turned to run after the ball, then stopped to talk with two of her cousins who were heading to the water with their surfboards.

Perfect timing.

"Hey," I said, approaching Ruth from behind. "I wasn't sure if I was ever going to get you back from my family."

Ruth spun around and smirked. "Looks like I'm all yours. What are you going to do with me, now that you have me, Nicky?"

I swallowed hard, wondering if this was another one of those trick questions.

I could answer it a thousand different ways, but I just needed to choose one.

Just one . . .

Come on, think of something good.

Nothing.

My brain froze up from the pressure of coming up with the perfect response and also from being caught off guard by how delightful Ruth was and how much she had changed outside of her professional environment.

In the end, my intelligence and my mouth betrayed me as I spewed out something completely ridiculous that I immediately regretted. "I can introduce you to a few of those eligible bachelors I told you about yesterday."

Ruth hesitated, basically letting me know that it was the furthest thing from her mind. "Oh . . ." She nodded and shrugged. "Okay."

I'm such a fool.

What was I going to do now?

CHAPTER TWENTY-ONE

NICK

If there were such a thing as an Idiot Hall of Fame, I would have been unanimously voted in and inducted this week.

"No need to wait, Mr. Morris," someone would have told me, escorting me directly to the front of the idiot line. "You deserve this more than anyone else we have ever met in the existence of the world."

I wanted to bury my head in the sand and scream from the top of my lungs because I was a certified bonehead of epic proportions.

I can introduce you to a few of those eligible bachelors I told you about yesterday.

Why the hell had I told her that?

What was I thinking?

You weren't thinking at all.

We walked toward the food area to meet my cousin, Jay, who has been in charge of the barbecue every year. It felt like I was heading to death row, my head down, my energy low, each step getting slower and slower, wondering how I got myself into this mess and how I could have flubbed-up a fantasy open invitation from such a beautiful woman.

What are you going to do with me now that you have me, Nicky?

I might as well have said, "Well, since I'm a bozo, I guess I should take you and introduce you to the competition and watch as one of them sweeps you off your feet and out of my life forever."

Too late to take it back now.

We stopped in front of the barbecue grill and checked out the various meats grilling: hot dogs, hamburgers, and sausages. Jay also had pork smoking in the smoker next to the barbecue that was always to die for. He had started cooking at eight that morning.

Jay had his back to us and was grabbing a few hamburger patties from the cooler under one of the tables. Then he pulled more buns from the bag.

He flipped around and dropped some patties and buns on the grill. "Hey, Nick."

"Hey. I wanted you to meet a friend of mine. This is Ruth."

Jay pulled off his gloves and dropped them on the table. "Any friend of Nick's is a friend of mine." He smiled and came around the table to hug Ruth. "A pleasure to meet you."

Why was everyone hugging her except for me?

"A pleasure meeting you as well." Ruth smiled and eyed the food on the barbecue. "This all looks amazing."

Jay slipped his gloves back on. "Thank you. There's going to be lots to eat in a couple of minutes."

Ruth pointed to the smoker next to the barbecue. "What do you have going on inside the smoker?"

"Nothing now because I already took it out." He pointed proudly to the big piece of pork on the cutting board. "This will be the first thing that will disappear when I let everyone know it's ready. Do you like pork?"

"I *love* it."

"Well, you have great timing then. Hang on . . ." Jay shredded some of the pork with a fork. He pulled a slider bun off the grill, placed the shredded pork on top, and squirted his secret sauce on top. Then he topped it with the other half of the bun, placed it on a paper plate, and handed it to Ruth with a napkin. "Try this."

"Thank you." Ruth took a bite and stopped chewing, her eyes opening wide. "Wow." She chewed a little more. "Double wow. What is this?"

"A pulled-pork slider. Twelve hours marinated, eight hours smoked, honey butter slider buns, plus my secret homemade whiskey barbecue sauce on top. Voilà!"

"This is incredible."

"Thank you. I'm glad you like it."

Ruth licked her fingers one by one. "Are you a professional chef? You must cook for a living."

Jay chuckled. "No, no. Many moons ago I had thought about doing it as a career. Unfortunately, things didn't pan out, but that's okay because I have a solid job. The family ropes me into doing this every year for the reunion." He winked. "Okay, they didn't have to convince me. I love cooking for people."

There was no way anyone, especially me, could compete against Jay in the cooking category. Sure, I could hold my own against the average person, but Jay was a master in the kitchen and on the barbecue.

He could have easily wooed Ruth with his food alone.

I glanced down at her plate.

It was empty.

Not good.

I wouldn't have been surprised if they were married before the end of the reunion.

All because I decided to be a nice guy and introduce her to him.

Maybe I would also get a star on the Idiot Walk of Fame.

Ruth wiped her mouth. "Seriously, you may want to rethink your career. What do you do now?"

I patted Jay on the back, hoping Ruth didn't like nerds. "He's a rocket scientist."

Jay shook his head. "A slight exaggeration . . . I work for Mathors Aerospace. We design unmanned drones that are able to carry emergency medical supplies to remote locations, as well as other things."

"That's wonderful," Ruth said. "I admire that you're—"

I tuned them out for a little bit, trying to come up with a plan to stop this dating game in its tracks and do something fun with Ruth. Something to get her away from anyone who was male, single, and good-looking.

If I had to introduce her to one more cousin, I could

choose the lowliest of the bunch to ensure there was no possibility that they would connect.

That was the problem I was faced with.

I wasn't lying when I had told Ruth they were all catches.

All of my cousins were gainfully employed, smart, kind, and good-looking.

I was in trouble.

And the only person I could blame was myself.

Uh-oh.

I think they were talking to me, because both Ruth and Jay were staring, waiting, like they wanted me to respond to something they had said.

"Where were *you*?" Ruth tapped the top of my head. "You sure were deep in thought."

"Me? Not at all. I'm right here. Sorry, what did you say?"

"I didn't say anything. Jay asked if you wanted to have one of the pork sliders before he gets bombarded by everyone."

I nodded. "Absolutely. You don't have to ask me twice."

Ruth smirked. "Actually, we *did* ask twice."

Jay laughed and shredded more pork with a fork. He pulled a slider bun off the grill, placed the meat on top, and squirted his secret sauce on top. Then he stuck it on a plate and handed it to me with a napkin.

"Thank you." I turned to Ruth before taking a bite. "Let's grab a drink and relax over there for a moment in the shade." I pointed to the chairs farthest away from where Jay was.

"Sounds like a plan. Nice to meet you, Jay."

"You, too! Hopefully, we can chat more later when things slow down here."

Ruth smiled. "I'd like that."

I wouldn't.

"Hang on a second," Jay said. "Let me give you one more before they all disappear." He prepared another pulled pork slider and placed it on Ruth's plate, smiling. "Since you like them so much."

"I do. And thank you."

A few seconds later, Jay yelled out, "Grub's on. Come and get it!"

Everyone converged on the barbecue area, as Ruth and I grabbed a couple of drinks and potato salad. We sat down to enjoy our food.

She turned to me, smiling. "I *adore* your family."

I choked on my first bite of the pork slider because I thought she was going to say that she adored Jay.

That would have been the death of me.

Ruth slapped me on the back. "Are you okay?"

I nodded. "Yeah. Fine."

"Try chewing next time. It's amazing how it breaks down the food and makes it easier to swallow." She leaned closer and studied me. "You seem different."

"Me? I'm fine!" I held up the pork slider. "I got a little too excited about eating this."

I was about to take my second bite of the pork slider when my cousin, Alex, sat down in the chair right next to Ruth.

Coincidentally, he was another one of the bachelors I was supposed to introduce Ruth to.

Just my luck.

"How am I the last one to know that you have a girlfriend, Nick?"

"She's not my girlfriend," I said, but then regretted it, even though it was the truth. Next time, I'd stuff the slider in my mouth whole. I'd just opened the door for Alex to swoop in and love her until the end of time.

Love her until the end of time?

Okay, now I was starting to sound like Brandon.

"Aunt Jan says you two are an item," Alex continued. "You're telling me that's not true?"

Ruth smiled, but didn't answer, glancing over like she was waiting for me to respond.

I had to tell the truth.

We weren't an item, even though I wanted us to be one.

"We're almost best friends." I winked at Ruth. "Isn't that right?" I leaned closer to her, playfully bumped her with my arm and knocked her food off her plate and into the sand.

What was left for me to achieve as an idiot?

This was going downhill fast and I was screwing up everything.

Ruth glanced down at her pork and potato salad, both now covered with sand. "Now, look what my almost best friend did."

I stood and grabbed it from the sand. "I'll get you another plate of food. Be right back."

Walking back toward Jay, I shook my head in disgust at my behavior, then tossed her plate in the trash.

Lindsey grabbed my arm and pulled me to a stop before I could reach the barbecue area. "Dad, *what* are you doing?"

"What are you talking about?"

"Come here. You're really, really blowing it big time." She yanked me away from the family.

"Is this about me not telling Ruth that you existed?"

"No!" Lindsey looked around and then leaned closer, whispering. "Brandon says you're introducing Ruth to all the single guys in our family? Have you lost your mind?"

"Apparently."

"You need to snap out of whatever funk you're in and conquer that woman."

"*Conquer* her? What century were you born? Ruth isn't a country."

Lindsey sighed. "She's *more* than a country, Dad. She's everything you need."

"Who are you?"

"I'm serious. Grandma and I both agree that Ruth is *amazing*. And she *likes* you."

"How do you know that?"

"Because when we were going around introducing her to everyone, she couldn't stop talking about you. *Nick this, Nick that, Nick this.*"

I glanced back over to Ruth, who was deep into a conversation with Alex, smiling like she was enjoying his company.

Lindsey blew out a deep, frustrated breath. "First, you introduce her to Jay and now Alex? You need to do something *now*. You're out of practice. Get over there and tell her how you feel. It's obvious."

"If it's so obvious, then she would know."

"Yes, but women want to *hear* it. And you need to *show* it with actions."

I couldn't believe I was getting dating advice from my daughter.

She was right, I knew that, but still . . .

I liked Ruth a lot. I could picture myself falling in love with her, especially seeing this other side of her that was so alive and playful.

She was a completely different person.

"Nicky!" My mom marched toward me, giving me that glare she had perfected over the years to let me know I was in serious trouble. "We need to talk. Now."

Great.

Something told me the schooling wasn't even close to being over.

"I'm guessing by the look on your grandmother's face that she knows, too?"

"Of course, she knows. We're women. We know everything."

That appeared to be the case.

My mom grabbed my arm, almost knocking the pork slider off my plate. "Ruth is not your girlfriend? Why did you tell me that she was?"

"I never told you that."

"Well then, she should be then! Heavens to Betsy, what are you doing?"

I shrugged. "Not enough, according to your granddaughter."

"Well, she's right. Do you know how wonderful Ruth is?"

"I do."

"And do you know how fast someone will snag her off the market and put a ring on her finger if you're not smart enough to do it first? How do you think that will make you feel if it happens? Would you *like* that to happen?"

I glanced over at Ruth and she happened to look my way.

We smiled at each other.

I shook my head. "No. I don't want to see that happen."

"Well, then? What are you waiting for?"

My mom was right.

They both were.

I needed to quit thinking.

I needed to quit analyzing every little thing.

Asking Ruth out on a date would be the perfect way to let her know my intentions.

"Dad? Why are you still standing here? Go! Conquer her!"

"I told you that she's not a country."

"Are we going to argue semantics?" my daughter interjected.

I didn't answer, walking past my family members in the barbecue line to grab Ruth another pork slider to replace the one I knocked over.

"No cutting, Nicky!" Uncle Steve said.

"I'm not *cutting*. I'm just *looking*." I glanced down at the empty cutting board where Jay had been shredding the pork. "Do you have more pork sliders?"

Jay placed a hot dog on a bun and handed it to my Aunt Julie. "You snooze, you lose. Back of the line or you're going to start a riot."

Crap.

I glanced down at the pork slider on my plate, knowing what I had to do.

I headed back to Ruth and sat down beside her, picking up my pork slider and holding it toward her. "Open up."

"I'm not going to eat yours," she said. "I can go get another one."

"No, you can't. This is the last one."

"Then I'm *definitely* not going to eat it."

"Open. Now. You know you want to. And I want to give it to you."

Ruth arched an eyebrow. "Pardon me?"

"That didn't come out right, but you know what I mean. Let me share this with you. It would be a pleasure."

And I truly meant that.

Ruth hesitated, smiled, then leaned closer to me. "Just a nibble and that's it."

"A nibble is fine. Two or three nibbles is even better."

She opened her mouth and I swear I couldn't take my eyes off her lips.

My heart banged against my chest, just watching her smile, and her waiting for me to feed her. Like I had done in the sushi restaurant.

I slowly fed it to her, watching her take a tiny bite on the end. She chewed slowly, moaning, her eyes on me, then glancing down at the pork slider again like she was okay having a little more.

Watching her lick the sauce off her bottom lip was damn near the most erotic exhibition I'd ever seen. How could eating pork be such a turn-on?

It was a pig.

I guess it didn't matter.

She wanted more.

Good.

I held it closer to her lips and she took another little bite.

Ruth moaned again as she chewed.

She needed to stop doing that. It was killing me.

Ruth finished the last bite and then polished off the potato salad before I could even blink. "Oops. I guess I was hungry."

I chuckled. "No need to apologize. I'm sure I enjoyed feeding you much more than you enjoyed eating it."

"I doubt that."

"Believe me."

"I don't."

"You have to."

We locked gazes, like we had done before.

We were in our own little world.

Just the two of us.

Ruth glanced at my lips.

I glanced at hers.

We were communicating without words.

It was amazing.

This had to be the unspoken language of—

Alex cleared his throat. "I *knew* you two were an item.

Look, I'm going to go get something to eat. It was nice meeting you, Ruth."

I totally forgot he was sitting there.

Judging by the pink color on Ruth's face, I'm guessing she had forgotten as well. "Nice meeting you too, Alex."

After he walked away, I couldn't help laughing.

Ruth covered her face with her hands, laughing with me.

"What am I going to do with you, Ruth?" I surprisingly asked.

She stood, grabbed the plate from my hands, and tossed it in the garbage. "I have just the idea. Take off your clothes."

"Pardon me?"

"Not *all* of them, Nicky. Take off your shirt. We're going for a swim." She grabbed the bottom of her dress, pulled it up over her head and off, dropping it on the chair next to me.

Ruth stood there waiting for me in her sexy black bikini.

I swallowed hard, watching her.

There was that confidence of hers that was my kryptonite.

She crossed her arms. "I can go get Jay to swim with me, if you're not interested."

I jumped up, practically ripping my shirt off, and flinging it into the air.

It landed on top of one of the umbrellas.

Ruth smirked. "That's what I thought."

CHAPTER TWENTY-TWO

RUTH

I left Nick standing there by the chairs and walked toward the water. I giggled on the inside, loving the expression on his face when I pretended I was going to go ask Jay if he wanted to swim with me. I had no intention of doing so and had a pretty good idea of what Nick's reaction would be.

Men were so predictable.

The truth was, I wanted to spend time with Nick.

I didn't care about those men he was introducing me to.

I cared about Nick.

And even though I didn't have a clue of how this could possibly work out between us, I wanted to explore the prospect of it.

Screw the online dating.

Screw the speed dating.

Taking matters into my own hands was the only way to go.

Smiling, I walked past a cute girl building a sand castle, while her mother took pictures.

"Who are you?" Nick asked, finally catching up with me at the edge of the water.

I laughed, walking past a couple of teenagers playing catch with a football, stepping into the ocean up to my ankles. "What are you talking about?"

I knew exactly what he was talking about.

He walked into the water up to his calves, and then turned around to face me. "I invited you to have some fun and spread your wings, but honestly I was skeptical that you would actually do it."

"Ahhh . . . did you underestimate me, Nicky?"

He chuckled. "By a mile. And I think I've created a monster."

I placed my hands on my hips. "And does this monster scare you?"

Nick grabbed a piece of seaweed floating next to us and tossed it. "Not even a little. I like what I see." He glanced down at my body, then looked back up and held my gaze. "A lot."

I got those goosebumps again on the back of my neck.

"Well, looks like that makes two of us." I returned the favor, running my eyes over his body and enjoying every inch of it.

Nick was in great shape.

No six-pack abs or ripped muscles, but he definitely took care of himself.

Glancing at the scar on his chest, I couldn't help feeling lucky that he survived the heart attack and surgery and was standing with me here today.

I quickly looked away, so he wouldn't feel self-conscious.

"It's okay," he said. "You can look."

I nodded, glancing at the scar again.

Sympathy and compassion filled my senses.

I wanted to reach out and touch the scar, but I resisted. "What happened exactly? You mentioned stress was involved, but I don't know the whole story. Would you mind telling me? I want to know."

Nick thought about it before he spoke. "I don't mind. It happened back when I owned a different landscaping design company before the one I own now. My ex, Crystal, pushed me into growing the company. I resisted at first because the business at that time was in my comfort zone. I could easily control everything, especially since I enjoy getting my hands dirty."

I nodded, letting him continue.

"I had no stress. I could be selective with the clients I wanted to work with because my services were in demand. I could take time off whenever I wanted. It was an ideal situation, although the time off wasn't as fun as I had hoped since all my wife ever wanted to do was work. I ended up having days off by myself." He gestured to me. "You know what the life of a workaholic is like."

I nodded again, feeling a little embarrassed. "Yes . . . I do."

"Anyway, she kept pushing me, saying I could grow the

company to a size where I would be able to let someone else manage it for me, but *I* would still make good money. She said that could easily pay for Lindsey's college and lead toward an early retirement for both of us. I ended up expanding the company, not because of Crystal's reasons, but because I was tired of arguing with her. I took on more employees, other designers, a bigger office, labor workers, etcetera. The company was getting huge and big money started coming in. Deep down it didn't feel right, because I was never motivated by money, but I kept moving forward. Part of the problem was that I never did like the business side of things. The money, the numbers, the paperwork."

I nodded, letting him continue.

"I loved designing and seeing my creations come to life before my eyes. But I was doing less and less of that as the company grew. I no longer enjoyed my job. With more responsibility came more stress, which led to me working way more than I wanted to on things I didn't like, which led to more stress and eating unhealthy foods. Then came the high blood pressure and abnormal cholesterol. And *that* led to even more stress because I was worried about my health, too. Everything kind of spiraled out of control and my body finally said enough is enough. That's when I had the heart attack."

"Wow."

He nodded. "Yeah. Five days in the hospital and I got *this* as a souvenir." He touched the scar on his chest. "And *this* after I fell from the heart attack." He pointed to the scar on his chin. "It wasn't a fun time in my life."

"It doesn't sound like it."

I knew stress was bad, but what happened to Nick was horrible.

I reached out and grabbed Nick's hand, squeezing it. "I'm sorry you had to go through that."

"Heads-up!" someone yelled.

Startled, we jumped back as a football landed in the water next to us, splashing us both.

Nick grabbed the football and tossed it back.

It landed perfectly in the hands of the teenager.

"Pretty impressive throw there."

Nick grinned. "I could've gone pro in the NFL. I gave it up to dig ditches."

I stared at him. "Really?"

He shook his head and laughed. "No. Not even close."

Laughing, I reached down and stuck my hands in the water. I moved them around and then stepped deeper until the water was up to my knees. "If you could choose any job in the world right now, what would it be?"

"That's easy. I'm already doing it."

I arched an eyebrow. "Seriously?"

"Of course. I knew early on what I wanted to do with my life. I graduated from Cal Poly with a degree in landscape architecture." His eyes lit up with pride. "I worked for a few companies, got my experience, and then branched out and started my own business. With the exception of my big mistake of trying to expand, followed by the heart attack, everything has gone according to plan. This is my passion and I wouldn't change it for the world."

"I'm impressed. You knew what you wanted to do at a young age, and you went for it."

"So did you."

I shrugged. "Not quite. My original goal was to also have my own business."

"You're going to be managing partner, the top dog of the company."

"True, but I wouldn't actually be the owner outright. The other partners underneath me would still own shares in the company. That will never change. When you have a board of directors and multiple partners, it's not the same as owning a company with nobody to answer to but yourself. I like to be in control."

Nick grinned. "I believe that. You're a pro at bossing *me* around."

I laughed. "Stuff a sock in it, Nicky."

Nick threw his hands up in defense. "I should know better than messing with you."

"Heads-up!" the same person yelled.

The football landed in the water next to us again.

Nick grabbed the football and tossed it back, another perfect toss. "Then let me ask you . . . if you could choose any job in the world right now, what would it be?"

I crinkled my nose. "Honestly, I don't know."

"Well, you're a smart woman. I have no doubt that you'll figure it out."

"Thanks." That was sweet of him.

"And beautiful," he added.

I love the way you look at me, Nicky.

"Incoming!"

I felt a painful thud against the side of my head.

I yelped and flapped my arms as I fell backwards.

277

Nick's arms surrounded me to keep me from falling, but a wave crashed into his back, pushing us both into the water and under. He gripped my waist with both hands and pulled me up to my feet, holding me tightly against his body. "I've got you."

I wiped the water from my eyes and blinked a couple of times. "Was that the football?"

Nick cleared some hair from my face. "Yeah. Are you okay?"

I nodded, even though I was a little fuzzy-brained. "I think so."

"Well, relax. There's no hurry. I've got you."

You certainly do. And why would I be in any type of hurry when your body is pressed up against mine like this?

"Sorry, lady," The teenager grabbed the football and jogged away.

"I think I'm good." I took a deep breath and laid my hands on Nick's chest.

My gaze shot to the scar over his heart.

I blinked a couple more times, staring at it.

My right hand had a mind of its own, sliding down his chest, and then gently and slowly tracing the scar over his heart with my index finger.

I glanced up at Nick, who was watching me intently, his eyes dark.

Oh, how I want to feel your lips on mine right now.

There was no doubt he wanted it as bad as I did, but the difference was that I wasn't going to wait around for him to make a move.

I stood on my tiptoes until our lips met. Wasting no

time, I opened my mouth and let him in, wanting to feel his tongue against mine. Nick didn't disappoint me, taking the lead, and pulling me even closer, deepening the kiss.

I couldn't even remember the last time I had kissed a man.

Years ago? Decades?

It didn't matter.

This was divine.

Nick pulled away from the kiss, his eyes locked with mine, our chests heaving, completely out of breath like we had run a marathon.

Now *that* was a kiss.

We remained silent.

I wasn't sure why he said nothing, but I couldn't think straight. All I could hear was the blood pumping at my temples, beating out a frantic pace.

I was still pressed up against his body, enjoying every second, aware that he was enjoying this as well, and much more than I thought.

Do it again.

His forehead was creased, though.

Something was on his mind.

I was finally able to speak. "What are you thinking?"

"Is this a trick question or do you really want to know?"

"I want to know."

He swallowed, searching for the right words. "What is happening here?"

"That's a very good question."

"And do you have a good answer?"

"Not at the moment, but it was like my dream."

What *did* happen there?

Something spontaneous?

Something primal?

Something I hoped would happen again?

Okay, the answer to the last question was a *yes*, for sure, but I had other questions.

What were we doing exactly? How could this possibly work out between us when we were so different from each other? Were we both crazy, or was it just me?

Doubts flooded my mind and I didn't know how to respond to Nick.

"Ruth? Talk to me. What do you make of what happened between us?"

I sighed. "It was a momentary lapse of concentration."

"On whose part?"

"Quite possibly we're both to blame, getting caught up in the moment . . ."

He nodded. "What are you saying? The kiss was a mistake?"

"I didn't say that. *You* said that."

Nick shook his head. "*I* didn't say that, but you may be right."

That's not what I wanted to hear.

"Or you may be wrong."

Much better.

I traced the scar on his chest again with my index finger. "Nick-fil-A . . ."

Nick moaned like he was in agony. "You're killing me, Ruthless."

"Is that right?" I smiled and continued to trace the scar.

"You may want to stop doing that soon or there will be a good chance that we're going to have another one of those momentary lapses of concentration that quite possibly is or is not a mistake."

I nodded, thinking about it, still tracing. "Okay then, let me ask you this . . . if there's a possibility that the kiss was a mistake, *why* are you still holding me against your body like you don't want to let go?"

Good luck answering that one, Nicky.

"That's just it . . ." He pulled me so close, my breath caught in my throat. "I don't want to let go."

Now, we're getting somewhere.

CHAPTER TWENTY-THREE

RUTH

The next day while I prepared lunch, I danced around my kitchen as the stereo in my family room blasted "Girls Just Want to Have Fun" by Cyndi Lauper. I didn't care that Nick occasionally glanced toward the house and shook his head, laughing at me.

He was the reason I even felt like dancing.

I couldn't remember the last time I had felt so alive. It was like I had been sucked into a big black hole for ten years and had forgotten that the sun even existed.

Nick was my sunshine.

He made me smile, for many reasons, including the pot of Black-eyed Susans on the kitchen counter that he had given to me first thing this morning.

"No charge," is what he had told me, winking.

I argued with him that I was going to pay him for the

flowers since he said he'd plant them for me, but Nick said they were a thank you gift for my business.

What a bunch of bull.

Especially since there were five more pots on the ground outside.

How could such a stubborn man make me smile?

Thoughts of that kiss in the water played nonstop in my head.

I had never been more distracted in my entire career. I still hadn't gotten much work done, unless you counted the time I took to plant organic tomatoes and red bell peppers in my new planter boxes while Nick watched and gave me even more goosebumps on the back of my neck.

"Dancing Queen" by Abba started playing and I began to dance again.

Nick yelled from the backyard and waved his finger at me. "No, no, no!"

I walked over to the screen door and slid it open, hands on my hips. "What seems to be the problem?"

"Your music selection. If I'm going to be subjected to your tunes while I work, I would like to hear something different."

"I'm not taking requests. And what's wrong with Abba anyway?"

"Everything. I can put up with Cyndi Lauper and Aretha Franklin. And what was that other song? The one where you were waving your arms in the air and singing about being *afraid* and *petrified*."

"That was "I Will Survive" by Gloria Gaynor. And you were watching me?"

I knew he was, but I wanted to hear him admit it.

Nick blew out a breath, like he couldn't believe I had to ask. "Of course, I was watching you. Have you seen yourself in the mirror?"

"Not recently," I lied.

"Well, go look. Then you'll know why I can't take my eyes off of you. How could I *not* watch you?"

"Am I supposed to answer that?"

"No. Anyway, where was I?"

"Abba."

"Right." Nick crossed his arms. "Abba is where I draw the line."

"Duly noted. Are you going to work today or just criticize my excellent taste in music?"

"I hope he's going to work!" Brandon yelled from the back of the yard, as he tried to position a new palm tree in the huge hole he had dug. "I could use some help over here."

Nick took a few steps toward me. "Of course, I'm going to work." He leaned in and whispered, "I used the music as an excuse to come over here and kiss you."

He kissed me on the lips.

Oh, my.

Nick grunted and clapped his hands. "Good! I'm glad we got that straightened out!" He winked and turned to go help Brandon.

"Nice try," Brandon said. "I saw you kiss her."

I laughed as another Abba song came on after the first one.

I turned it up louder and continued to dance in the

kitchen, glancing out the window as Nick shook his head again, smiling.

I blew him a kiss.

A few minutes later as I ate my sandwich, I grabbed my buzzing phone from the kitchen counter.

I hadn't heard from Dee today yet, but she had a good excuse since she had been at the dentist all morning. She joked that she chipped a tooth falling on the beach after witnessing our kiss in the water. The truth she was getting a root canal.

Dee: I'm back from the dentist. Root canals suck.

Ruth: You poor thing. Are you in pain?

Dee: Lots, but I'll survive.

Ruth: I will survive! I was dancing to that song in the kitchen.

Dee: You were dancing at home?

Ruth: And singing.

Dee: Wow, this is serious. I want to be your maid of honor.

Ruth: You're putting the high heel before the garter.

Dee: Sounds like your head is still in the clouds from that kiss.

Ruth: You should see the view, it's great from up here.

Dee: Well, don't forget you have the company party tonight at six.

Ruth: Crap. I forgot.

Dee: That's why you pay me the big bucks. To remind you of things, which includes how amazing I am.

Ruth: Nick and I had plans tonight. Not good.

Dee: Looks like you'll have to take him with you.

I had hoped that Nick and I would be doing something romantic this evening, a real date, since it hadn't happened last night. We both had wanted to spend more time together after the reunion, but I had to get back to work and Nick had spent almost three hours helping clean up and break down everything on the beach after the reunion was over.

I wasn't looking forward to the party, but unfortunately I couldn't skip it.

And taking Nick wasn't even close to romantic, but I didn't want to cancel on him either.

I wanted to see him.

Walking back over to the screen door, I slid it open and stepped outside.

Brandon and Nick were finishing up the soil around the first palm tree they had planted.

Nick glanced toward me and waved me over. "I've got something for you."

"What is it?"

"You have to come here if you want to find out."

I followed him to the gazebo and waited while he opened a cardboard box, pulling out beautiful wind chimes with long silver tubes. He undid the fasteners that held them together inside the box and carefully hung it on the hook above his head.

He stood back and grinned. "It's a Himalayan echo wind chime."

"It's beautiful."

Nick nodded. "Many practitioners of feng shui believe a wind chime's sounds can have a positive effect on the energy around your house."

The timing of the ocean breeze was perfect, moving the wind chimes enough to give off a pleasant, peaceful melody that made me want to kick off my shoes, close my eyes, and listen for a while.

I smiled. "It's working. I feel positive."

"Me, too."

I stepped closer to Nick and hugged him. "Thank you."

"My pleasure. No charge."

I smacked him playfully on the arm with the back of my hand. "Quit saying *no charge*."

"Hey—I like to have things crystal clear with my clients, so there are never any misunderstandings."

"Your clients . . ."

Nick hesitated and leaned closer. "That's not all you are to me, but we can discuss that when I see you this evening." He winked.

"Speaking of that . . . I completely forgot about a work event that I need to attend. Actually, it's a party."

Nick's face went blank. "Oh . . . okay."

"I want you to come with me. It's Stansfeld's company cocktail party to celebrate closing two of our deals, Amsterion and Caltonic. It's customary for us to have a party after every big transaction and milestone and this time it's for the two deals that I collaborated on."

Nick ran his fingers through his hair, sighing, not looking very excited about the idea at all. "I'll be honest with you; I've been to those types of parties before in the past and they're not my thing."

"I can appreciate that, but *you* have never been to one of those parties with *me*, so it would be a different experience."

"I don't know . . ."

I crossed my arms. "Don't make me beg. I want to see you tonight, and it was my fault that I forgot about the event. I promise that if it gets too boring, we can leave early and do something else alone. How's that?"

Nick nodded. "Really?"

"I promise."

"I do want to see you . . ."

"Well, then? Come with me. We don't have to stay till the end."

"Okay, okay. Count me in."

"Great!" I reached up and kissed Nick.

I felt better that he agreed to come after I made the mistake of double-booking my evening.

And maybe it wouldn't be that bad.

It was just a party.

What could possibly go wrong?

CHAPTER TWENTY-FOUR

RUTH

I jerked my head back in surprise when I opened my front door and saw Nick standing there in a charcoal suit, crisp white shirt, and a black tie.

Every time I had seen him since we had met in person for the first time, he had been wearing shorts and a polo shirt with his company logo on it. Short pants were the norm all-year-round for most people working outdoors in gardens, since Del Mar's climate was considered to be like the Mediterranean with warm, dry summers and mild, humid winters.

But still . . .

Nick cleaned up well.

He looked dapper, debonair, and delicious.

I smiled. "I'm beginning to understand why the women in college called you Nick-fil-A."

Nick grinned. "Thank you." He glanced at my black cocktail dress and my four-inch stilettos, grinning. "And *I'm* beginning to wonder why you don't have a nickname like *Babe* Ruth. Maybe we can skip the party and stay right here."

I patted him on the chest. "That's more tempting for me than you'll ever know, but I'm required to be at the party, and I don't want to be fired before I become managing partner. Sometimes a girl's gotta do what a girl's gotta do." I motioned to his truck on the street. "Now, let's get out of here before I change my mind."

Nick drove us to the Hilton San Diego near the Del Mar Fairgrounds and Racetrack, just five minutes away from where I lived.

We passed through the lobby and down the hallway, following the arrows on the signs that said, "Stansfeld Investments Celebration - Courtyard Terrace."

"I forgot to ask, what did you do with Karma for the evening while we're here?"

"She's with my mom." He chuckled. "And she says she'll let me know if she's ever going to give her back to me or not."

I laughed. "I like your mom."

He smirked. "Me too, but she's not keeping my dog. I've become attached to her rather quickly. She's a good girl, and very sweet."

Nick and I both glanced through the open doors of a banquet room as we walked by it, the music from the DJ, the colorful lights, and the packed dance floor catching our attention.

He grabbed my hand and pulled me to a stop. "I think this party will be *much* more fun. Let's crash it. What do you say?"

I shook my head. "I say *nice try*. You're not getting out of this now. Let's go." I walked toward the door leading out to the Courtyard Terrace and the pool.

Nick passed me, pushing open the glass door. "You can't fault me for trying."

I smirked and walked by him. "It was a valiant effort."

The Courtyard Terrace had white lights strung above the heads of my coworkers with the swimming pool illuminated behind them. Jazz music played in the background and waiters walked around, offering drinks and appetizers. There were no chairs, just tall cocktail tables that everyone hovered around as they ate, chatted, and drank their favorite alcoholic beverages.

I led Nick through the crowd, stopping to say hello to many of the other partners in the firm. A waiter stopped in front of us with a tray of champagne, but we both declined, opting to head to the bar for a beer.

I clinked my Heineken bottle against Nick's Corona bottle. "Thank you for coming."

"You're welcome."

Another waiter stopped in front of us with a platter. "Crispy coconut shrimp with orange marmalade sauce?"

I nodded. "Yes, please." I grabbed a napkin and one of the shrimp, dipped it in the sauce, and ate it. "Ooh, that's good. You have to try this, Nicky."

Nick followed my lead, grabbing one of the shrimp, dipping it in the sauce, and eating it.

He chewed and nodded his head. "You're right. Amazing."

The waiter started to walk away.

"Wait," I practically yelled.

He turned back around and grinned. "One more?"

"Yes. Please." After eating another shrimp, I licked my fingers, and took another sip of my beer.

Nick chuckled. "I like a woman who eats."

"You won't ever see me being shy or self-conscious about it."

"I like that. And speaking of women . . . are you the only one here?"

"I'm the only female partner at the company."

Nick glanced around the Courtyard Terrace. "But *you* brought a date. Why didn't any of these guys bring their significant others? Or were they all smarter than me?"

I laughed. "You're smart because you know how to get on my good side. But all the women are together on the far side of the courtyard. They're known as the Abandoned Wives Club and they do everything together, like widows. They're always as far away from their spouses as possible since the guys only talk about business at our parties."

"I'm expecting a hundred-grand bonus," the voice said behind me.

"Me too," said someone else. "I've had my eye on the new Jag. Have you seen that baby? That's why I work fourteen hours a day. I'm sporting wood just thinking about it."

Nick set his beer on the cocktail table, shaking his head.

"Everyone makes a lot of money but doesn't have time to spend it or enjoy it."

"That's a fair assessment."

"The company doesn't believe in a work-life balance."

"No. They don't."

He crinkled his forehead. "And *why* is this appealing to you?"

I opened my mouth and closed it.

"I guess I'm trying to see your point of view. Why you would sign up for this lifestyle in the first place?"

I sighed and lowered my voice. "Honestly, it's not as appealing as it used to be. And I blame *you* for that." I poked him in the arm with my finger.

He grinned. "You mean you *thank* me, not blame me, right? You got a taste of the good life and now you're hooked on Nick-fil-A."

I laughed. "You got that right." I took a step toward Nick and stood on my toes to kiss him, but then stopped myself, and pulled back after realizing where I was.

Nick held his palms up. "What? The company doesn't allow you to have feelings either?"

"Feelings are distractions. They cause us to take our eye off the ball."

"Please don't tell me you believe that."

"Sadly, I used to. Not anymore, though." I squeezed his arm.

"My stocks are rockin' right now," said another man walking by while on the phone. "I think I'm going to buy another boat. I'm telling you, they're chick magnets."

Nick shook his head in disgust. "A boat he'll never use . . ." He took a swig of his beer. "Is it time to leave yet?"

"No. Maybe you'll enjoy the evening more if you put all your focus on me. I guarantee you that I wouldn't have a problem with that at all."

"I don't have a problem with it either, but *he* might." He motioned behind me with his chin.

I turned, just as Mason stopped in front of me, crossing his arms. "Ruth."

"Mason."

"Gary's looking for you. There's an emergency staff meeting tomorrow with all the partners."

I glanced around for Gary. "Do you know why?"

"I guess you'll find out soon, won't you?" Mason walked away, looking satisfied as he gave me one of his go-to lines.

One of these days I was going to use that line on him and see how he liked it.

Nick watched Mason and then turned back to me. "What a jackass."

I nodded. "Good eye."

"What's his problem?"

"That's what you would call a bitter partner who can't handle that he wasn't the one being groomed to become managing partner."

"But why would he act that way with you if he knows *you're* the one who will be managing *him* soon?"

"The one thing he has going for him is that he's a partner, which is essentially part owner of the firm. Unless he does something that's strictly against company policy or illegal, he's protected, even when he's being an idiot. It would take a lot of legal action and a recommendation from a disciplinary committee to have him removed. But hey, don't worry about Mason. I can handle him. And he's nothing compared to some of the men I've had to deal with in my career. The one thing I won't do is take crap from any of them."

Nick grinned. "Well, he's a jackass, but *you* are a badass, Ruthless. With all this testosterone around, I'm impressed with the way you handle yourself."

I clinked Nick's bottle. "Thank you."

A waiter stopped in front of us with a tray of shot glasses filled with something that wasn't liquid. I had no idea what they were.

I pointed to them, curious. "What are those?"

"Shrimp cocktail shooters."

"Really?"

"Oh, yeah. You have to try one."

Nick and I both grabbed a shot glass, clinked them, and sent the shrimp cocktail shooter down the hatch.

I set the empty shot glass next to other empties on his tray and grabbed another. "You're right. Delicious." I slammed the next one and nodded. "Mmmm."

Nick laughed. "I agree. One more for me, too."

After that, we sampled crab cakes, pork pot stickers dipped in soy ginger sauce, and tandoori chicken skewers. Then we grabbed a second round of beers.

"I'm stuffed." Nick pointed to the door. "Okay, I guess we can go now."

"Behave. Especially since my boss is coming this way."

Gary approached and held his glass toward me, smiling. "Ruth. Congratulations on the acquisitions. You're having a banner year."

"Thank you."

He turned to Nick. "Gary Stansfeld, managing partner."

"Nick Morris. A pleasure to meet you."

"And you as well." Gary shook hands with Nick and then turned back to me. "You didn't tell me you had a boyfriend."

I had no idea how to respond to that.

I smiled. "I was planning on sending a company-wide email in the morning to let everyone know I'm dating."

Gary laughed. "Good one." He glanced at Nick. "She's a keeper."

Nick grinned. "I can't argue with you there."

"Speaking of the morning, we have an emergency staff meeting with all partners first thing tomorrow. Eight o'clock. You need to be there, of course." He glanced at Nick and then got his eyes back on me. "I can fill you in on what's going on before you leave tonight."

"Is there a problem?"

"Nothing you can't handle." He turned to Nick. "A pleasure meeting you. Enjoy the evening."

After Gary walked away, Nick turned to me. "He seems like a decent guy."

"We don't agree on everything, but Gary is honest and plays by the rules. I can't ask for much more than that. How are you doing? Are you bored yet?"

"I'm hanging in there, but . . ." Nick placed his beer

bottle on the cocktail table next to us. "I need to go find the restroom. I'll be right back."

"Sounds good." I watched Nick head back into the hotel, grateful he'd said yes and came with me to the party.

He didn't look very happy to be there, and I couldn't blame him. If it weren't for the food, the beer, and Nick's company, I would have been bored myself. Maybe we could stay a little bit longer and then sneak out to do something more exciting.

Another partner, Steve, placed his beer on the cocktail table next to me. "Was that Nick Morris you were talking to?"

I was surprised by the question. "Yeah."

Steve looked impressed. "Wow. He looks good. How do you know him?"

"I hired him to design my new backyard."

He arched an eyebrow. "Really?"

"Yes. In fact, he's almost done with the project. How do you know him?"

"Well, I don't know him directly. I know *of* him. He was hired to design the courtyard and employee area for a company I worked for a few years back before I came to Stansfeld."

"He's got a great eye for design and detail."

"That's an understatement. Nick has been compared to Frederick Law Olmsted."

"Who?"

"He's the guy known for helping design Central Park. He also designed Stanford University and the University of Chicago. Nick used to be a big deal."

"Used to be?"

Steve frowned. "Well, yeah . . . Our company hired him, but he never actually ended up starting the job he was contracted for. We had to hire someone else to take over."

"That's odd. I wonder why."

"We found out he'd had a heart attack. I heard he ended up selling his company for over twenty million dollars. That's why I was surprised when you told me he was working for you. The man doesn't have to work. He's loaded."

I tried to play off my shock. "Some people work for fun, because they love what they do."

"Right! Good one!" Steve laughed, grabbed his beer from the table, and waved goodbye, walking away.

I stood there, still surprised by what he had told me.

Nick had sold his other company for twenty million dollars?

Was that why he gave me such a great deal when he gave me the quote to work on my backyard? I had no doubt he could have charged me double for what he was doing.

Dee told me he was the best, and the best companies usually charged a premium for their services because they were in demand. Was that why he kept giving me freebies, even though I kept telling him to charge me for them?

If what Steve had told me was true, I would have an even greater respect and admiration for Nick and his generosity, which would lead me to wanting to kiss him more.

But the kissing would have to wait for later since I was still at a work event.

My mind was going a million miles a minute as I walked toward the restroom.

I looked for Nick on the way but didn't see him.

Hopefully, he didn't sneak out on me.

He would never do that.

At least, I hoped he wouldn't.

CHAPTER TWENTY-FIVE

RUTH

A few minutes later, I came out of the bathroom and pushed open the glass door that led out to the garden terrace. I made my way through the other partners and consultants, searching for Nick since someone had stolen the table where we had been hanging out earlier.

Where are you, Nicky?

As I searched for Nick, I noticed something odd.

A few people snickered as I walked by them.

A handful of other coworkers whispered, watching me.

One partner even pointed at me.

What was going on with them?

Were they talking about me?

It was like they knew something that I didn't.

Or maybe I was part of an inside joke that I would find out about later.

I finally spotted Nick on the other side of the Garden

Terrace near the gate that went to the pool area. He waved me over, a concerned look on his face as I approached.

Something definitely happened.

What could have possibly happened while I was in the bathroom for a few minutes?

I threw my palms up in confusion. "I don't understand what's going on here. Everyone including you is acting weird all of a sudden."

"Come here for a second." Nick slid his hand around my waist to my lower back and guided me around to the other side of the cocktail table next to the tree.

We were almost completely out of view.

Did he want to sneak me a kiss?

I was all for it, but this was not the time nor the place.

Nick suddenly yanked the side of my dress. "There you go. All good."

I glanced down to my side, confused. "What just happened?"

"Your dress was stuck in your panties. You were flashing a good portion of your leg to everyone. I didn't mind the show, but I'm guessing you didn't do that on purpose."

Now I knew what all the snickering and whispering was about.

I blew out a frustrated breath and covered my face with my hands. "Why does every possible embarrassing moment of my adult life happen when I'm with you?"

"I guess I'm here to keep you humble."

"Mortified is more like it."

Nick chuckled. "I've seen you at your worst."

"There's no doubt about that. What's your point?"

"I'm still here."

I let out an audible sigh.

My heart is going to melt.

I reached up, kissing him on the cheek.

"Careful, you're going to get in trouble."

"Screw them."

"Can I tell you something else?"

"Of course."

"It pisses me off that I had to witness ten or twelve of your coworkers, all watching you walk across the terrace with your dress stuck that way, and not one single person had the decency to stop you and let you know. They just watched! I don't know how you can work with these people."

I glanced around the courtyard and shrugged. "I can handle them."

"I have no doubt about that, but you're different when you're around them. Too serious. Uptight. Cranky, even."

I sighed. "Behind every cranky woman is a sweet girl who's a little tired of everyone's bullshit."

"Well, I love seeing that sweet girl when she makes her irregular appearance." Nick thought about it. "And don't get me wrong, being in this toxic environment is making me feel uptight, as well. Your coworkers leave a bad taste in my mouth. Can we go?"

I stared at him for a beat.

"You promised me we could leave if we were bored."

I had promised him that and I wouldn't go back on my word. "Yeah. We can go." I glanced around the courtyard, trying to figure out an escape route. "But we need to leave separately, so it doesn't look like we're actually leaving. Nobody will notice. I'll meet you in the foyer inside."

"Roger that."

I pulled my phone from my purse. "Okay. Here I go."

Pretending to talk on the phone, I avoided eye contact with everyone and walked back inside the hotel, waiting by the large painting of a beach sunset. I slid my phone back into my purse and glanced back toward the glass door that led to the garden terrace, expecting Nick to come through right behind me.

A minute later, he came through the same door, spotting me, and walking my way.

I smiled. "Ready?"

"More than you know," he said.

I surprised myself by grabbing his hand. "Let's go, then."

I loved the way his hand felt wrapped around mine.

We walked down the long hallway toward the front of the hotel, Nick glancing down at our intertwined hands. "Holding hands, huh? Looks like this is getting pretty serious."

I smiled. "It is for me."

"Good." He pulled me toward the open door of the banquet room with people dancing inside. "In that case, we can't leave until you dance with me."

"Nick, we can't go in there."

"Yes, we can. Just one dance. Listen, they're even playing our song."

I did my best not to laugh. "This song is going to haunt me for the rest of my life."

It was "Shake Your Booty" by KC and the Sunshine Band.

The song that was playing when I got the wedgie at the gym.

The same day I met Nick but didn't know one day I would have feelings for him.

"Turn that negative memory of a wedgie into a positive one."

"That's impossible. That wedgie will be stuck in my—"

Nick laughed.

"Okay, poor choice of words." I couldn't help laughing with him. "This is me being serious now. We're going to get kicked out of the hotel if we crash this party."

"We were leaving anyway. The difference would be we would have a private escort out of the place. Like royalty." He grinned and gestured toward the banquet room with his head.

I laughed. "You're crazy."

A woman approached us from inside the banquet room, waving us in. "You can come inside and dance. We're finishing up, it's okay." She headed back to the dance floor and waved at us again to come inside.

Nick grinned. "Wasn't that nice of her? *That's* the kind of person you should be working with, not those egotistical suits who don't care about you and are obsessed with money."

"Did you pay her to do that?"

Nick chuckled. "No. Never met her before in my life. This was meant to be." He held out his hand. "Shall we?"

I stared at his hand for a moment and then placed my hand in his.

He led me to the dance floor and spun me around.

We danced to the last minute and a half of the booty-shaking song.

It felt good to be with Nick.

No, it felt *great*.

I could feel my shoulders relax.

Just like that, I forgot about work again.

"Okay, last chance to dance!" the DJ said. "One more song before we say goodnight."

Nick glanced toward the DJ and crossed his fingers. "Please be a slow one."

I want it to be slow, too.

And it was.

The song was "Heaven" by Bryan Adams.

"Yes!" Nick pumped his fist in the air and pulled me in close.

I sighed and rested my head on his shoulder, enjoying being in his arms again.

We swayed to the music, a smile on my face, as I listened to the lyrics that hit home, talking about meeting someone who turned your life around.

That's what it felt like Nick was doing for me.

"*This* is our song," I let slip out before I could stop it.

"I couldn't agree more." Nick caressed the side of my face. "I've seen glimpses of the real you, an amazing person that I'm addicted to. You're playful. You're sweet. You're funny. And when you're in that blissful state, with no work on your mind, that makes you even more beautiful than you already are. So beautiful my heart can barely handle it."

"You do that to me, Nicky."

He kissed me again.

I melted a little more.

Looking into his eyes, I was curious about what Steve had told me. "Can I ask you something?"

"Anything."

"Why did you not charge me enough when you submitted the bid to work on my backyard?"

He studied my face for a moment. "What makes you think I didn't charge you enough?"

"Nicky?"

He chuckled. "Fine." He sighed, thinking about it. "Honestly, I don't need the money."

Wow.

Steve was right.

"And if you don't need money, why do you work?"

I was pretty sure I knew the answer but wanted to hear from him.

Nick shrugged. "I love working outside and getting my hands dirty, you know that. I love helping people and I want to stay active. I enjoy creating magical places for people to unwind. Continuing to do what I love accomplishes all those things. I charge enough money to pay Brandon's salary, plus have a little extra to pay for a sushi meal here and there." He grinned. "Okay, more than a few sushi meals, but you know what I mean."

"Nicky . . . that is so sweet and—" I kissed him on the lips.

He pulled away from the kiss, grinning, his eyes still on me. "If I asked you a question, will you tell me the truth?"

I smirked. "You can't spell truth without Ruth."

He chuckled. "I can't believe you're that corny."

"But you love it, don't you?"

He chuckled. "I do." He hesitated, staring into my eyes. "My question is . . . what do you think about *us*?"

"Wow, this is getting deep, isn't it?"

"It is."

We continued to sway back and forth as Bryan Adams sang about being in heaven.

I was in heaven.

"Ruth?"

I laughed. "Sorry. I was listening to the lyrics of this song." I thought about his question. "What do I think about us? Well, things can happen a lot faster at our age, because we have the experience to know exactly what we want and what we don't want."

"Uh-huh. I can appreciate that. And what do you want?"

I was known for having the confidence to say what was on my mind at any given time without fear of what people thought, but my heart rate picked up speed as I anticipated the words that were about to come out of my mouth. "I want *you*."

Nick grinned. "What a coincidence."

And his lips were on mine again, this time with more passion, more feeling.

He pulled me closer, tighter.

I felt my legs getting weak and—

"Okay!" the DJ said on the microphone, causing me to jump and bump teeth with Nick's. "That's the end of the night for us. Thank you for coming. Good night!"

I pushed back a little from Nick's arms. "Do you want to go back to my place?"

"I think I *have to* go back to your place since I drove you here, remember?"

I squeezed his arm. "You *know* what I mean . . . do you want to go back to my place *and* come inside?"

Nick nodded. "There's nothing more I would rather do." This time, Nick grabbed my hand. "Let's get out of here."

We thanked the woman for inviting us to dance with her and walked out of the banquet room toward the front of the hotel.

"Ruth," Gary said. "There you are."

Crap. Talk about bad timing.

I stopped and flipped back around. "Hey, Gary. What's up?"

"I've been looking all over for you for the last ten minutes." He glanced back at the banquet room. "What were you doing in there?"

I decided to tell him the truth. "Dancing."

"Oh . . ." He studied me, glanced at Nick, and then got his eyes back on me. "Were you leaving?"

This time I decided to lie. "No, just going out to the car to get something."

He nodded, looking skeptical. "Can I talk to you for a moment?"

"Of course." I turned to Nick. "Excuse us for a minute."

"Not a problem." Nick pointed to the set of chairs over by the front door in the lobby. "I'll wait for you over there."

"Sounds good."

Gary waited for Nick to leave before speaking. "I wanted to give you the rundown on what was happening tomorrow. Remember I mentioned in the board meeting that we needed to come up with some fresh ideas on new revenue streams for the company?"

I nodded. "I remember."

"Well, *that* is our number one priority moving forward and that's why we're having an emergency staff meeting tomorrow. Nobody is satisfied with income predictions for the next two quarters. We need to dig deep and come up with new ideas that are going to wow them. I admit it feels a little odd to even think of growing the company when I'm about to retire, but I'll still be a shareholder. And I have a fiduciary responsibility to the other shareholders and investors. I'm counting on *you* to grab the bull by the horns and take the lead. I need something huge."

"Okay . . ."

"And you have *tonight* to come up with it. You can present it at the meeting tomorrow morning." He pointed toward the lobby. "I know you said you weren't leaving, but you may actually want to head home now since you'll most likely be pulling an all-nighter." He patted me on the shoulder. "No rest for the weary, but this is your time to shine and show everyone why you're going to be the new managing partner. See you in the morning."

"You got it."

I walked toward the lobby, hating myself for what I was about to do.

I had no other choice, and I already knew how Nick would react.

He wasn't going to like it one bit.

And how could I blame him?

Nick stood and stepped toward me, rubbing the side of my arm. "Is everything okay?"

I nodded, even though it wasn't.

How was I going to tell Nick?

I avoided eye contact, trying to come up with the right words.

"Ruth. Talk to me."

I sighed and looked him in the eyes. "I'm going to have to take a raincheck this evening."

Nick's jaw and shoulders stiffened. He glanced down the hallway, even though Gary was probably already back in the Courtyard Terrace.

"I have to work," I added, even though I was sure Nick already was aware of that.

"I'd better get you home then," Nick said coldly.

He walked past me and—

"Wait," I said, grabbing his arm. "I want you to know how sorry I am about this. I was looking forward to the rest of the evening."

He nodded but didn't say anything.

I swallowed, not enjoying the big lump that had formed in my throat. "It's just . . . we have an emergency staff meeting in the morning and I have to work all night."

"That's what you do, Ruth. You work and work and work."

"I *do* have a job, you know. What do you want me to do? Quit?"

Nick shook his head. "I would never tell you to do that. *You* are the only one who gets to decide how you want to live your life."

I blew out a frustrated breath. "It's *one* night of work. Tonight. I asked for a raincheck, so you know I want to see you again. We can even get together tomorrow night."

"But what if something else comes up tomorrow night and you have to cancel on me again? And then something else comes up the day after that? Every day we have something planned I'll be wondering if it's actually going to happen or not. I've lived this life before. It didn't work. That's one of the reasons I'm divorced."

I honestly didn't know how to respond to that.

"And I'll be honest with you, this was the only negative thing I could see coming between us if there was going to be a relationship of any kind. How could I love a woman when she's never around?"

I stared at him. "Love? Who's talking about love?"

Yes, I was falling for him, but this was not the time to mention that.

"I was being hypothetical, but it's like you said . . . things can happen a lot faster at our age because we have the experience to know exactly what we want and what we don't want. We've already been through a lot of the crap that young people have yet to experience. Under ideal conditions, I could fall in love with you in a heartbeat if it wasn't for that one question that keeps popping up in my head. Will your work get in the way of us having something meaningful?"

"And your answer is obviously *yes*."

Nick shook his head. "I didn't have to answer the question, actually. You answered it for me."

CHAPTER TWENTY-SIX

RUTH

I thought of last night's party for at least the hundredth time over the last ten hours. Except for the food and dancing with Nick in the banquet room, the party was a complete bust. The look on Nick's face when I told him I wanted to take a raincheck broke my heart. It was almost enough to make me cry.

He didn't deserve that.

And I did truly understand his point of view and couldn't blame him for the way he felt.

We were silent in his truck when Nick took me home from the hotel. When he pulled into my driveway, he told me he would be finishing up the job in my backyard tomorrow, and he would get out of my hair and give me time to think about things.

I didn't need time to think.

And I loved having him in my hair.

Lucky for me, I was never one to back down from a little adversity.

A bump in the road wasn't going to slow me down.

I would repave the road if I had to.

I was confident things would work out well. Especially after I shared with Nick my idea for the company. He helped me come up with it and he doesn't even know it.

It started during our conversation over dinner when he and I ate the leftover Italian food at my house. Nick had asked me if I was happy and what I did for a living. It was obvious at that point that he didn't approve of my chosen career. The thing that hurt the most was when he said that we were complete opposites because he built things and I tore them apart.

I hadn't wanted to hear it, but it was the truth.

Then Nick asked me a wise question.

Why don't you go in there and help them turn the company around instead of gutting it?

I had answered Nick by telling him because it wasn't my job.

It wasn't what my company did.

But why not?

Why couldn't Stansfeld Investments jump into the arena of salvaging companies instead of buying them and piecing them out? With my idea, nobody would lose their job. Gary wanted a new revenue stream for the company, and this would be the perfect time to implement it.

Staying up all night wasn't as easy as it used to be. With the help of six cups of coffee and plenty of determination, I had accomplished my goal of coming up with an idea that I was sure the company would love. An additional revenue stream for Stansfeld that could actually lead us in a completely different direction after I took over.

I was positive that my plan would also get Nick back into my good graces since it was because of his advice and his cousin, Jay, that I came up with the idea in the first place.

Arriving at the Stansfeld office, I said a quick hello to Dee and entered the conference room before most of the other staff had arrived.

I wanted to prepare and go over my notes one last time.

As everyone filled in the seats around me, we were just about ready to begin.

I took a few seconds for some positive affirmations.

I've got this. I'm ready to go. This is going to be flawless and well-received. They are going to love my idea.

Mason was the last of the partners to enter the conference room for the board meeting, sitting right across from me and sporting his usual cocky smile.

And as usual, I wanted to wipe it off his face, but I had bigger fish to fry.

Bagel Barney would have been proud of my food idiom.

I smiled, thinking of how different Nick was from Barney or any of the other losers I had met while trying to find the perfect match. I had come up with that ridiculous list of character traits when I had no clue that the man of my dreams was right under my nose the entire time.

"What are you smiling for?" Mason asked, crossing his arms.

"I guess you'll find out soon, won't you?"

Mason flared his nostrils and looked away.

Gotcha, bonehead.

Gary walked to the front of the conference room and grabbed the pen from the ledge of the white board. He pulled the cap off the pen and wrote, "New Revenue Streams for Stansfeld." He dropped the pen back on the ledge and turned around, glancing around the room at all of us.

Here we go.

Gary held his hand in the air to quiet everyone down. "Okay, I've briefed you all on what's going on and what we need to accomplish today. As you can see on the board behind me, we need some fresh ideas on new revenue streams to keep everyone happy. We're looking for the *wow* factor here and I'm confident that you are going to come up with some winners. Ruth, let's start with you."

Showtime.

There was no need for more coffee now.

I was running on pure adrenaline.

"You got it." I stood, grabbed my folder of notes, and walked to the front of the room, standing in front of the whiteboard facing the staff.

This is going to be flawless and well-received. They are going to love my idea.

I set my folder down on the table next to me, grabbed the pen from the ledge, and wrote on the white board, "If You Build It, He Will Come."

"*Field of Dreams*," Steve yelled out proudly.

I stuck the cap back on the pen and turned around, pointing to him. "That's right, Steve. This was the famous line and premise from the movie *Field of Dreams* with Kevin Costner. How many of you have seen that movie?"

Just about every hand when up in the air.

I nodded. "Almost all of you. Me, too. *Great* movie. Well, *in* that movie, Kevin Costner's character believed that if he built a baseball field on his property, it would attract legendary baseball players who would want to play there. Everybody thought he was crazy, but he did it anyway because he believed in the idea with all his heart and all his soul. Nothing was going to stand in his way. In the marketing world, that baseball field was essentially a product, designed to attract something."

Many of the heads nodded.

Everyone else watched me eagerly, intrigued looks on their faces.

All except for Mason.

You have their full attention. Keep going. Knock 'em dead.

"As we all know, sometimes having the right product is not enough. That's why our company exists. We find undervalued companies with superior products, but inferior management or marketing skills. We buy them at a fraction of what they're worth, then gut them and sell the good pieces for a profit. This business model has worked well for us."

I took the cap off the pen and wrote on the white board, "Rebuild It and They Will Stay."

I placed the pen on the ledge and turned back around, glancing at my notes on the table. "But what if we tried a new approach? What if, instead of tearing apart a company, we rebuilt it? It sounds a lot more positive, now doesn't it?"

Some people nodded.

"It also sounds like a lot more work," Gary said.

A few others nodded at his comment, agreeing with him.

I expected pushback, but I wasn't finished yet.

"Unless you know what you're doing," I corrected Gary. "With my idea, we return to the roots of our company, consulting. There's no overhead since we're not technically acquiring the company, which means we have a bigger profit margin plus additional future revenue from owning shares in the company as part of the deal. The company we help will recover from its doldrums and nobody loses their jobs."

Gary sat forward in his chair. "Give us an example."

I smiled. "I would be glad to."

Nick is going to love it when he finds out this will help his cousin, Jay.

I grabbed the pen again and wrote on the board, "Mathors Aerospace" and stuck the cap back on and placed the pen on the ledge of the white board.

"Mathors Aerospace is a company on the cutting edge of technology. They design unmanned drones that are able to carry emergency medical supplies to remote locations. They have a hundred other patents and are waiting for FAA clearance to move forward with many of them. But while they wait, they're bleeding money. Normally, we would go into a company like this, get rid of the broken pieces, keep what's working, and resell the company for a profit. We could make ten million dollars on the deal without batting an eye. But Mathors Aerospace is missing out on the big picture, and so are we. What if, instead of ten million dollars, we made *a hundred* million dollars? Ten times more."

"Now you have my attention," Gary said, as laughter filled the room. "How exactly do we do that?"

"It's simple. Mathors Aerospace needs to use the existing patents they already own with products they already sell instead of creating brand new products that need approval and FAA clearance. They would be updating, not building from scratch. The commercial drone market should reach twenty-five billion dollars in the next five years and the biggest downside to drones is the downtime for recharging. Mathors Aerospace has a patent for a drone battery that recharges itself using the air that keeps it up in the first place. Imagine that? A drone that doesn't need to stop to recharge? Imagine long distance drone flights? We can help them move in this direction without any money out of our pockets and I know exactly how to do it."

I smiled, proud of my idea. I had never been more excited about my job and taking it in another direction. I wasn't tearing something apart. I was building something.

Like Nick.

Gary nodded, thinking about it. "Very interesting. Thoughts everyone?"

Not a surprise that Mason was the first to raise his hand.

Gary pointed. "Yes, Mason."

Mason turned to me. "We have evolved into something bigger and better since the beginning when Gary had started this company. Returning to our roots is like taking a step back."

I crossed my arms. "I disagree. It's a matter of implementing a new plan that—"

"We already have a proven plan that works. What guarantees can you give that we can make ten times more money?"

"I have the numbers to show that the market—"

"Market factors can change the course of a company," Mason interrupted again. "For instance, you can tell Mathors Aerospace to market their drones to Europe, but then Europe can outlaw the same drones. Where will the earnings come from then?"

"That's highly unlikely and the additional income comes from sales of shares that we acquire from the company. Essentially, we would be part owners."

"They could offer us a million shares or ten million, for that matter, but what if the stock market takes a dump and those shares are suddenly worth pennies now?"

"I've done the research and—"

"I doubt any of us are willing to take such a huge risk with the future of the company."

Gary cleared his throat. "Okay, looks like this needs a little more research."

I held up my index finger. "But I think—"

"It's okay, Ruth. Let's revisit this again soon."

My blood pressure was shooting through the roof.

Mason blindsided me.

He probably had it planned the entire time.

What a bastard.

I grabbed my files and sat down, dejected.

This outcome wasn't what I expected.

I had worked hard on this for almost ten hours. I still believed it was the right thing to do. I had worked out all the numbers and was sure my plan was perfect for the company.

For the next hour, other partners presented their ideas, but I had no idea what they were. I had blocked them all out and had been replaying what happened with Mason over and over again in my mind, coming up with things I should've said to shut him up.

After the meeting, I pulled Gary to the side.

"Mason was right," he said before I could say a word. "Your idea wasn't bad, but it's also not worth the risk. We have a proven method that works for companies that are in trouble, like Mathors Aerospace. Anyway, make it happen, and you can come up with another revenue stream idea this week. There's still time."

I stared at Gary, confused. "What do you mean *make it* happen?"

"I mean, talk with the CEO of Mathors Aerospace and look into us acquiring them."

"I'm not going to do that."

"Why not?"

"Because that's not what my idea was about."

Gary walked over to the door and closed it, the two of us the only ones left in the conference room. "I don't understand what the problem is."

I decided to tell him the truth. Surely, Gary would understand.

"I know someone who works at Mathors Aerospace."

He nodded. "Your boyfriend?"

Gary kept calling him my boyfriend, but I wasn't going to correct him. "No. His cousin."

"And?"

"*And* if we acquire Mathors Aerospace he's going to probably lose his job. His department would most likely be the first to go."

Gary crossed his arms. "And?"

I sighed. "Gary. I *know* him. I can't do that to him."

"Your first mistake was making this personal, because it's not. It's business. If he's talented he'll bounce back, no problem. He'll find another job and thank you in the end."

I had to put my foot down. "No."

Gary blew out a breath. "I don't like where this is going. This is not like you."

Just because I was showing compassion and didn't want someone to be fired? Just because I was finally starting to have a life?

I had something I was sure would make Gary change his mind. "There are two other potential companies we can acquire instead of Mathors Aerospace."

Gary leaned against his desk. "You said we could make a ten-million-dollar profit off Mathors Aerospace without batting an eye. Now you're telling me we should flush that money down the toilet?"

"I'm telling you we'll get that money from a different source. Why does it matter where it comes from? And that wasn't even the purpose of this meeting. You wanted *new* revenue streams."

"But that doesn't mean we give up on the old." Gary shook his head, the first time I had ever seen him so disappointed in me in ten years. "Ruth, there's a lot of pressure on me from the board to bring in more income."

I couldn't believe I was hearing this from him.

I sighed. "I can't, Gary."

He nodded, deep in thought. "Sounds like you need time off to think about things."

Unbelievable.

Another man who wanted me to take time to do some thinking.

"This will give you time to clear your head and think about your role at Stansfeld," Gary added. "You need to figure out what's most important to you and reevaluate your priorities. Take a couple of days off and let me know what you come up with."

I placed my hands on my hips. "You can't be serious."

"I am." Gary sighed. "Maybe your priorities have changed, and if that's the case, there's nothing I can do about it. But I need to know ASAP where your head is. I need to make an informed decision about the future of this company. The ball's in your court. Let me know what you decide."

Gary turned and walked out of the conference room.

Staring at the back of the door, I stood there deep in thought.

What just happened?

I had come into this meeting with high hopes of showing everyone an amazing new revenue opportunity, something that should have made the company happy, and Nick as well.

It was supposed to be a slam-dunk.

In the end, my idea got bounced to the curb like a basketball.

Maybe I did need time to think about why this was all happening to me.

I needed to tread carefully with Stansfeld and with Nick.

One wrong move and I could lose everything I had worked so hard for.

CHAPTER TWENTY-SEVEN

Two Days Later . . .

RUTH

I flipped over the pancakes on the griddle, smiling as my mom cooked bacon, and my dad prepared the coffee. I hadn't done this in years and had forgotten how much I enjoyed it.

It was my second day off, and I still hadn't been able to process my thoughts and figure out what my next step was. The pancakes would make up for it, or at least they would give me temporary pleasure until I had to start thinking about work again.

Yesterday, Nick called to chat briefly. He said he wanted to hear my voice, which was a good sign after what had happened at the party. He was busy helping his parents with some home project for most of the day, but then his mom got on the phone and invited me to have dinner with them this evening. It was a little awkward, but there was no way I was going to say no.

Other than the brief phone call with Nick and two other chats with Dee, I did absolutely nothing except read all day, with a break in the middle to take a nap in my new gazebo.

It was blissful.

I have to do it again soon.

How I was able to keep my mind off work was a wonder to me. It helped that I had started the day by doing Nick's water-listening exercise by the fountain in the morning.

I had even told Dee to take two paid days off, since I didn't think it was fair that I had the time off, but she didn't.

Funny how she didn't argue with me at all.

In fact, at this very moment she was headed to Dana Point to catch the ferry to Catalina Island to spend the day there with Brandon.

Today was the opposite of yesterday for me because I had breakfast with my parents, and then dinner with Nick, his parents, and Lindsey.

"The bacon is done." My mom used the tongs to pull the last few strips from the pan, placing them on the serving plate. "Ready with the coffee, honey?"

"All ready." My dad poured the last of the three cups of coffee and placed them on the table with cream and sugar. "And *I'm* ready for some pancakes."

"You're in luck because they are ready to be eaten!" I

scooped the last of the pancakes with the spatula onto the platter and placed it in the center of the kitchen table next to the butter and syrup. "Okay, let's eat." I rubbed my hands together, excited, and then took a piece of bacon from the plate and ate it with my fingers.

"This is all so wonderful." My mom helped herself to pancakes and added the butter and syrup on top. "Like old times."

I nodded, finishing off my first piece of bacon and diving into the pancakes. "I agree. This feels good. I think we should make it a regular thing. Maybe once a month? What do you say?"

"Twice a month is fine with me." My dad took a sip of his coffee. "Or once a week."

My mom shook her head. "Honey, let's not scare her away after we've gotten her back."

I wagged my finger at them. "You don't have to worry about that. I'm back for good. I let Gary's mentality take over my life and it won't happen again. No matter what happens going forward, I'm going to make time for you on a regular basis." I felt my eyes burn. "And I'm sorry."

"You need to quit apologizing. Life is a learning process." My dad grinned. "And I've learned that *everything* gets better when you have pancakes and bacon."

We shared a laugh together and had a wonderful group hug.

As odd as it sounded, I was back.

My parents were amazing.

I had left and done my own thing with my career while they carried on with their lives, but there was no resentment on their part. They weren't mad. They didn't give me crap about it. It was like that break never existed. They had told me they were happy if I was happy, and that was the only thing that mattered.

After breakfast, Mom and I cleaned up.

Dad went to Home Depot to get light bulbs.

I was deep in thought, thinking about my mom's life and how she gave up her career for me.

My mom leaned forward, trying to get a look at my face. "Everything okay, sweetie?"

I wiped down the top of the pancake griddle. "I guess."

"Something seems to be on your mind."

I nodded. "Yeah . . . I was curious, actually."

"What is it?"

I stopped wiping and turned to her. "Why did you give up on your dreams when I was born?"

She stared at me for a moment. "Who said I did?"

"I know the whole story, mom. You had a bright future ahead of you as a painter. Then you gave it all up."

We had never talked about this before.

"Sweetie, where is all this coming from? I didn't give up a single thing when you were born."

"You're telling me you didn't give up an amazing career?"

She sat down on the chair in front of the easel. "I love painting, but I always considered it secondary because the only thing I wanted was to have a baby girl. Ask your father! When I had you, I was set. I didn't need *anything* else to be fulfilled. And I have no regrets. Not one."

"But you gave up painting for me."

"No, I didn't. Your dad made plenty of money to take care of us and I was all for it. All I wanted to do was take care of *you*. I don't know *where* you got that from or why you think I gave up anything, because it couldn't be further from the truth. I'm fortunate to be one of those people in the world whose life turned out the way I wanted it to."

"You're not just saying that?"

Mom laughed. "No, sweetie. Follow me. I want to show you something."

I followed her upstairs and down the hall to the guest bedroom in the back. I couldn't remember if I had stepped in that room this century.

My mom pushed open the door and motioned for me to go in.

I stepped inside and froze.

The room was full of paintings.

There must have been a hundred of them.

Rows and rows of paintings were on the floor, leaning against each other ten deep.

Including one unfinished painting on an easel.

All were signed at the bottom by my mom.

I spun around to look at everything. "What's all this?"

"A new passion project of mine that I started this year. This is what *you claim* I gave up."

I blinked a couple of times, more confused than ever. "I don't understand. What exactly is going on here? What are you doing with all the paintings?"

She smiled. "I have my own business now. Well, maybe *business* is not the right term."

I flipped through the paintings leaning against the wall.

I didn't know much about art, but I loved the colors and the simplicity. There was a young girl looking up into the stars in the sky, smiling. She actually reminded me of me when I was young. The odd thing was, they were all identical.

"Why are all the paintings the same?"

My mom pointed to them proudly. "That has been my bestseller by far. I have been mass-duplicating it. I call it, 'The Girl with Stars in Her Eyes.'" She smiled. "It's the story of a young girl who dreams big and shoots for the stars. She isn't ever afraid to go for it, whether it's learning to whistle, riding a bike, or playing soccer." My mom kissed me on the forehead. "That's you, sweetie."

"Me?" I stepped closer to the unfinished painting on the easel, deep in thought.

"Of course. Ever since you were a little girl, you've always gotten whatever you wanted when you put your mind to it. And that has continued into your adult life, even today. I've always believed in you, but more important than that, *you* have always believed in you."

I nodded. "It's beautiful. I love it." I turned to her. "Why didn't you tell me you were doing this?"

She shrugged. "You've been busy."

My BS detector was sounding a full alert with my own mom.

This may have been a first.

"Mom, there's something you're not telling me. What is it?"

She sighed. "Fine." She thought about it. "It's just . . . I didn't want to make you feel bad."

"Why would I feel bad that you portrayed me in a beautiful piece of art like this?"

"Well . . . you've been obsessed with your career—"

"Motivated," I corrected her.

"Right. Motivated. Anyway, you've been so focused on rising to the top and making all that money that I didn't think you would like it very much if I was doing the complete opposite, giving all my money away."

"Okay, wait, what do you mean you're *giving* all your money away?" I glanced around the room again. "You don't make any money when you sell these?"

She shook her head. "Not a single penny. I've been selling these paintings for years and donating all the money to charities. Meals on Wheels. The Wildlife Conservation Society. And a few other charities that are near and dear to my heart."

I never knew this side of my mom existed.

"It's such a joy to help others." She shrugged. "And I don't need the money."

Now, she sounded like Nick, which made me feel worse.

So many people were doing good in the world and I suddenly felt inadequate for not doing my part to contribute to something, anything.

My mom was right.

I had been obsessed.

"Are you mad at me, sweetie?"

I stared at my mom, shocked that she would ask such a thing. "What? No! How could I be mad at you, Mom? What you're doing here is beautiful. It's wonderful. It's kind on so many levels. I'm so proud of you, you have no idea." I hugged her and then pulled away, thinking about my own life. "I'm beginning to realize that the last ten years of my life have been a huge mistake."

"There are no mistakes, only lessons."

"Well then, my lesson is that I have to pay more attention. I thought you had given up everything and my only goal since then was to make sure that I didn't do the same. And oddly enough, I thought that would make you happy and that you could live vicariously through me."

"Oh, no, honey. I would never want to have your life. I would die from the stress or maybe something caused by the stress. I don't know how you can live like that, but you seem to love it. Who am I to judge or make you feel bad about your lifestyle?"

Ouch.

That was like a slap in the face.

My mom put her arm around me and squeezed. "You shouldn't have to live your life for me or anyone else. The most important thing is happiness. And love, of course. I pray every day that you'll have someone special in your life. When are you going to meet a man?"

"Actually, I've met someone."

My mom's eyes got wider. "That's wonderful, sweetie! Do you love him?"

I thought about it. "That's a good question. I'm not sure if I'm there yet, but I'm falling for him, there's no doubt about that."

My mom hugged me. "Well, if he fills your heart with joy and happiness, don't you dare let him get away. And make sure you tell him how you feel."

She was right.

Nick did fill my heart with so many positive emotions.

And I was going to tell him exactly how I felt when I met him for dinner.

~

After getting home from having breakfast with my parents, I ended up reading for three hours. Then I ate a light lunch, tidied up the house, read for another hour, and napped for almost two hours. Once again, it was pure bliss, but this time I had a big problem.

I had completely lost track of time.

Now, I was scrambling to get to the restaurant to meet Nick and his family, without arriving late.

My phone vibrated, but that would have to wait.

"Not now!" I ran from the closet, tossed my dress on the bed, and took off my jeans and blouse. "I'm late, I'm late, I'm late."

After slipping into my dress, I moved quickly to the bathroom to apply a little makeup, and to quickly fuss with my hair.

My phone vibrated again, and I ignored it.

It must have been Dee sharing photos from her day with Brandon on Catalina Island. I couldn't wait to hear about her day trip and see the pictures.

I grabbed a pair of pumps from the closet floor, slipped into them, grabbed my purse and keys, and flew out the door.

"You're not going to be late," I mumbled to myself.

333

The clock in my dashboard told me I had six minutes to get to Yanni's Bar & Grill, my favorite Greek place. "Okay, I'm cutting it close."

I would only be a few minutes late, no big deal.

My phone vibrated again.

There was no way I was going to check it now while I was driving. "Leave me alone!"

Why was I nervous?

"Relax." I took a few deep breaths, like the ones Nick taught me. "Everything is going to be fine. There's no reason to be nervous."

Yes, there was.

Tonight, I planned to profess my love to Nick.

I had made the decision and was going for it.

He needed to know how I felt and there was no more denying it. I didn't want to lose him over a job that didn't make me happy after all.

I love him.

The thought made me smile.

Nick was a special man. I wanted to make him a priority in my life.

When I visualized my future, I saw him there.

Us.

He was right when he said people needed to have a work-life balance.

It was important and I knew that now.

My priorities had changed after meeting Nick and especially after what I had learned about my mom this morning at my parent's house.

She hadn't given up anything when she had me.

And neither would I.

I pulled into the parking lot at Yanni's and turned off the engine.

I checked my hair and face in the mirror.

My phone vibrated again.

"Not now."

Why was Dee going crazy with the text messages today?

Had Brandon proposed?

I got out of the car, taking a deep breath before entering Yanni's. I spotted Nick, his parents, and Lindsey at the first table on the right.

"Hey, everyone." I smiled, a little out of breath. "Sorry, I'm late."

Nick looked over at me first and did a double take.

His face was rigid.

He wasn't blinking.

Come on. Technically I'm only five minutes late.

That was nothing at all. There was no way he could be mad because of that.

Nick's parents, Jan and Ralph, were avoiding eye contact with me.

His daughter, Lindsey, was glaring at me.

What the heck was going on?

I glanced down to make sure my dress wasn't stuck in my panties again.

Nope. All good.

Something had happened.

Nick stood and turned toward me. "What are you doing here?"

I blinked and looked around. "What do you mean?"

Something was seriously wrong, and I had no idea what it was.

He crossed his arms and blew out a breath. "You didn't listen to my message?"

I shook my head. "No. I heard my phone vibrate a few times, but I was running late and didn't check it. What's going on? Why is everyone so serious? Did I get the time wrong?"

Maybe someone died, but who?

Something wasn't right.

I glanced over at Nick's parents again.

They were still avoiding eye contact.

Lindsey looked like she wanted to jump over the table and strangle me.

This was bad, whatever it was.

Nick placed his hands on his hips. "You need to leave."

"But—"

"Now. You're not welcome here."

What the hell?

The lump in my throat was big.

I couldn't swallow.

Something horrible was going on and I had no clue what it was.

I lifted my foot to turn back toward the door to leave, but then changed my mind.

I wasn't going anywhere until I found out what was going on. "Why are you acting this way? Tell me what happened."

"Like you don't know."

My heart was racing with fear. "I'm totally in the

dark here."

"Better than being on the street, like my cousin, Jay. I hope you made a lot of money buying Mathors Aerospace. It didn't take you long to put your armor back on, did it? You ripped his life apart."

"Mathors . . . What?" I practically yelled, startling a passing waiter.

I was able to fill in the blanks quickly and figure out what had happened.

I had told Gary that we needed to leave Mathors Aerospace alone, but he obviously hadn't listened.

Just when I thought things couldn't get any worse.

I took a step toward Nick. "I had no part of that transaction. I had no idea it was even happening."

"Then, it's just a coincidence that your company bought Mathors Aerospace three days after Jay told you he worked there? Three days after *he told you* that the company was having a few problems? You never mentioned it to a single person?"

I couldn't lie. "Well, I did bring it up, but that was because my company was looking for some new—"

"Enough."

"Let me explain. It's not what you think."

"I knew your nickname was *Ruthless*, but I never expected you to use my family for your own financial gain. I thought we had something between us, but apparently it was one-sided."

"Nicky, please."

His jaw tightened. "*Don't* call me Nicky. That name is reserved for people who care about me and who care about the people in my life. Obviously, *you* don't fit in that category. Leave. Now."

He turned and sat back down, avoiding eye contact like his parents were, making it crystal clear that our conversation was over.

Things went from worse to catastrophic, just like that.

I exited the restaurant and got in my car, staring through the windshield.

Things had unraveled so quickly.

Covering my face with the palms of my hands, I tried with all my strength to keep my burning eyes from turning into an ugly cry.

It hurt so bad.

The last thing I would ever want to do was hurt Nick.

I would never forget that look on his face.

Disappointment. Anger. Regret.

I could see them all in his eyes.

My life was falling apart.

I couldn't think straight.

What was I going to do now?

I was desperate.

I took two deep breaths, thinking of the fountain in my backyard.

Then a couple more breaths.

I sighed. "Suck it up. This is not the time to fall apart."

Giving up was never an option.

I would need to dig deep because this was the most painful thing I had ever gone through.

Dee could help me.

Pulling out my phone, I saw that I had five messages.

"That was stupid," I mumbled to myself, realizing I could've avoided the confrontation with Nick if I had checked my messages earlier.

Too late now.

I had one voicemail message from Nick and four text messages from Dee. I didn't need to listen to what Nick said in his message because he had already drilled that into me in person inside the restaurant. I scrolled through Dee's text messages.

Dee: Big trouble. Call me.

Dee: Where are you?

Dee: Okay, here's the deal. Mason convinced Gary to give him the go ahead to make a deal with Mathors Aerospace behind your back. They screwed you over.

Dee: There's only one way to fix this. I'll keep digging to see what else I can find out. Let me know if you need backup.

My pulse pounded hard in my temples as my pity party suddenly turned into exasperation. I was furious that someone on my own team would stab me in the back like that after all I had done for the company.

Mason messed with the wrong person.

I tapped my reply to Dee.

Ruth: On my way to the office. It's better if you don't get involved. This could get ugly.

I was going into full-on warrior mode.

No backup from Dee was necessary.

I knew what I had to do—the decision wasn't difficult.

The consequences, on the other hand, were huge.

I had no other choice.

CHAPTER TWENTY-EIGHT

RUTH

Twenty minutes later, I entered Stansfeld and walked directly to Mason's office, pushing open the door without knocking.

Mason swiveled around in his chair, grinning, squeezing a stress ball. "*There* you are."

I took a step toward him, hands on my hips. "You think this is funny?"

He nodded. "Absolutely. I *am* a little surprised that it took you so long to get here."

I studied him for a few moments, analyzing what I knew, and what he had said.

It didn't take long to figure out what was going on here:

* Mason was expecting me.

* The bastard set me up.

* He wants me to get fired.

* The only way for me to lose my job was to break the law or do something against company policy.

* That would only happen if I took matters into my own hands and tried to pull the plug on the Mathors Aerospace deal.

* If I was out of the picture, *Mason* would be next in line for a promotion.

His grin got bigger. "You figured it out."

"If I get fired, you're the new managing partner."

He laced his fingers together and held his hands behind his head. "Bingo."

Two could play this game.

I took a few steps toward him, placing my palms on his desk, leaning forward. "And what if I walk away now and leave the Mathors deal the way it is? Things will stay the same. You'll still be partner and *I* will be managing partner, above *and* all over your ass."

"Tsk, tsk." Mason kicked his feet up onto his desk. "*You* would never do that. Gary told me you know someone who works at Mathors. You don't want the deal to go through because he'll lose his job. You've gone soft. You'll do anything to keep him from being laid off."

"There's not a one hundred percent chance that he'll lose his job."

"Sure, there is. This is my baby. When the deal goes through, I will personally fire him."

"Nice try. You don't even know who he is."

"Hmm. Well, your boyfriend's name is Nick Morris and his cousin is Jay. How's that? And it doesn't matter how many Jays there are in the company because I'll just fire them all."

My pulse started pounding in my temples again. "You piece of—"

Mason held up his hand and laughed. "I was about to tell you to not get your panties in a bunch, but that may be asking a lot, based on what I saw at the party." He lowered his feet back to the floor and smacked the top of his desk, laughing again.

The man was trash and there was nothing I could do about it. The sad part was that there were many other men like Mason who were working at Stansfeld. Why would I want to work in a toxic, unethical environment like this? That was just it.

I didn't.

My priorities had changed.

Managing partner didn't have the same appeal it had had when I first started working there. Now, I knew with absolute certainty that I had no desire to be a part of this organization.

The only goal at the moment was to beat Mason at his own game.

I shook my head in disgust. "What a heartless bastard you are."

"Maybe so, but I'm going to be managing partner soon."

"Not if I can help it." Dee entered the office and walked toward me, with all the confidence in the world.

"What the hell are *you* doing here?" Mason asked.

She smirked. "Helping Ruth put you in your place."

Dee turned to me and handed me a note, smiling. "We can talk about my raise some other time." She smiled and walked out the door.

I wasn't the least bit surprised when I unfolded the piece of paper and read it, because Dee always delivered the goods.

Mason bought 10,000 shares of Mathors Aerospace BEFORE the deal.

I nodded, and folded up the piece of paper, smiling.

Dee never ceased to amaze me.

I love that woman to death.

The only thing she was missing was a superhero cape.

She was worth her weight in gold.

That's why she was my best friend. She had my back. I had hers.

I've said before that I could attribute the success in my career to hard work, determination, experience, and knowing how to deal with men's super-sized egos. It was also about having the right information available to make the right decision at the right time.

Mason was going down.

And that made me giddy with laughter.

"Why are you still here?" Mason stared at me. "What's so funny?"

I walked over and sat on the edge of his desk, pushing some papers aside. "I've got some bad news, Mason."

He let out a nervous chuckle. "What are you talking about?"

I held the piece of paper in the air. "It seems as if a certain douchebag partner in our firm bought some shares in Mathors. Now, *who* could that be?" I pretended to think about it.

Mason froze and turned white, at a loss for words.

"What do you think will happen when the Securities and Exchange Commission finds out about this very clear case of insider trading? Sounds like *someone* I know had better turn in their resignation, unless they want the SEC to find out. I mean, you must know you could go to jail for this, right?"

"You bitch!" Mason jumped to his feet, his chair slamming into the wall with a loud bang, and then falling over in the process.

Gary rushed into the office. "What's going on here? Everyone in the office can hear you."

Mason pointed at me. "Ruth is . . ." He poked the inside of his cheek a couple of times with his tongue.

I slid off the desk and glared at him, daring him to say something.

I didn't care either way at this point.

"Ruth is . . ."

Gary held his palms up. "Ruth is *what?*"

Mason's gaze bounced back and forth between Gary and me. "Ruth is blackmailing me!"

And there it was.

Mason was officially going down.

Gary walked over to the door and closed it, before turning back around. "What are you talking about?"

"Wait!" Mason paced back and forth, running his fingers through his hair. "You know what? Forget about it."

I shook my head. "Too late." I turned to Gary. "Mason purchased ten thousand shares of Mathors Aerospace before you signed the contract to acquire them."

Gary whipped his head in Mason's direction. "You did *what?* That's insider trading, you jackass."

"It was . . . a coincidence—really. I'll cancel the sale. I'm pretty sure I can do that."

I waved my finger at him. "Tsk, tsk. You can't *undo* the purchase of the shares. And there's a record of it." I turned to Gary. "This type of behavior from a partner is unacceptable not to mention, against the law. I doubt you would condone such a thing."

Gary crossed his arms. "Of course not. Mason, you're such a fool. Go home. We'll talk about this later."

He didn't budge. "Gary, I—"

Gary pointed to the door. "I said go home." He walked toward the door. "Ruth—in my office. Now."

I followed him to his office and closed the door behind me.

Gary walked toward his desk and flipped around. "I can't believe this crap. I should've known that something would eventually happen between you and Mason, the way you two are always at each other's throats. But I *never* expected this." He went around to the other side of his desk and sat down, thinking. "I'm going to recommend to the disciplinary committee for his immediate removal. Let's hope there are no other repercussions from the SEC. I need to talk to our legal team, just in case."

"I assume that with this new revelation, you'll be pulling the plug on the deal."

"Not at all," Gary said. "Nothing there has changed."

I wasn't expecting that. "Why not?"

"I told you before. The company needs the money. There's no way we're going to throw away millions of dollars. I'll take care of Mason, but Mathors Aerospace is a done deal. Let it go, Ruth."

I blew out a deep breath. "Sorry, Gary. I just can't do that."

"I'm not asking you."

I took a few steps toward his desk and crossed my arms. "I. Can't. You always tell me this is business, but that couldn't be further from the truth. This is one hundred percent personal. These are people's lives you're messing with. And that's why I'm going to personally make sure this deal doesn't happen."

Gary stood and came back around to the front of his desk. "I don't understand where this is coming from. This is like any other deal you've been associated with in the past. Nothing has changed."

"*I've* changed. I can't do this anymore."

"Ruth, you know the consequences if you mess with this deal. You'll lose everything. Your job. Managing partner. Your future. *Everything.*"

I wasn't listening. "This is the right thing to do."

I felt at peace with my decision.

Stansfeld had sucked the life out of me.

No more.

I grabbed a yellow sticky note and pen from Gary's desk.

Leaning over, I wrote two words on it.

I QUIT!

I handed the note to Gary.

He read it and shook his head. "Please. Don't do this. Think about what you're throwing away."

"That's just it, Gary. I *have* thought about it. And I'm not throwing away anything that's worth keeping." I walked toward the door.

"Ruth . . ."

I stopped at the door and swung around.

Gary blew out a breath. "It looks like you've made up your mind."

I nodded. "I have."

He took a step toward me. "You're the best damn partner this firm has ever had—I want you to know that. You'll be an asset to any company who's lucky enough to have you, but keep in mind that the door is always open if you change your mind."

I nodded, smiling. "Thank you, Gary. I appreciate that very much."

I turned and walked out the door, knowing I would never return.

CHAPTER TWENTY-NINE

Three Days Later . . .

RUTH

I smiled at Judy as we finished our fish sandwiches on a bench in the middle of the Oceanside Fishing Pier, marveling at how she was a completely different woman. I had told her in the airport that we both needed to get a life, and she hadn't wasted any time.

At least one of us succeeded.

Honestly, I was happy for her, but I couldn't help being jealous at the same time. Judy's social calendar was completely full. The woman had new boundless energy and spunk for an eighty-year-old. We talked about getting together again next week, but there was one big problem. She couldn't seem to fit me into her busy schedule.

On the other hand, my schedule was wide open after quitting my job.

I had no regrets for making things right with Mathors Aerospace. They walked away from the deal with Stansfeld and jumped at the chance to work with me after I had offered my consulting services at no charge to help turn around their company. The plan was to apply the exact strategy that was shot down by Mason and rejected by Gary during the board meeting.

I had no doubts that it would work, and they even offered me 50,000 shares if my ideas came to fruition, which I had no doubt they would.

But it wasn't about what I was getting out of the deal. It was a matter of principle and doing the right thing for Jay and Mathors Aerospace. I'd essentially tossed ten years of hard work in the trash dumpster, but the truth was, I knew I could easily find another job.

What I couldn't find was another Nick.

Could I blame him for not returning my phone calls? It was obvious that he wanted nothing more to do with me. I just wished that he would forgive me.

Judy wiped her mouth with her napkin and scrolled through the calendar on her phone. "Yeah, Tuesday is not going to work for me either. I've got bingo from nine to eleven, then lunch with Penelope, my new friend from the Mira Mesa Senior Center. After my afternoon nap, I've got a ukulele lesson, and an early dinner with Samuel, who teaches the computer class on Saturday mornings."

I smiled. "You met a man?"

Judy blushed. "Not just *any* man. A younger man!"

"How much younger is he?"

She leaned closer and whispered, "He's seventy-five."

I pretended to be shocked, putting my hand on my chest. "Judy—you cradle robber!"

She laughed. "I know! Isn't it wonderful? And he's *such* a gentleman. He's always wiping my computer screen for me with a microfiber cloth he said he uses *just* for me. Isn't that the sweetest thing you've ever heard?"

"It doesn't get much sweeter than that. He sounds like a wonderful man. And I'm glad to see you took my advice about getting a life. You're such an inspiration."

"I couldn't have done it without you." She patted the top of my hand. "What about you, dear? Do you have a life yet?"

I sighed and watched a fisherman cast his line into the ocean. "Well . . . not exactly. It wasn't a good week for me, but we don't need to talk about that."

"Of course we do, dear. That's what friends are for." She gave me a knowing smile. "Give me the Reader's Digest version since I'm going to need to take off soon for bingo."

I turned to her. "I thought you said bingo was on Tuesday mornings."

"Who said I only played once a week?" Judy laughed and squeezed my hand. "Now, tell me, what's going on with you?"

Funny how the tables had turned.

Now it seemed as if Judy was ready to give *me* advice.

I shrugged. "My life imploded this week. I'm suddenly unemployed *and* I lost a very special man."

"And what are you going to do about it? Sit around and mope?"

The question surprised me, but it wasn't far off target. "Basically. Yes."

"Well, that doesn't sound like the Ruth *I* know."

I laughed, fully aware that the history between me and Judy didn't go that far back in time. "I thought grieving was part of the natural healing process."

"How long have you been down in the dumps?"

"Three days."

"Boy, you're *really* milking it!"

I couldn't believe Judy made me laugh again. "Yes, I'm *such* a drama queen. If it makes you feel any better, I've been getting a lot of reading done. I hadn't read a single book in over ten years, but I just finished my third novel in less than a week. I'm obsessed and can't stop reading now. *And* I also have a newfound appreciation for napping."

"Oh, I just love my afternoon naps." Judy squished the wrapper from her fish sandwich into a ball and stuck it in the bag. "What kind of books are you reading?"

"Romantic comedies."

She lit up. "I *love* romantic comedies! There's nothing better than a little laughter with a happy ending."

"I agree." I lost my smile, thinking of Nick. "Too bad I didn't get *my* happy ending."

"That just means the end of your story hasn't been written yet. But you *do* need to make a little effort, you know? What's his name?"

"Nick." I smiled. "I liked to call him Nicky."

She lit up. "I *adore* that name. And do you love him?"

I nodded.

"And does he love you?"

I sighed. "*That*, I don't know. He told me that under ideal conditions, he could fall in love with me in a heartbeat."

"What kind of ideal conditions are we talking about here?"

"He didn't like my job, plus the fact that I was a workaholic."

She nodded as she ate one of her french fries. "I'm no brain surgeon, but it's very clear to me that you have no job, which would make it *impossible* for you to be a workaholic. Especially with all that reading and napping goin' on." She winked. "I wouldn't give up on him yet. But if for some reason the stars are not aligned for you and Nicky to be together, that means there's someone else out there better suited for you."

I nodded. "Yeah . . ."

Judy gestured across the pier. "Maybe even someone like that man right over there. You *certainly* have caught his attention. He can't take his eyes off of you."

I followed the direction of Judy's hand and froze.

My breath caught in my throat. "That's Nick."

Judy squeezed my hand. "Then it looks like *this* is my lucky day. I'm going to have a front row seat to your happy ending. If only I had some popcorn."

I swallowed hard, my eyes starting to burn. "I don't know what to say to him."

"Speak from the heart, dear. And remember, he came

here to find *you*. Hear him out and let him say what he has to say."

Nick started walking my way and my heart pounded in my chest.

I stood and took a few steps toward him.

He stopped and jammed his hands in his pockets. "Hey."

"Hey . . ." I could barely get the word out. "How did you know I was here?"

"Dee," we both said at the same time.

He chuckled. "The all-knowing one."

"*That* she is."

"These birds are voracious!" Judy stood up from the bench and walked toward us. "It's like I'm in that Alfred Hitchcock movie. I'm taking off or they'll steal my fries. Sorry to interrupt, I'm Judy, by the way. It's a real pleasure to meet you, Nick."

Nick hesitated. "The pleasure is all mine." He was probably surprised she knew who he was since I hadn't introduced them.

I gestured to Judy. "We met at the airport the same day I met you, and we've become good friends."

"And I have to go now, dear, but we'll catch up again soon. And by the way, you did it!" Judy winked at me. "Watch out!" She pointed behind Nick.

A seagull flew right above Nick's head.

He ducked at the last second, avoiding it. "Whoa. That was a close call."

"Yeah . . ." I watched the seagull fly away. "That bird almost took your head off."

He nodded and thought about it. "Kind of like what I did to you in the restaurant, right?"

I sighed. "I deserved it."

"No. You didn't." Nick looked like he was searching for more words.

I wanted to say so much, to tell him how sorry I was, how bad I felt.

Remember, he came here to find you. Hear him out.

Nick ran his fingers through his hair. "What you did was . . ."

"It was wrong," I blurted out, not having the patience to wait any longer to speak and apologize. "I know. I'm sorry. Please forgive me."

He shook his head. "I'm not talking about that."

"Oh . . ." I was confused but needed to let him finish. I took a deep breath and waited.

"I'm talking about what you did for Jay, saving his company and his job. Hell, how did you even *do* that? It doesn't matter. I can't believe what you sacrificed. Dee told me you quit your job."

I nodded. "I did what I had to do."

"My point is that you did something out of the kindness of your heart. The nickname *Ruthless* doesn't even apply to you anymore. It's not fair you had to sacrifice your job."

"It was my fault all this happened in the first place."

He held up his hand. "Please, let me finish."

I nodded.

Nick blew out a deep breath. "The thing is, I overreacted. It wasn't fair. I was taking out my frustrations, some of the baggage I had with my ex-wife, and lumping it together with what had happened with you. I should've let you explain yourself in the restaurant instead of jumping all over you. Then I found out that you were really trying to help Jay, and that you were screwed over by your own company. I didn't know that, and I apologize for not giving you the benefit of the doubt."

"I'm the one who should be apologizing here." I rubbed my forehead. "What else did Dee tell you?"

"Everything." He locked gazes with me. "She told me how you feel about me. Is it true?"

I swallowed hard as my heart began to pound again.

I could feel my face getting hot.

Why would she tell him that? It was the truth, but that wasn't the point!

I finally nodded. "It's true. I love you."

Please tell me you love me back or I'm going to die right here on the spot.

Nick took a step closer to me. "The thing is . . . I promised myself I would never fall in love with someone like you."

Definitely *not* what I was hoping to hear.

"I was mad when it had happened because I didn't think there was any way for us to have a future together. I'd convinced myself of that, but I was wrong."

"Wait, wait, wait." I held up my hand and then placed it on top of my head, more confused than ever. "I'm sorry. Back up. Please. You're killing me right now." I rubbed my temples with my fingers. "When you say you were wrong, is it because you don't love me, or were you wrong thinking there could be no future between us, or wrong because you were convinced, and now you're not convinced?"

"I love you, Ruth."

I blinked twice and whispered, "Please say that again."

"I love you."

Tears of joy and relief streamed down my face. "*Why* didn't you start with those three words from the very beginning? Do you know what you were doing to my heart?"

He chuckled. "I happen to be an expert in the ways of the heart." He grinned and grabbed my hand, placing it against his chest where the scar was. "And *this* heart is all yours."

Nick stepped closer, grabbed me by the waist, and pulled me against his body.

I love this feeling.

Then he kissed me.

Heaven.

Nick broke off the kiss and looked into my eyes. "What was Judy talking about when she said *you did it*? What exactly did you do?"

"I got a life, Nicky." I smiled and pulled him closer. "I got a life."

EPILOGUE

One Year Later . . .

RUTH

Life can change or end in a heartbeat. One minute, I was falling off a bike trying to remove a wedgie at the gym. Three months later, I married the stranger who was kind enough to help me off the floor.

Getting a life had been my goal after the near-death experience on the plane, but I had gotten much more than I had bargained for.

I got the man of my dreams.

But I wasn't the only one who was lucky in love. In fact, there were three weddings in twelve months. I enjoyed being in the bridal party for two of the weddings, but nothing beat being a blushing bride who was madly in love.

It was amazing how fast everything happened.

"When you know, you know," Judy had told me.

She was right. She was also the first of us to get married.

Two weeks after she had gone out with Samuel, her computer class teacher, he'd proposed. They'd made it official a few weeks later on a Hornblower Yacht on the San Diego Bay. The wedding celebration included dinner, dancing, and bingo, of course.

The next wedding had been for me and Nick.

My heart still skips a beat when I think of how he had proposed to me in front of my now fully healthy roses in my backyard.

He'd handed me a velvet box and asked me to open it. Inside the box was my grandma's locket that he and Karma had found. It was polished, completely restored to its former beauty, and attached to a new silver sterling necklace that I absolutely loved.

Inside the locket was a little note that said, "Marry Me."

Then he'd gotten down on one knee and pulled out a diamond ring.

I screamed *yes*, jumping into his arms, and kissing him.

We were married two months later in an intimate ceremony on the beach in Del Mar, right in front of Lucy and Ricky Ricardo's old summer home. The reception took place at Bernardo Winery with Jay's famous pulled pork as the main meal.

Our first dance song was "Heaven" by Bryan Adams.

Nick and Karma moved in with me, and our first home project together was painting the kitchen yellow, my favorite color.

As for my professional life, it had done a complete one-eighty after I had quit Stansfeld. My new job was wonderful and rewarding. It had also been the least stressful year of my life.

I started my own consulting firm to save companies who were going through difficulties. I used the same strategy that saved Mathors Aerospace from going under and left me walking away with 50,000 shares that had quadrupled in price in twelve months.

Dee was still working for me, because only a fool would let someone of that caliber go. I gave her another raise and a title worthy of her talent: Vice President.

As for my former company Stansfeld, Dee had informed me that Steve had been promoted to managing partner after Gary retired. Mason had been fired from the company, as expected, and was subsequently fired from his next two jobs after that. He was never caught by the SEC for his insider trading but was now being investigated by the IRS for tax fraud.

As for me, I had the perfect work-life balance.

I no longer tore things apart.

Shutting down my computer every day at five on the dot was pure joy. Plus, I didn't work on the weekends.

I had a wonderful life.

By the way, Nick's cousin also had thousands of shares of Mathors Aerospace that quadrupled in value. After catering our wedding, Jay ended up quitting his job to pursue his passion of being a chef. He eventually opened a cute cafe near Balboa Park. People lined up around the corner, waiting for the best pulled-pork sandwiches in San Diego County.

As for the third of the three weddings, Dee got married yesterday, here on Catalina Island. I couldn't be any happier for my best friend. Brandon was the best guy I could ever wish for her. Of course, my hubby and I were thrilled to be matron of honor and best man.

Nick and I decided to spend the week on the island. We rode tandem bikes with Dee and Brandon on Pebbly Beach Road by the water.

Dee pointed toward Lover's Cove as we approached on the bikes. "There's the spot! I married my sweetheart there!"

"What a coincidence!" Brandon said on the tandem bike seat right behind her. "I married my sweetheart there, too!"

After stopping to take a few more pictures and talking about their gorgeous wedding yesterday, we looped back around to return to town.

Nick was starving and I anticipated him suggesting for us to stop for lunch soon.

"Anyone ready to eat?" Nick said, from the seat behind me on our bike.

I know my husband well.

"Me!" I raised my hand and almost fell off. "Whoa!"

Nick chuckled as he kept the bike from toppling over. "Didn't you learn your lesson? We don't need another episode of you falling off the bike again."

"I agree. That was a close call."

At least he didn't mention the wedgie.

Speaking of which . . .

I wiggled my butt in my seat, realizing I had gotten another wedgie after almost falling off the bike. It was getting more uncomfortable with every minute that went by.

Wait until we return the bikes, then nonchalantly pull that sucker out. Nobody will ever know.

I shifted my butt in the seat again, but the wedgie went even deeper, like it was looking for a place to hibernate for the winter.

"What's going on with your wife, Nick?" Brandon laughed. "She looks uncomfortable. Does she have what I *think* she has?"

You have got to be kidding me.

"Remember my rule." I turned my head and glared at Nick. "Don't say it."

"Say what, wedgie girl?" Brandon laughed again.

"Pull over the bike, Nick. Your best friend is going to get it."

Dee intervened, "How dare you threaten my husband like that?"

Nick laughed. "Lift your butt up, my love. I'll pull it out for you."

"No!" I peddled faster.

Nick laughed harder. "You can't get away from me. We're on the same bike, remember?"

Now, I was laughing as well as I turned my head to the right, checking my peripheral. "Nicky, you keep your hands away from my rear. Do you hear me?"

"Come on, shake your booty."

"Not funny!"

Okay, maybe it was.

The four of us laughed all the way to the bike rental

shop, where we got off the tandem bikes, and turned them back in.

I walked quickly toward the building, flipped around, and gently removed the wedgie.

The three of them were still laughing.

I shook my head in amazement as I joined them again. "Why does every possible embarrassing moment of my adult life happen when I'm with you?"

Nick stepped toward me and kissed me. "I told you before—I'm here to keep you humble. Now, let's go eat."

We walked down the sidewalk toward the Mexican restaurant, holding hands, and peeking inside the quaint shops as we passed them.

I pulled Nick to a stop when a painting in a gallery window caught my eye.

"Oh, wow."

He eyed the painting in the front display window. "That's beautiful. Do you like it?"

I nodded, almost in shock. "I *love* it. And I know who painted it."

Nick leaned closer to the window to read the signature at the bottom of the painting. He turned to me. "No way . . . your mom painted that?"

I nodded again with a mixed feeling of joy and admiration. "She's been selling them and giving all the proceeds away to charity."

Dee and Brandon moved closer to the window.

"Your mom is an amazing painter," Dee said.

"I agree." Nick continued to admire the painting. "It's

wonderful." He leaned forward again to read the title of the painting. "The girl with stars in her eyes?"

I gestured to the painting. "That's me."

"Really?"

I nodded. "She said she could see the passion I had at an early age. That there wasn't anything I couldn't do if I applied myself. Education, career, meeting the love of my life."

Nick kissed me. "I especially love the last part." He grinned. "Well, looks like it's settled then. We need to buy this painting."

"Wait . . . What?"

"I want it for our home."

"I'm sure my mom would be happy to give us one for free."

"But if I buy it, you said all the money goes to charity, right?"

"True. Minus the gallery's fee, I would assume."

"Then, what are we waiting for?" He pulled me into the gallery and closed the door behind us. He told the salesperson that he wanted to buy the painting, without asking the price.

And just like that, I fell in love with Nick a little more.

We waited for the salesperson to remove the painting from the window display and wrap it for us.

I pulled Nick close and hugged him. "I love you so much. You turned my life around." I reached up and kissed him.

A few seconds later, Nick broke off the kiss, looking into my eyes. "You were smiling while we kissed."

"Maybe . . ." My tone was flirty. "It's just . . . I can't believe I found love in my own backyard."

He kissed me again and grinned. "You certainly did."

THE END

<<<<>>>>

Ready for more fun? Go to the next
page for your FREE romantic comedy.

FREE romantic comedy!

Subscribe to my newsletter and receive free stories, fun giveaways, and the latest news on sales and new releases! Plus, get a FREE copy of my fun story, *Happy to be Stuck with You.*

http://www.richamooi.com/newsletter.

You can also browse my entire list of fourteen romantic comedies on Amazon:

Author.to/AmazonRichAmooi

ACKNOWLEDGMENTS

Dear Reader,

I hope you enjoyed *It's Not PMS, It's You.* I enjoyed writing this story about a strong, confident woman who doesn't take crap from men. Go Ruth! I admit that I had SO much fun torturing her with those bad dates. I know, I'm so cruel. LOL.

By the way, my hot Spanish wife was the inspiration behind the infamous wedgie scene in the first chapter. Yes—she really did hurt her wrist while trying to remove a wedgie during a spinning class at the YMCA. We laugh about it all the time, and I told her one day that I would have to use the incident in one of my romantic comedies. She agreed!

I would like to take a moment to thank you for your support. Without you, I would not be able to write romantic comedies for a living. I love your emails and communication on Facebook and Twitter. You motivate me to write faster! Don't be shy. Send an email to me at rich@richamooi.com to say hello. I personally respond to all emails and would love to hear from you.

Join me on Facebook here for more fun:

https://www.facebook.com/author.richamooi/

If you would like to get an email update from me when I have a new release or sale on one of my books, sign up for my newsletter here. You'll get a free romantic comedy just for signing up.

https://richamooi.com/newsletter/

Please consider leaving a review of the book on Amazon and Goodreads! I'd appreciate it very much and it helps new readers find my stories.

It takes more than a few people to publish a book so I want to send out a big THANK YOU to everyone who helped make *It's Not PMS, It's You* possible.

First, thank you to my amazing wife, the love of my life, Silvi Martin. She's the first person to read my stories and always gives me the best feedback to make the story better. She cracks me up, too. I loved her reaction when she was reading the first draft of this story and saw that I had brought back Bagel Barney in another scene to annoy Ruth.

She had said, "No! Not Barney again!" Hahahaha. I LOVE MY WIFE! I couldn't publish a book without her. Thank you, my angel! I love you, love you, love you!

Thank you to Sue Traynor for another amazing cover!

Thanks to Meg Stinson for editing.

A big thank you to Paula Bothwell, Graham Toseland, and Sherry Stevenson for proofreading. You rock!

Thanks to Teresa Carpenter and Hannah Jayne for helping me with the brainstorming before I started writing the story.

Special thanks to my beta readers Robert, Cheryl, Maché, Silvi, and Deb for giving me great feedback.

Thanks to San Diego Romance Writers of America, Author's Corner, and Chicklit Chat HQ.

With gratitude,

Rich

ABOUT THE AUTHOR

Rich Amooi is a former Silicon Valley radio personality and wedding DJ who now writes romantic comedies full-time in San Diego, California. He is happily married to a kiss monster imported from Spain. Rich believes in public displays of affection, silliness, infinite possibilities, donuts, gratitude, laughter, and happily ever after.

Connect with Rich!
www.richamooi.com
rich@richamooi.com
https://www.facebook.com/author.richamooi
https://twitter.com/richamooi

Made in the USA
Coppell, TX
30 June 2020

29705245R00218